LOVE'S FIRST BLOOM

This Large Print Book carries the
Seal of Approval of N.A.V.H.

LOVE'S FIRST BLOOM

DELIA PARR

THORNDIKE PRESS
A part of Gale, Cengage Learning

GALE
CENGAGE Learning

Detroit • New York • San Francisco • New Haven, Conn • Waterville, Maine • London

GALE
CENGAGE Learning™

LIBRARY OF CONGRESS CATALOGING-IN-PUBLICATION DATA

Love's first bloom / by Delia Parr
    p. cm. — (Thorndike Press large print Christian historical
  fiction)
    ISBN-13: 978-1-4104-3463-0 (hardcover)
    ISBN-10: 1-4104-3463-X (hardcover)
    1. Clergy—Fiction. 2. Trials (Murder)—Fiction. 3. Children of
  clergy—Fiction. 4. Journalists—Fiction. 5. Large type books.
  PS3566.A7527L68 2011
  813'.54—dc22   2010045476

Published in 2011 by arrangement with Bethany House Publishers, a
division of Baker Publishing Group.

Printed in Mexico
1 2 3 4 5 6 7 15 14 13 12 11

Dedicated to
"The Shell Point Girls"
on
Anna Maria Island, Florida,
who welcomed me into their homes
and now have a special place
in my heart.

ONE

March 1838
New York City

Ruth Livingstone had very little time left to change her father's mind.

After a hasty ride through dark, deserted streets, she parted the curtains on the coach window while waiting for Capt. Grant to arrive. Moonlight rested on the *Sheller,* a packet ship that was lying at anchor in the harbor. She blinked back tears. Unless Ruth could sway her father's decision, the morning tide would carry her far from home, along with Lily, the sleeping toddler now nestled against her father's chest.

She dropped the curtain and swiped at her tears. Even though he had rejected every one of her arguments since rousing her from bed two hours ago and telling her she had to leave, she prayed she still might get him to agree to let her stay home with him.

"Please, Father," she whispered. "When

7

Capt. Grant gets here, tell him your plans have changed so you can take another day or two to find someone else."

Seated directly across from her, Rev. Gersham Livingstone cradled the sleeping child and shook his head. "I don't have another day or two, Ruth."

"But I don't understand why I must go when you have so many supporters who would be better suited —"

"You're the only one I can trust to take Lily away and keep her safe," he insisted, keeping his voice low.

"But what if Capt. Grant questions me? What am I supposed to say if he sees that I'm not this . . . this Widow Ruth Malloy that he expects?"

"I told you. Capt. Grant never meets any of the women he helps me to relocate before sailing. At least you get to keep your given name," he added.

Frustrated, Ruth found it hard to be grateful for keeping her first name when she was giving up so much else. "What about the Garners? Surely they'll suspect that I'm not —"

"Elias and Phanaby Garner will accept you without question when you arrive. In turn, they'll introduce you to the community as a distant relative whose period of mourning is over and is in need of a home. I explained all this to you on the way here," he gently chided.

Dropping her gaze, she swallowed hard. According to her father, the Garners did not know that the real name of the woman they were expecting had been Rosalie Peale, the well-known prostitute found murdered some days ago. Or that the child in the reverend's arms was in fact Rosalie Peale's secret daughter.

The very idea they would think Ruth was a former prostitute . . . Oh, it both shamed and humiliated her as a woman of faith. Being the daughter of a controversial minister who devoted his life to the fallen angels of the city had never been easy, but Ruth found it terribly ironic that the only way she could support him now was to become one of his reclaimed fallen angels herself.

Desperate to change his mind, Ruth tried another tack, keeping her voice to a whisper to keep from waking the little girl. "The constable can't seriously think you could have killed Rosalie Peale," she argued, unable to fathom that anyone would consider him capable of murder.

"Indeed he shouldn't, but the press has fueled public clamor for an arrest that should have been made days ago."

She snorted. "The reporters who've surrounded our house from dawn to dusk for the past two days are even worse than the scoundrels you allowed inside to interview you. Have they no sense of decency?"

"Decency doesn't sell newspapers," he replied. Her father placed a hand on her shoulder. "Instead of being angry about a situation we can't control, we should be grateful that my lawyer was able to persuade the constable to give me time to put my affairs in order before arresting me."

She placed her hand on top of her father's and blinked back more tears. "But you're innocent! It isn't fair!"

"It's not fair for Lily to bear the stain of her mother's sins, either, but she will — unless we can get her out of the city before anyone finds out about her, especially one of those reporters. Unfortunately," Rev. Livingstone added wistfully, "many people, even people we know well, actually believe everything they read in the newspapers. They don't need to wait for a trial to convict me."

Ruth's heartbeat slowed to a thud that pounded against the wall of her chest. She tried not to think of their several neighbors who had closed their hearts, as well as their doors, to both her and her father in recent days. Even Harrison Steward, her father's closest friend, had abandoned him, refusing any contact.

For several long moments she allowed herself a time of self-pity, until she realized her father would pay a far greater price, even beyond losing the affection of their neighbors or even his dearest friend.

He would pay with his very life.

Her father edged forward in his seat to get closer to her. "The path God chooses for each of us to follow isn't always an easy one, but we all have to decide whether or not we're willing to trust in His wisdom and embrace His will. I can't risk letting the glare of scandal that's already churning in the press to shine upon this innocent child. Can you?" He gently urged the sleeping child into Ruth's arms.

Ruth awkwardly cradled the little girl close for fear she would wake up. "No, I-I can't. I'll go. I'll take care of her," she whispered, then tensed when she heard two soft raps on the coach door.

Her father answered by parting the curtain only long enough to nod and drop the curtain back into place before cupping her cheek. "It's time to go now, Ruth. With God's grace, I'll be exonerated quickly. Then I'll send for you, and we'll make more permanent arrangements for Lily. Until then, God will take care of you both. Trust in Him."

Ruth managed half a smile. As more tears slipped free, she kissed the palm of her father's hand, pressing the memory of this moment deep within her heart. When he turned her hand over and kissed its back, she felt his tears, too.

Quietly, without saying another word, he disembarked. Ruth gathered her courage. Once she stepped out of this coach, she would have to swallow her pride and silently bear the mantle of a sinful past she had not lived.

Two

Toms River, New Jersey

"Please don't throw your food, Lily," Ruth cautioned for the third time, gritting her teeth to keep from crying out in frustration. As she wiped a glob of soggy bread from her own forehead with the tip of her apron, she laid her other hand atop the toddler's hands to keep them still.

Three weeks ago when she first arrived here, Ruth knew her faith would be tested while she waited anxiously for her father's innocence to be recognized in a court of law.

Hiding the truth of her real identity, and allowing the middle-aged couple who had opened their home to her to believe she was a former prostitute, had been just as hard as she had expected it would be.

She'd had no idea, however, that her greatest challenge would come from twenty-two pounds of pure mischief disguised as the eighteen-month-old toddler sitting directly in front of her. With bright blue eyes and a mop of unruly blond ringlets, the slender toddler was a pretty, delicate little girl who had a mind of her own, a will to match, and one favorite word: *no.*

With her eyes dancing, Lily tugged her hands free and smeared bread soggy with gravy all over her face and through her curls.

"Mercy!" Ruth cried. "You need another bath for certain now."

Giggling, little Lily clapped her hands, sending drops of gravy in all directions. "Bath! Me. Bath!"

Out of the corner of her eye, Ruth caught a glimpse of the smile on Phanaby Garner's face and heard the woman catch a giggle of her own before turning back to stir the pot of fish chowder bubbling on the cookstove.

Exceptionally tall and uncommonly thin, the middle-aged woman was still just as patient and good-humored as she had been from the moment she and her husband had welcomed both Ruth and little Lily into their home. The heat from the cookstove today added a flush of pink to her cheeks, and wisps of hair that escaped from the tight bun she wore at the nape of her neck curled around her narrow face to soften her sharp features.

Without a word of complaint, Phanaby set down her spoon and gracefully side-stepped her way around the food Lily had thrown to the floor. After moistening a fresh rag, she carried it back with her, stopped in front of Ruth, and smiled. "There's a bit of gravy in your hair, too," she said and gently dabbed at Ruth's hairline. "There! All gone now," she pronounced and handed the cloth to Ruth. "I'll heat up some water for Lily's bath while you clean up her tray and the floor."

Truly exhausted, although it was barely midday, Ruth groaned. "I'm so sorry she's made such a mess again."

"Bath! Bath!" Lily cried and smacked both palms on the tray of her baby chair, splashing gravy onto the sleeves of the last clean gown Ruth had left.

Phanaby giggled out loud this time and gazed at Lily. "I never knew a baby who loved a bath as much as you do."

"Or needed one so often, I suspect," Ruth quipped as she swiped at the mess on her sleeves. Wondering if she would have the energy to keep up with this little mite the rest of the day, she got down on all fours and started wiping up the floor.

"I don't know about that," Phanaby argued as she pumped fresh water into a pot.

15

"Jane Canfield used to dunk her three boys in the river several times a day to clean them up when they were about this age, or so she claimed."

Ruth sat back on her haunches and pushed back a lock of hair that escaped to block her view. "In the river?"

Phanaby carried the pot over to the cookstove. "The river's warm enough come full summer."

"Have I met Mrs. Canfield?" Ruth asked, resuming her task.

"No, the Canfields moved west a long time ago. Jane was a sweet woman and a good friend. Mr. Garner enjoyed her husband's company, too. They had a cabin on the south side of the river at the time, but she brought the boys to visit whenever they came into the village." She set the pot on the cookstove. "She had the prettiest little flower garden not too far from the cabin on a little finger of land that poked into the river. Her flowers bloomed there from spring until fall. I still look for them each spring, but the garden and the cabin have been empty since they left."

"Bath! Bath!" Lily cried as she tried to squirm out of her seat, interrupting a flash of Ruth's own childhood memories. She fondly recalled the tiny flower garden her

16

mother had kept behind their home in the city before death had claimed her — and a series of housekeepers had let the garden go to weeds.

"A bath you shall have, little miss, and then you'll be off to take a fine nap so we can all eat our dinner in peace. I hope," Ruth added.

Once she had both Lily and the tray wiped clean, she set the dirtied cloth aside, then hoisted Lily to her hip and covered another yawn. "I'm sorry Lily was so restless again last night," she said, offering one more apology to the countless ones she had given for the past three weeks for Lily's behavior.

Phanaby offered Ruth a gentle smile. "It's no bother. Like I've told you, Mr. Garner wouldn't wake up if a hurricane swept through the house, and I sleep nearly as soundly. She'll surely take a good nap this afternoon, and you look like you might need a bit of rest today yourself. You couldn't have gotten much sleep last night, either."

She lifted Lily out of Ruth's arms and into her own. "Poor Lily," she said, rocking from side to side. "She's probably teething a bit. Did you use the remedy Mr. Garner made for her?"

Ruth nodded. "I rubbed it on her gums whenever she woke up, just like he said, but she still didn't fall back into a sound sleep for very long."

"Then she's probably still not accustomed to sleeping in a trundle bed," Phanaby murmured before pressing her cheek to the top of the toddler's head. "Do you miss your crib, sweet baby? I'll try harder to find one for you," she crooned as Lily relaxed against her shoulder.

"Please don't bother yourself. The trundle bed is fine for now," Ruth offered, hoping and praying that her father's trial, which had started just last week, would soon end with his acquittal and he would send word that it was safe to bring Lily back to the city.

"It's no bother. In fact, I'm a bit embarrassed that we didn't have a crib here for you when you arrived. It's just that . . . well, we thought Lily was a bit older than she is," she murmured as she stirred the chowder and Lily played with the collar of her gown. She glanced over her shoulder to look at Ruth. "You're quite a bit younger, too," she said, without a glimmer of judgment in her voice.

Blushing, Ruth dropped her gaze. With every bone and muscle in her body yearning for a good night's sleep, Ruth felt like ninety-two instead of twenty-two, yet the love and understanding in the woman's eyes was so intense, she nearly forgot how physically tired she was.

Instead, her spirit ached and tugged at her heartstrings, yet again, for deceiving this generous, loving woman and her husband and not telling them the truth: Ruth had not been a fallen angel, selling her body to anyone with enough coins while living at Mrs. Browers's brothel. A brothel where no one, even Mrs. Browers, knew she'd had a child. And she had not paid another woman to take Lily into her home and care for her for the past year and a half.

She was Ruth, Rev. Livingstone's daughter, a woman of virtue and faith who longed for the life she had left behind and the father she dearly loved.

"You're a good woman, Ruth, and you can be a good mother to Lily," Phanaby encouraged. "I know it's been hard learning how to care for her yourself," she said, reminding Ruth that she knew about the arrangements under which she and this little one had allegedly lived, without judging her for it. "It'll get easier once the two of you really get to know one another. Just trust yourself. Trust in God and know that both Mr. Garner and I are here to help you, too, so you won't ever have to be separated from each other again."

"I-I know . . . and I thank you both. For . . . for everything," she managed, humbled by the example of faith and generosity this woman and her husband had set before her.

Phanaby's eyes misted. "You're very, very welcome," she managed before turning away. "This water still needs a good bit of time to warm. I'll keep an eye on this little cherub for you. While I do, why don't you go downstairs to the apothecary and remind Mr. Garner that dinner will be ready in about half an hour. Otherwise he's likely to leave to deliver some compound or another, especially now that the weather has turned fair again. By now, I'm sure you've noticed how oblivious he can be to the hour when he's working."

Ruth smiled. Mr. Garner was so devoted to his customers, he might seem almost possessed by his work at times, but his girth alone provided ample evidence that he was never too devoted or too preoccupied to forget to be at the table at mealtime. "Of course. I'll be right back. By then the water should be warm enough that I can give Lily her bath and get her settled down before dinner."

Lily turned and stretched toward the sink.

"Bath! Bath!"

Ruth patted Lily's back. "Yes, baby. As soon as I get back," she promised and headed for the stairs at the end of the hallway that led to the back of the family's living quarters above the apothecary. She paused and smiled as she looked out the window at the top of the enclosed staircase that led down to the first floor.

Finally, after ten long, gray days, the relentless rain that had pelted the village had stopped. The sun, sitting bright and high in a cloudless blue sky, reflected off the bows of several packet ships sitting heavy in the river, waiting to be unloaded at the docks several blocks away.

She had no interest in any of the goods from the city that would soon appear in the various shops in the village, even if she had any coin to spend. She was only interested in one thing: news about her father's trial, which had dominated the city newspapers that were usually delivered twice a week to the village.

After ten days without any shipments arriving at all, every single copy of those newspapers would be scooped up as soon as they arrived. Even here, readers were obsessed with the scandalous, even licentious details of the life of Rosalie Peale and the controversial minister who was on trial for her murder.

Hopeful that Mr. Garner would get copies of the newspapers at some point today, Ruth opened the door to the staircase, looked down at her apron and gown, and sighed. She'd had no idea that taking care of a young child would take such a toll on her clothing, and she sorely needed to launder the few clothes she had managed to bring with her.

The steps were uncommonly steep, and after she picked up her skirts with one hand, she held tight to the railing with the other. She descended very, very slowly, and hoped that the time she had spent on her knees praying would help to stem the growing fear within her that her father would be wrongly convicted.

THREE

Ruth opened the door at the bottom of the staircase and stepped into the storeroom. She took a deep breath of the warm, fragrant air, but ended up in a bit of a coughing fit. She remembered too late that unlike the pristine shop itself, the storeroom was a magnet for dust and disorder.

The paned window next to the rear door was covered with grit and grime, which ten days of rain had failed to remove, allowing only dim light to enter the room. Baskets filled with dried flowers, roots, and herbs used as remedies or compounded into healing tonics lined a number of rickety shelves. Even the overhead beams were laden with drying bunches of healing herbs, and she crouched to avoid disturbing them.

Since arriving here, Ruth had only helped Phanaby with housekeeping tasks upstairs, but as she neared the curtain that separated the storeroom from the shop itself, she made a mental note to offer to help Mr. Garner tidy up the storeroom as one way to repay him for his kindnesses, too.

Once she reached the curtain in the doorway, she stopped and cocked her head. Relieved that she did not hear any voices, meaning Mr. Garner was not busy with a customer, she parted the curtain and peeked into the apothecary itself.

Mr. Garner, however, was not there. She discovered him standing outside on a ladder, apparently so intent on washing the paned window next to the front door that he did not even see that she was waving to him to get his attention.

Unlike his wife, Elias Garner was average in height, although his weight might be appropriate for a much larger man. The dull brown hair on top of his head was rather unremarkable, but the mustache he took such pains to groom was quite streaked with gray and red hair.

She had come to know him as a gentle, quiet man, a man devoted to his God and his faith, as well as his wife and his customers. Elias was but a single example of the large network of believers her father had developed to help those fallen angels who sought to reclaim their faith. Humbled again by the generosity of the Garners, she swallowed hard. She moved closer to the window to capture Mr. Garner's attention.

When he finally smiled and waved back, he pointed to the one pane on the window that was still dirty and held up one finger to indicate he would be back inside as soon as he finished.

Smiling a reply, she took advantage of this unusual opportunity to be in the apothecary by herself and looked around. Unlike the storeroom, the shop itself was a vision of order and cleanliness, the scent of the room more medicinal than herbal. Four substantial wooden shelves, separated in several places by vertical pieces of wood to create the look of bookcases that stood side by side, ran horizontally along the wall to her left. In front of the shelves, a counter widened as it reached the rear of the shop to create a workbench where several mortars and pestles of different sizes stood next to a small brown parcel.

Instead of open baskets filled with herbs that lined the shelf in the storeroom, however, dozens of bottles and jars organized by color and shape and filled with sundry healing preparations sat on the top two shelves. The third shelf contained patent medicines, while the fourth and lowest shelf contained all sorts of gadgets and tools for preparing compounds. Graters in several different sizes nestled next to wooden and ceramic bowls and pitchers, as well as two rolls of brown paper and several balls of twine.

Turning, Ruth noted that there was a narrow workbench, not much more than a ledge, on the wall directly behind the counter. When she noted the mirror hanging on the wall over that workbench, she walked over and gazed into it. When she looked beyond her own reflection, she had a full view of the shop and realized Mr. Garner must have placed the mirror there in order to keep an eye on his shop when he turned his back to work.

Once her gaze settled back on her own reflection again, she quickly looked away and blinked hard. There was nothing she could do to add more height to her short stature, but she could ill-afford to lose any more weight without looking as gaunt as Phanaby. Helping to feed Lily at mealtimes, however, often meant that Ruth had little time to think about eating herself.

Pressing her eyes closed, she massaged them with her fingertips and tried not to think about the circles under them that were nearly the same gray color. "Sleep. I need sleep," she grumbled. She opened her eyes, removed the comb in her hair, and used it to smooth her hair back into place again without bothering to use the mirror. She had always worn her hair very simply, and she did not need a mirror to make sure she pulled the sides up into a comb at the top of her head, leaving the back to fall in waves to the middle of her back.

She barely had the comb in place again when Mr. Garner opened the door and came back inside carrying a ladder with one hand and a bucket with the other. Grinning, he held up the bucket and waved his arm toward the sparkling window as he approached her. "One task done and done well, wouldn't you say?"

"I would," she agreed. "Mrs. Garner asked me to come downstairs —"

"To remind me that dinner will soon be ready," he said and set the ladder down to lean against the counter. When he tried to put the bucket down, he inadvertently hit the side rung on the ladder. Apparently panicked that the dirty water would hit her or perhaps the brown parcel sitting on the counter, he yanked the bucket back toward himself.

Ruth managed to jump out of the way, but nearly all of the dirty water ended up soaking his canvas apron, as well as parts of his shirt and trousers, before the water puddled on the floor.

Groaning, he shook his head and stepped out of the water pooling at his feet. "Now, that's a fine mess I've made of myself and my shop. I hope I didn't get any of this on you."

"No, I'm fine."

"That's probably because you're young and nimble enough to get out of harm's way," he said as he untied his apron and peeled it off himself. Frowning, he dropped it into the now-empty bucket. "I can't very well go anywhere without changing into dry clothes first, and I can't even do that until I mop up all this water."

"I can help," Ruth said quickly. "I can mop up the water for you."

He sighed. "It's not the water I'm concerned about. Mrs. Sloan, down at the general store, is especially upset with me because I didn't remember yesterday to give her twice the remedy anyone else normally asks for, and I promised I'd have the extra in her hands before she sat down for dinner today."

"She always gets twice the normal amount? Why?"

He chuckled. "Simply put, because she likes to have extra on hand, regardless of the cost." He pointed to the brown parcel lying on the workbench. "Would you be a dear and take that parcel over to her for me?"

Ruth moistened her lips. On the few times she had gone walking about the village, she had always been with one of the Garners or both. Reluctant to go alone, she hesitated. "I-I really shouldn't leave right now. Lily made a mess of herself again. I'm afraid she needs another bath and —"

"Lily isn't the only one who made a mess, now, is she? Don't worry. As soon as I mop up this water, I'll head right upstairs and tell Mrs. Garner that I needed you to run an errand for me. She won't be very pleased that I'll be dripping wet when I do, but I think I can safely promise that she won't mind starting Lily's bath."

When she caught her lower lip, he captured her gaze and held it. "The village is your home now. Sooner or later you'll need to venture out on your own, without either Mrs. Garner or myself," he said. "The people here have their faults, like we all do, but for the most part, they're all good folks. Some of them might end up as friends while there are others you might want to avoid. Maybe it's time you discovered which ones are which, without having one of us with you all the time to do that."

Ruth swallowed hard, caught between the advice he offered and the difficult reality of actually taking it. She was still uncomfortable with her adopted identity, and she missed the anonymity she could find in New York City. Here, the number of people who lived and worked in the village was so small, she could never hope to go anywhere at any time without being recognized. "I-I suppose I could, but —"

"That's the spirit," he said and handed her the parcel. "While you're there, you might as well get a couple of those lemon sticks Lily favors so much. And get something sweet for Mrs. Garner and yourself, too. Mrs. Sloan can just put it on my account."

Ruth held on to the parcel but looked down at her apron, which was badly stained and a bit crusted with the remnants from Lily's breakfast as well as her dinner. "I'd have to change my apron first."

"Nonsense. Just toss it into the bucket with mine. Besides, if you don't go now, I'm afraid you might be too late."

She furrowed her brow. "Too late?"

He smiled. "Mrs. Sloan won't have any trouble selling every one of those city newspapers that should have finally arrived today. Even folks here have gotten caught up with Reverend Livingstone's trial. I was hoping to get copies of the newspapers while I was there. You must be as anxious as we are to find out if the good Lord has answered our prayers and Reverend Livingstone's finally been found innocent of murdering that poor woman."

"Indeed I am," Ruth agreed and slipped off her apron, as well as any hesitation she had about going to the general store alone.

Ruth walked up Water Street and noted that the village was quiet as most folks gathered at home to share the midday meal together. She paused at the corner, where the small roadway intersected Main Street, to shake the mud from the hem of her skirts and grimaced. She had more to worry about than a few stained aprons and soiled gowns waiting to be laundered. Her mud-soaked slippers were probably beyond saving, her feet were numb, and the sun that warmed the top of her head only served to remind her that she had forgotten to wear a bonnet.

Anxious at what she might learn from the newspapers, and nervous about being out and about all by herself, she glanced across the street. The stable to her left, where patrons of Burkalow's Tavern and Inn kept their mounts, added a pungent smell to the air that nearly dominated the more fragrant dinner odors emanating from the inn itself.

Tears welled unexpectedly, and she blinked them back as she carried the parcel to the general store. She did not know if anyone was taking meals to her father or providing him with fresh clothing while he was imprisoned, but she prayed that some of his supporters were seeing to his needs in her absence.

Sloan's General Store was two full squares away, directly opposite the bank, and she smiled when she saw there were no customers going in or out of either establishment. When she approached the front door to the general store, it opened so abruptly, she quickly took a step back and gripped the parcel she was carrying for fear she might drop it.

She recognized the young man who nearly ran into her. On her first journey into the main of the village with Mrs. Garner, she had met Silas Simms. The young seaman worked on one of the packet boats, such as the *Sheller,* which routinely traveled between Toms River and New York City twice each week, carrying charcoal, lumber, and farm goods from the village and returning with all sorts of commercial products.

Barely fifteen, with a long face pocked with scars, Silas was all arms and legs and had yet to learn how to control them, which made her wonder how he managed when he was at sea. "Oh, sorry, ma'am. Excuse me." He rocked back on his heels, nearly tripping over his own two feet in the process.

Blushing, he managed to untangle his feet and catch the stack of newspapers that slipped out from beneath his shirt as well. When he finally met her gaze, his blush deepened. "Dailies. They're recent up to yesterday," he explained, quickly shutting the door behind him and shoving the papers back under his shirt.

He looked around, as if making sure no one else would hear him, and lowered his voice to a whisper. "That minister's trial's gettin' real interestin' now. The captain brought more newspapers for the general store today than usual, and I brought a few of my own. I'm hopin' I can sell some down to the inn, but please don't say nothin' to Mrs. Sloan. I don't think she'd favor me doin' that, even if she's bound to sell out her own papers," he admitted.

Ruth nodded, disappointed to learn that her father's trial had yet to end. She stared at the bulge of newspapers hidden beneath his shirt. When her heart began to race, she shifted the parcel she had been carrying. "Are you just now delivering the newspapers to Mrs. Sloan?" she asked, if only to confirm her assumption that the newspapers for Mr. Garner were waiting for him inside the general store.

"Yes, ma'am," he replied. He pulled several newspapers out from underneath his shirt and handed them to her. "You can have these. I got plenty more."

"No, thank you," she said and offered them back to him. "I just wanted to make sure that Mr. Garner's newspapers hadn't been sold."

"No, you keep those, ma'am. They're for you. They're good readin', too," he said and leaned close as he lowered his voice yet again. "Seems like the good minister mighta murdered somebody else, too. Anyway, I'll be back the end of the week with more newspapers. Maybe by then they'll have found the other body."

"Wh-what other body?" she managed before her throat tightened with fear.

"Accordin' to those papers, none of the officials or reporters have been able to find his daughter since the trial started, so they decided he musta killed her, too. They're lookin' hard, but they say she's got no family to take her in. One newspaper claimed

34

she's just hidin' out somewhere. Not that I blame the poor woman. I'd hide, too, if that wicked minister was my father."

FOUR

New York City

After living a self-imposed, but well-deserved, exile for the past two years, Asher Tripp returned home prepared to confront his past and to ask for the opportunity to make amends and redeem his reputation.

With his carpenter tools and travel bag at his feet, he stood under the eaves of a bookstore that would not open for several hours yet. The early morning flurry of activity across the street at the cellar office of the *Galaxy* was achingly familiar. Yet it inspired difficult memories of his very public, very humiliating failure — one that had put the newspaper itself at great risk of shutting its doors.

Encouraged by the volume of the day's daily newspapers that had been picked up for delivery to homes throughout the city, he also found the large number of boys carrying away newspapers to hawk on street corners very reassuring. Judging by the size of the papers themselves, which were half of what they used to be, he realized that the paper's primary focus had completely changed in his absence from politics and commerce to crime and other more sensational topics that had greater appeal for the masses.

Obviously, the newspaper he had abandoned was now thriving as one of the new daily newspapers that sold for a penny, a full nickel less than the larger newspapers that appealed to the city's political and business elites. Tripp only hoped that this change would not have a negative impact on both his decision to return and his chance of success.

He drew in a long breath and picked up his tools and travel bag, but waited for a carriage to pass by before crossing the street. As he descended the cellar steps, he noted that the sign over the cellar door was exactly the same. The name of the newspaper had not changed, and he was pleasantly surprised to see that his name, as co-owner and co-editor, had not been removed but remained just below his older brother's.

For as long as he could remember, Tripp had walked willingly in his older brother's shadow. Still, he had never been as driven or as focused as his brother, especially after their father's death and their mother's remarriage, which prompted their move to New York City.

Now both his mother and his stepfather were gone. Clifford was the only family he had left. Clifford was also one of the very few people here in the city who had known him long enough and well enough to call him Jake, the middle name he preferred to Asher, the given name his brother insisted be used professionally.

Jake took a deep breath and prayed that the bonds of brotherhood they shared were still strong enough to allow his brother to forgive him and welcome him back into his life. If not, he had no hope his brother would allow him to try, yet again, to be the man he wanted to be.

Pausing at the bottom of the steps, he set his travel bag down just long enough to open the door. Assaulted by the smell of ink and paper that inspired even more bittersweet memories, he had both his bag and his tools on the floor and the door closed again before the echo of the bell over the door had stopped ringing.

Straight ahead, two large wooden desks littered with papers, pens, and inkwells, as well as stacks of newspapers, stood side by side. Behind them, a partition separated the front office from the printing area that was now silent, waiting only for the afternoon when the day's news would be written and then put to press overnight.

"I'll be with you in just a moment."

Jake stiffened as his brother's hurried footsteps drew nearer. When a door in the partition opened, he clenched and unclenched his fists, anticipating the moment when he would come face-to-face with his brother for the first time in two very long, very difficult years.

Without looking up, Clifford walked into the room to greet his caller, wiping his ink-stained hands with a gray cloth. He was still quite a bit shorter in stature than Jake, but the auburn hair they had in common was now tinged with just a hint of gray and his face was lined and shadowed by overwork.

"I was hoping to get more of this ink off before I —"

Looking up, he stopped abruptly and stared at Jake, while the cloth lay motionless in one of his hands.

For several heavy heartbeats, Jake met his brother's gaze and held it. "They say you can judge a man quickly by looking at his hands, in which case I would venture to say that you're still a man completely dedicated to his work." He felt oddly embarrassed by how rough his own hands had become over the past two years.

Clifford walked forward, but stopped behind the desk he had claimed as his own when they first opened their newspaper four years ago with nothing more than belief in themselves — and a line of credit from the bank to augment their mutual investment of funds they had inherited from their stepfather. He tossed the cloth to the top of his desk. "They also say you can judge a man by his actions, in which case I would venture to say that you are —"

"A coward? An incompetent, irresponsible cad?" Jake offered quickly before his brother could utter the words.

Clifford nodded. "At the very least, although I could add a few more negatives, if you've a mind to listen," he countered as he walked around the desk and stopped directly in front of him.

Jake braced himself by locking his knees and straightening his shoulders. "I'll listen. I deserve anything and everything you have to say to me."

"Probably more, if truth be told, although I must admit that I'm quite at a loss to simplify into a few words what you did to me and to the business we started together when you walked away, leaving nothing more than a note for me to read."

"I know," Jake offered. "I'm sorry —"

"Unfortunately," his brother continued, without allowing Jake time to completely apologize, "I had no choice but to stay here and try to clean up the mess you left behind if I had any hope of recouping the losses we suffered." His voice reflected a deep hurt that tugged at Jake's conscience.

Glancing down at the tools on the floor, Clifford shook his head. "Did you ever once think about me while you were traipsing anywhere and everywhere, earning your keep as a common handyman with our father's old tools? Or were you too busy feeling sorry for yourself to give me a single thought?"

"Of course I thought about you," Jake said.

"And just how would I know that? You never wrote. Not even once. If it hadn't been for Capt. Grant, I wouldn't have even known you were still alive, though I suspect you might have been back sooner if it hadn't been for him."

"Under the circumstances, I wasn't certain you'd even care or be willing to read a letter from me," Jake replied, without defending the man who had given Jake free passage on his ship whenever he needed to move on from one town to another along the eastern seaboard.

Clifford sighed. "Circumstances? I didn't create those circumstances. You did, the moment you took up the cause for that woman and stirred up public interest in her, even though I warned you to investigate more thoroughly. And when the reporters for the *Herald* and the *Transcript* and the *Sun* uncovered the fact she was a swindler, you didn't even have the courage to stay and face the truth: Because of your incompetence, that woman and her accomplices disappeared with thousands of dollars. All because you assured the public that rescuing an elderly woman who had allegedly been the victim of her own vulnerability was a worthy cause."

Clifford paused and shook his head. "The *Galaxy* became a laughingstock. I couldn't even give copies of it away for months," he admitted, his voice crackling with anger. He braced both hands on his desk and leaned forward. "You didn't even have the courage to stay and help me to rebuild what was left of the newspaper. Did you know I had to move a cot into this cellar because I didn't have enough money to live anywhere else? Of course not. You didn't even stay long enough to face me, not even once, did you?"

Jake swallowed the lump in his throat. "No. I-I couldn't. I never meant for you to carry the burden of what I'd done. I'm sorry. I'm truly sorry, Clifford."

His brother stood up straight. "I'll never be able to forget what you did, Jake, and I'd be less than honest if I said that I'd ever be able to forgive you, either. So if that's why you're here, I'm afraid you'll just have to be as disappointed in me as I am in you."

Stung, Jake nodded stiffly. Shifting his weight from one foot to another, he struggled to choose the right words to say so that his brother would not refuse his request to return to work, in spite of how unforgiving he claimed to be. "You have every right to be angry with me —"

"How good of you to admit it to my face," his brother snapped. "Not that you care, but I've worked long and hard for the past two years without your help. The *Galaxy* is second only to the *Sun* at the moment, thanks to the Livingstone trial, and I'm determined to top their circulation by year's end. If it's money you want, I'm willing to return your initial investment, but frankly, I don't think you deserve any of the profits I've managed to accumulate."

Jake cleared his throat. "All I want is to

come back and work with you."

"Work here again? Are you daft?"

"You just admitted that I still own an interest in the business," Jake insisted. "I don't want money or any of the profits you've earned over the past two years. I just want a chance to prove myself, to you and to the readers I disappointed."

"I've worked very hard to regain the people's trust," his brother countered. "Readers have a long memory, especially when they've been hoodwinked out of their hard-earned money. And just in case they've forgotten how you led them down that ill-fated path, there are reporters for the other penny dailies who will be more than happy to remind them, even if I decided to take a risk and let you return to work here."

"Then don't tell anyone I'm back here working again," Jake argued. "Give me an assignment outside of the city. Anything. I'll travel anywhere, for any length of time, to investigate the background of any story you choose. Just let me prove to you that I can pursue a story and investigate it until I've uncovered the whole truth of the matter and not just the truth I hope or want to see."

"And if you fail?" Clifford asked.

Jake stiffened. "I won't fail."

"But what if you do? What then? Where

44

will you run off to this time?"

"I won't fail. No matter how long it takes or how hard I have to work, I won't let you down again. Please, Clifford. I just want one more chance."

Clifford's gaze hardened. "If you fail this time, you'll sign over your interest in the newspaper to me, leaving me free to find a more suitable partner. That's the best I can do."

Jake extended his hand. "Agreed."

Instead of shaking his brother's hand, Clifford walked over to the desk Jake once used and sorted through a bunch of newspapers lying on top. "Are you familiar with the Livingstone trial, or have you been living in total oblivion for the past few weeks?"

"Actually, I've been living for the past few months in a very small town in New Hampshire, helping to rebuild a church that was destroyed by fire. They have absolutely no interest in anything beyond county lines and barely support their local newspaper."

Clifford snorted. "What about the Jewett case two years ago, right after you left?"

Jake nodded. Headlines up and down the East Coast had roared with the Jewett case for a good year after the trial ended. "That I remember."

Clifford paused for a moment and looked

at his brother.

Jake shrugged. "I was living in Philadelphia at the time, and the papers carried the story there, too. As I recall, despite overwhelming evidence, the young man was obviously guilty of killing Helen Jewett, but he was acquitted — a case of where the victim's ill-fated life as a prostitute mattered less to the jurors than the status of the man who killed her."

"Exactly as the *Galaxy* predicted long before any of the other newspapers, which helped reestablish the paper's credibility," Clifford noted with pride. "The Livingstone trial, which shouldn't reach the jury for at least another two weeks or so, is generating even more interest than the Jewett case did, because the man charged with killing this particular prostitute just happens to be a minister. I'm sure you remember him and his organization, Prodigal Daughters, which was designed to bring the city's 'fallen angels' back to the faith. He was rather controversial even before this poor woman was found murdered only hours after he left her."

"He's the minister who confronted those women on the street and tried to convert them," Jake offered.

"And visited the brothels regularly at night

to see them, which did not endear him to the owners of the brothels or the city elites who frequented them," Clifford added. "Here. Read these," he ordered as he shoved a handful of papers into Jake's hands. "Learn everything there is to know about the case."

"If the trial is right here in the city, it's going to be hard to hide the fact that I'm back working here, assuming that's what you have in mind," Jake stated.

"But you won't be here. Not for very long, although I expect you to keep a very low profile while you're here," his brother said. "There's no doubt that Reverend Livingstone is guilty, and the city will not accept his acquittal like they did for Jewett's murderer, which means his fate is sealed. But right now, the big question that's fueling public interest isn't about the trial itself. It's the mystery surrounding Livingstone's daughter, Ruth. She's gone missing, and no one, including two of my best reporters, has been able to find her."

"What do you think happened to her?" Jake asked as he began skimming the headlines on the four-page newspapers.

"Speculation seems to favor the idea that she didn't go into hiding to avoid the scandal of the trial, but that her father may have killed her, too."

Jake abruptly stopped reading and met his brother's determined gaze. "You actually think he killed her?"

"I don't know, although in all truth I suspect he didn't. He doesn't seem to have many supporters left, but it wouldn't surprise me to learn that one of them is giving her a place to hide from the press as well as the officials who would dearly love to speak to her. If you're serious about redeeming yourself, then that's your assignment. Find her."

"Find her," Jake repeated, envisioning days, if not weeks, spent traveling again, risking all that he owned to meet his brother's challenge.

"If she's dead, you need to find her body and have it positively identified," Clifford demanded. "If she's alive, you need to find out why she went into hiding and whether or not she has evidence that would help to convict her father. Either way will suit both our needs. Just find Ruth Livingstone before anyone else does. Otherwise you're finished here. Permanently."

Jake swallowed hard. His brother had given him a challenge almost impossible to meet, but it was a challenge he could ill-afford to turn down. "Is there anywhere I can stay while I'm in the city?"

"I still have that cot in the back storage room. You can sleep there. Just be discreet. I want as few people as possible knowing you're back in the city again," Clifford snapped.

"I've slept on worse more than once during the past two years," Jake replied. He knew he would never again find a good night's sleep if he failed his brother professionally again. But he was determined to earn even more — his brother's forgiveness.

FIVE

Breathing hard, Ruth shut the bedroom door and leaned back against it for support. Her fingers were trembling so hard she had trouble unbuttoning the cuff of the sleeve on her work gown. When she finally managed to free the button and fold back the cuff, she blinked hard to clear her vision, stared at her forearm, and nearly gasped.

The circle of flesh just above her wrist bone was already turning purple. And she was just as shocked to see there were droplets of blood oozing from several places. She had never expected that Lily would actually bite her, but that was the least of her worries right now.

With Lily safe and secure in the crib Phanaby had borrowed from a member of the congregation, Ruth ignored the toddler's cries of protest and rushed to the kitchen. She moistened a cloth with cold water and gently pressed the cloth against the wound and winced. "She bit me. She actually bit me!"

As the throbbing finally eased into a dull pain, Ruth removed the cloth, looked at her forearm, and groaned. She would wear a small but nasty bruise there for a good while, but at least Lily had not bitten her on her cheek, which would be impossible to hide.

When Lily let out another burst of shrill screams, Ruth hunched her shoulders and cringed. There was no doubt that anyone downstairs in the apothecary would be audience to her crying.

Embarrassed by her inability to handle Lily and dreading the apology she owed to Phanaby for what Lily had done, which inspired this tantrum, she took a deep breath. After she checked to make sure the bleeding had stopped, she rinsed the cloth before setting it into the sink. She quickly rolled her cuff back into place again before she heard footsteps rushing up the back staircase.

Hurrying out of the kitchen and into the hallway, Ruth reached her bedroom door just as Phanaby and Elias came rushing through the door at the top of the staircase. Although she was grateful that Lily's screams had quieted to a whimper by then, she still felt guilty for the look of pure panic in their eyes. The poor woman's face was as pale as the full moon that had been shining last night while Ruth was rocking Lily back to sleep for the third time. Her husband, who hurried forward to stand alongside her, was panting for breath.

"What happened to Lily?" Phanaby gushed, her concerned gaze locked on the closed door.

Ruth managed a weak smile and battled tears that welled again. "I'm so sorry that we worried you both up here. She's fine. Just having a bit of a tantrum again. I-I put her into her crib, but as you can hear, she's quieting down now."

Elias furrowed his brow. "Are you sure she's all right?"

Nodding, Ruth moistened her lips. "I'm sure."

Phanaby let out a huge sigh and patted her heart. "I thought for certain she'd gotten hurt. She was screaming so loudly, I heard her outside. I dropped the laundry I was hanging up into the dirt and ran right back inside where I nearly bumped into Elias, who had left Reverend Haines in the shop to run up here to see if you needed help with the poor child."

Ruth cringed. "I-I'm so sorry. I'll wash everything again for you," she assured the woman before glancing at her husband. "Please ask Reverend Haines to forgive us for making him wait on our account," she said, although she was not worried overmuch. She could not think of anyone else in the village who would be more forgiving or more discreet than the pastor of the small church where the Garners had taken both her and Lily to attend services.

Elias nodded but glanced at the bedroom door before meeting Ruth's gaze again. "If you're certain she's all right, perhaps it might be best if I leave the two of you to sort through this . . . this difficulty."

"She's perfectly fine," Ruth insisted.

While he quickly disappeared back down the hall, Phanaby cocked her ear to the bedroom door and smiled. "She's quiet now," she whispered. "Do you think we could just check on her to make sure she's not quiet because she's getting into more trouble? She nearly climbed out of the crib a few days ago, remember?"

Ruth groaned, turned the doorknob, and eased the door open. She tiptoed into the room, with Phanaby right on her heels, but they did not need to cross the room to peek into the crib. Lily was sound asleep, lying at the top of Ruth's bed with her tiny arms wrapped around Ruth's pillow. The two fingers she liked to suck were still in her mouth, and she had Ruth's shawl gripped tightly in her other hand.

As annoyed as she was with the little imp, Ruth took one look at her and felt a hard, quick tug on her heart. Lily's poor little face was swollen and blotched with patches of red, the ringlets that curled about her face were wet with her tears, and all Ruth could think about was how very frightened and confused this little one must be after being swept from her caretaker and the mother she would never see again to live with strangers.

Silently, Phanaby took Ruth's elbow and led her out of the room, easing the door closed again before she started them both down the hallway. "Since Lily can climb out of that crib, it'll probably be best if we return it to Mrs. Martin before Lily has a chance to climb out again and hurt herself. She seemed so happy when I left you to go outside. Whatever happened to upset her so?"

Being careful to protect her wrist, Ruth took a deep breath. She stopped in front of the Garners' bedroom door, forcing Phanaby to halt her steps. "After you went outside to hang up the clothes you'd washed, I wanted to help. So I moved Lily's chair into the corner, sat her down, and gave her a few of her toys to keep her occupied while I emptied the washtub," she offered.

She paused as a warm blush spread from her cheeks down the full length of her neck and then poured out yet another apology. "The washtub was too heavy for me to lift, so I started taking out the water, a potful at a time, and . . . and I suppose I was trying so hard not to spill any of the water on the floor that I didn't notice that Lily managed to slide off her chair and disappear. By the time I realized she was gone and found her, I'm afraid I was too late. I-I'm sorry. I don't know how, but I'll find a way to make amends. Truly, I will," she insisted.

Phanaby dropped her hold on Ruth's elbow and furrowed her brow. "Amends? For what?"

She started to raise her hand to point to what Lily had destroyed when the woman walked past her and into the sitting room, her footsteps crunching on the debris on the planked floor.

The room itself was rather small, with only a small rosewood settee on the far wall flanked by tin sconces on the whitewashed wall, and a pair of mismatched, straight-back chairs that usually sat side by side in front of the fireplace with a very small mantel that held an old tin oil lamp. The only touch of luxury in the entire room was the heirloom crystal vase that used to rest on a tall wooden stand in front of the single window in the room.

Rays of sunshine that poured through the window's sheer curtain glistened on the shards of crystal on the floor, shining light on the damage Lily had done — damage which had inspired a tantrum when Ruth ran into the room and pulled Lily away before she could touch the fragments and hurt herself.

As the woman walked past the chair Lily had tugged over in order to reach the vase, Ruth watched with heart-thumping dread. Phanaby pressed her fingers to her lips and knelt down to pick up the pieces of the broken vase, and Ruth rushed to her side and knelt down alongside her.

She placed both hands on top of Phanaby's and did not let go to wipe away the tears that covered her cheeks. "I-I'm so very sorry, but please don't be mad at Lily. It's entirely my fault. I should have watched her more closely, but . . . but she's so quick and so determined. I know there's no way I could ever let you know how very badly I feel, but if there's any way at all that I can make amends . . ."

She paused to gulp down another wave of tears, and Phanaby pulled a hand free to swipe at the single tear of her own that trickled free and lay on top of her cheekbone. "The vase was a wedding gift to my great-grandmother, who gave it to my grandmother, who gave it to my mother, who in turn gave it to me before she died, hopeful I would marry one day," she whispered and tugged her hands free to pick up a large shard of crystal.

Ruth choked on the lump in her throat that she tried, in vain, to swallow.

Phanaby set the shard back down on the floor with the others, studied them for several long heartbeats, and turned to Ruth. As the rest of her tears finally fell free, she wiped Ruth's cheeks with the palm of her hands and cupped her face. "I'm not crying because Lily broke the vase," she murmured, her gaze as steady as her hands.

"But you just said —"

"I'm crying because I'm a foolish, foolish woman."

"But I don't understand. You're not foolish. That vase is very special to you —"

"Special? No," Phanaby countered and glanced down at the floor. "When I see that

57

vase lying shattered on the floor, I'm grateful to Lily because now I'll never have to look at it again, day after day, and be reminded that I don't have a daughter of my own who would put this vase in her home after she married. Over the years that Mr. Garner and I have been married, we've both come to accept that God's many blessings to us don't include having children."

She paused to take a deep breath. "Every time I caught even a glimpse of that vase when I walked past the sitting room, I lost a bit of my faith in His will, but I just . . . I just never had the courage to put the vase away, even after Lily tried several times to get her hands on it and I knew she could get hurt. Thanks to Lily, I don't ever have to look at the vase again, do I?" she said, smiling.

Ruth shook her head, unable to find her voice as she tried to comprehend the depth of faith and wisdom within this woman's heart. She also tried not to question God's will, but simply could not understand why He had given a prostitute like Rosalie Peale a child, yet withheld the blessing of a child from this woman of faith.

Phanaby took hold of Ruth's hands and leaned into her strength to get back to her feet before tugging Ruth up, too. "Are you certain Lily didn't cut herself? Did you check her carefully?"

Pain shot through Ruth's wrist, and she winced. "No, she's perfectly fine, but I'm afraid I didn't fare so well," she admitted as she tucked her injured wrist into the palm of her hand.

"You're cut? How badly?"

"Not cut. Bitten, I'm afraid."

Phanaby's eyes widened. "Bitten? Lily bit you?"

Ruth nodded. "Hard enough to draw a little blood. She was angry because I wouldn't let her play with the vase after she dropped it."

Chuckling, Phanaby turned Ruth toward the doorway. "Come along and let me take a look. Since she broke the flesh, you'll need to put something on that. I've got some ointment in the kitchen," she said, and shook her head. "That sweet little cherub has a bit of a temper, but don't worry. She'll only bite you once more and that'll be the end of it."

Ruth rolled her eyes. "Would you care to tell me why?"

Phanaby chuckled again. "Because the next time she bites you, you're going to bite her right back."

Six

New York City

Lured by the news that a verdict was imminent in the Livingstone trial, Jake managed to get to the courthouse just as the doors burst open.

Several men who were leading the hordes of reporters stampeding behind them shouted out the jury's decision in a single voice that cannoned through the thick hush of expectation: "Not guilty! Not guilty!"

Within seconds, wave after wave of full-bellied jeers and colorful expletives exploded from the crowd like the finale of cannon fire on the Fourth of July. The outcry reduced the few cheers from the minister's supporters to whispers.

Jake scanned the faces of the crowd of reporters, searching for his brother. The rush of urgency and excitement was palpable as reporters broke free, one by one, and charged off with their notes to get to their respective offices to write the articles for tomorrow's headlines, proclaiming two very important words: *not guilty.*

Now that the minister had been acquitted, Jake highly doubted Clifford would want him to find the daughter, which meant he had wasted the past few weeks reading everything the newspapers had printed since Rosalie Peale had been found murdered. He couldn't help but wonder: Would there be another chance to redeem himself?

Standing off from the angry crowd, where he was cloaked in night shadows, Jake had the anonymity he needed while he waited for his brother to appear. Clifford had an amazing, instinctive sense of timing that served him well. At any newsworthy event, Clifford was inevitably the last one to arrive so he could be the first to leave with facts in hand. Jake was more than a bit disappointed that his brother was still nowhere in sight.

As the crowd grew louder and turned unruly, Jake was glad he was far enough away to remain uninvolved. In point of truth, he really did not know or care if the jury's decision was a miscarriage of justice, which was obviously the opinion of the majority of the hundred or so men who surrounded him, or a fair and judicious judgment rendered by twelve good citizens who would probably be wise to leave the court-room tonight by the back door.

He was, however, thoroughly convinced that it was the power of the printed page that had shaped the opinions of the men and woman gathered here. It was also the power of the printed word that had inspired them to be here, waiting long into the night for the jury's verdict. But with tonight's shocking verdict, it would also take that same power to make them care about what-ever had happened to the minister's daugh-ter. He would have to harness all of his talents and intelligence to find out, assum-ing Clifford wanted him to continue.

"Jake!"

The sound of his name, followed by a hard nudge in the middle of his back, forced him to turn around.

"What are you doing standing here?" his brother demanded. His face was ablaze with the challenge of making the *Galaxy* the first newspaper to hit the streets in the morning with headlines announcing tonight's verdict. "Follow me," he instructed and charged off.

Jake caught up with him with two long strides. "How did you get behind me? I've been here since the courthouse doors flew open."

"I paid one of the bailiffs to let me out

the door the judges always use. Lucky for you, I just happened to see you from the alley," he replied as he increased his pace to a jog. "Keep up with me. I've got two of my men at the office waiting to set whatever I write into print."

"The crowd is definitely displeased by the verdict," Jake said.

His brother grinned. "A verdict rendered by the jury exactly two hours and forty-seven minutes after Judge Matthews told them to dismiss every single word of testimony from Mrs. Browers and the rest of the women who live at her brothel because they were 'unreliable witnesses whose testimony was flawed by their immoral characters.' "

Jake waited until they passed diners leaving a late-night restaurant before posing a question. "Do you still want me to find Ruth Livingstone?"

Clifford snorted. "Don't be ridiculous. With the acquittal, it's even more imperative. You heard that crowd back there at the courthouse. They're incensed that the jurors wouldn't convict that man. If you can prove he killed his daughter, then I can almost *choose* the headlines for his next trial . . . one that will most assuredly not end with an acquittal."

"But what if she's alive?" Jake argued when they passed the bookstore directly across from the office.

Stopping abruptly, Clifford turned to face him. "Then find out if she's hiding evidence that would have convicted her father of killing Rosalie Peale."

Jake shook his head. "That won't matter now. The man's already been found not guilty of killing Rosalie Peale, and the law is perfectly clear. He can't be tried again for killing her, no matter what kind of evidence emerges, and I don't think people will care to read anything about the trial now that it's over. Besides, what if she isn't in hiding for any other reason than she doesn't want her father's scandal to taint her?"

"People care about what newspapers tell them to care about, what *I* tell them to care about," his brother snapped. "The *Galaxy* isn't the only newspaper sending out reporters to find Ruth Livingstone, and none of them will be calling back reporters who are still trying to investigate Rosalie Peale's mysterious past, either. Readers have the right to know where Ruth Livingstone is, whether that's in some unmarked grave or not. And if she's alive, they'll demand to know if she was hiding evidence that would have convicted him. I don't have time to argue with you. If you're not up to the task, which you nearly begged me for, then say so and I'll send someone else."

Jake shook his head. "No, I'll do it."

"Then stop wasting any more of my time, as well as your own, and get it done. And don't forget to send me reports if you have to leave the city. With some cleverly written articles, I can keep public interest in this case brewing for months and finally make the *Galaxy* the top-selling penny newspaper in the city — provided you don't let reporters for the *Sun* or any of the other newspapers find her first. Please tell me I didn't make a mistake offering you a chance to redeem yourself professionally. Tell me you do have at least one solid lead about where she could be after spending the last two weeks looking for her," he said.

"I do have one that I got this afternoon that looks promising," Jake replied defensively. Capt. James Grant was an important man to know and call a friend. The accomplished seaman commanded respect from his crew, as well as all who knew him. He was just as comfortable socializing with the city elites and dining in the finest restaurants as he was in the seedier areas along the wharves. He knew this city and the people who lived there better than anyone Jake knew. Even more important, Capt. Grant was the one man he could still trust.

"I'm leaving again at first light before tomorrow's newspapers are even off the press. I won't be back to the city for a bit because I have a few things to take down to Baltimore first. Perhaps you should come along," Capt. Grant suggested.

Jake stared at the older man sitting across from him at a table in the back of a dimly lit tavern where the owner, a friend of his companion's, had already locked up the front door and gone upstairs to bed. The wrinkles that creased Grant's weathered face were deeper now than they were nearly fifteen years ago when they had first met, and the few hairs he had on his head back then were long gone. But he had never lost the generous heart he hid beneath the stiff exterior that his reputation, as well as his livelihood, demanded.

"Sir, you know I can't leave," he replied. "You know how important it is to me to be back at work with my brother," he added, reluctant to disappoint the man who had helped him after the debacle of his very public mistake two years ago.

Grant slurped the last of his soup and set

down the bowl. "I know how important you think it is to prove you're as talented and dedicated as your brother, but I was hoping that after spending two weeks back in the city, you'd have realized you don't need to prove yourself to him or anyone else. You're a far better man than he is, Jake. Always were. Always will be, unless he gets himself a conscience like the one I know you've got."

Despite the compliment and the fact that the captain addressed him familiarly by his preferred name, Jake cringed at the criticism that was aimed at both himself and his brother. Capt. Grant had often stepped in, settling arguments between the two brothers after they first moved to the city, but Jake and Clifford were not children anymore. "That isn't fair. You don't really know Clifford. He's the most amazingly talented newspaperman in the city."

"I see him often enough, and I still know him well enough. I read his newspaper." Grant tore the crust off the end of a loaf of bread and wiped up the last bit of soup in his bowl. "I don't suppose Clifford will turn his attention to another scandal now that the trial's over and Livingstone has been acquitted."

Jake waited until the man shoved the

soggy crust into his mouth before answering, hoping to have his say without being interrupted. "Reverend Livingstone's acquittal only means the reading public will demand more news about him, or more specifically, his daughter. She's still missing. Until she's found, there are too many questions that still need answers, and I've promised Clifford that I'd get them. And don't think I'll be out there looking for her alone. The man who finds her first will make a name for himself. I intend to be that man. I need to be that man if I have any hope of reclaiming my place with Clifford at the *Galaxy*."

Jake's words hung in the air, creating a wall that divided them. As anxious as he was to repay this man for all his help over the past two years, he was just as intent on reclaiming his professional career as Ashton Tripp.

When the man finished eating the entire loaf of bread, he washed it down with a pint of hard cider. After setting down the pewter mug, he locked his gaze with Jake's. "I was afraid you would confirm what a number of people said down at the courthouse and thereabouts after the verdict was announced."

Jake furrowed his brow. "You were there?"

he asked, although his question was rhetorical. The old sea captain had an uncanny knack for appearing in the most unlikely of places along the eastern seaboard where he regularly came to port. Why the man was at all interested in the trial, however, remained a mystery.

"I was there," he murmured, then let out a long sigh. "I was hoping I wouldn't have to do this, but I made a promise I'm bound to keep, which is why I was there for the verdict tonight. Given the sustained interest in the good minister and his daughter, I don't believe I have any choice but to agree that you should return to your newspaper work and do exactly as Clifford asked you to do — find Ruth Livingstone before any other reporter does."

"You do?" Jake replied, nearly choking on his own surprise. He had no idea how Grant's promise to someone had anything to do with Rev. Livingstone's trial or his daughter, Ruth, for that matter. But he was more confused by the man's abrupt change of mind about Jake's future plans.

His confusion mounted when the man pushed himself away from the table, stood up, and motioned for Jake to do the same. "Pack up your things and be back here in half an hour. Don't forget your tools. And don't argue. There isn't much time," his companion urged. He then lowered his voice to a whisper, even though there was not a soul around who could hear them. "If you're serious about wanting to find Ruth Livingstone, I believe I can get you close enough to find out what you need to know," he said, holding up his hand to keep Jake silent. "All I'm prepared to say right now is that our interests, at least for the next few weeks, seem to overlap. Several days before Reverend Livingstone was arrested, I delivered a small wooden chest for him to Mrs. Elias Garner in Toms River, New Jersey. If you go there, you should learn all you need to know."

Jake shook his head, as if he could shake off his confusion. "You want me to go? As a reporter?"

"Not as the reporter, Ashton Tripp. Not entirely," he said quickly. "Jake, I need you to go there because you're the only reporter I know with the strength of character and sense of righteousness that will help me to keep my promise to an old friend. On one condition," he added sternly.

Jake nodded. "Name it."

"You have to promise me that you won't give your brother access to what you learn about that young woman or her father, including anything contained within that wooden chest — anything at all — until you speak to me first."

"Agreed," Jake whispered without a moment's hesitation and then hurriedly followed Capt. James Grant out of the tavern.

SEVEN

Toms River

Ruth peeked down at Lily, saw her sucking on her fingers, heard the toddler's gentle, rhythmic breathing, and smiled.

She was not certain if Lily was sleeping more soundly these past two weeks because she was sleeping back in the trundle bed or because she had two new molars. All that mattered now was that the little girl slept peacefully through the night, giving Ruth some much-needed rest. Anxious to welcome the morning, she quickly slipped into a work gown, but carried her boots and a light shawl with her.

Once she was in the hallway and had the door to her room shut, she eased past the door to the Garners' bedroom and smiled again. From the moment she and Lily had arrived, this couple had offered nothing but love and acceptance to her, in spite of the life they thought Ruth had led before coming here. And they had completely accepted Lily, a child born out of wedlock to a prostitute, a child even many strong believers would judge harshly because of the circumstances of her birth.

When she reached the back staircase, Ruth opened the door, sat down on the top step, and donned the old boots Phanaby had given to her. Once she picked up the canvas bag she had left beneath the window next to the door, she slipped out into the alley behind the two-story clapboard structure and closed the back door. Greeted by spring morning air and the fresh scents of pine and musky earth and river, she took several long, deep, relaxing breaths before she slid the handle of the canvas bag over her shoulder.

She quickly wrapped her shawl around her shoulders before carefully making her way down the alley that separated the buildings and outbuildings planted along Water Street and the wild grasses and stands of pine trees that hugged the northern bank of the Toms River.

The sun was threatening to break across the horizon now, directly behind her to the east. With the world bathed in soft, gray light, she reached Main Street, which had yet to welcome the traffic of a new day.

She stopped to shift the strap of the canvas bag that was digging into her shoulder, and she looked around to see if anyone was out and about. As usual, the stable directly ahead lay dark and quiet, although it would soon burst with activity as travelers staying at the inn arose and sent for their horses and wagons. To her right, the planked sidewalks that ran on either side of the main thoroughfare in front of a variety of buildings were empty.

It would be a few hours before storekeepers made ready for another day of commerce. Their wives, however, would rise to prepare breakfast soon, adding soft light and fragrant aromas to the village. Nearby farmers and others who harvested the bounty of the pinelands that surrounded the village would not arrive until midday. By early afternoon, packet ships would arrive carrying cargo that would include a fresh set of city newspapers she was anxious to read for news of her father's trial. Once all the cargo was unloaded, local wares would be loaded onto the packet ships that would return to New York City the next morning.

She was not certain about the schedule for the stagecoach or even whether it would travel through here today. If it did, she hoped that none of the passengers on board would be reporters who had the village of Toms River as their final destination in their search for Rev. Livingstone's daughter.

Satisfied when she finally had the canvas bag in place that she could proceed alone and unnoticed, she turned left and crossed the bridge to get to the south side of the river. Although the day promised to be fair, a strong easterly breeze blew across the river, capping brackish waves with white foam, and she tightened her shawl around her shoulders.

She stopped when she reached the middle of the bridge to finish her morning prayers, a new ritual that seemed to make it easier for her to pray, despite the uncertainty of her father's trial and her own future. After she folded her hands and rested them on the wooden railing, she raised her face to the heavens and closed her eyes. As the breeze caressed her face, she acknowledged that if she had to be anywhere other than home, she was grateful that He had brought her here to this place and to this particular couple's home.

Because Phanaby and Elias Garner were such faithful followers of the Word and solid members of the community, most of the villagers here had accepted her. No one had ever questioned that she was exactly what she pretended to be: a young widow with a little girl to raise on her own.

Most simply offered their friendship and understanding. She did not know whether it was out of respect or pity, but they had never asked her about where she had lived before or how her husband had died, beyond the brief explanations either Phanaby or Elias had offered to them before she had even arrived: Ruth's husband, Martin, had owned a small stationery store in New York City, but was heavily in debt. After his unexpected death due to some unnamed illness, she only lasted a year on her own until it was necessary for her to turn to distant relatives for help.

Ruth sighed, bowed her head, and tried again to open her heart. "Heavenly Father, I come to you again this morning to praise your wisdom and to ask you to help me," she whispered.

Unbidden, tears welled, and she paused to blink them away and swallow the lump in her throat. "I don't understand why you would let my father suffer so cruelly," she murmured. "I don't understand why you chose me to protect Lily when I have to learn so much about caring for such a young child. Or why my burden has to get even harder now that reporters are trying to find me, which only places Lily at even more risk of being discovered. Please, Father. Help me to understand. Help me to be more patient. And please touch the hearts of the jurors, that they might truly believe in my father's innocence and set him free to continue the work he has been doing in your name so we can be together again very soon. Amen," she whispered and opened her eyes.

Less than a heartbeat later, she closed her eyes again for just a moment. "I forgot to ask you earlier to bless Phanaby for agreeing to take care of Lily until breakfast each day and giving me a very special place to spend that time. Amen," she finished before the first hint of golden light burst through the shadowed horizon.

Her heart began to race with anticipation once she reached the other side of the bridge. She turned down a narrow, sandy path that hugged the shoreline on the south side of the river, which had yet to develop as the village had done. She slowed her pace and meandered her way between the low vegetation that flourished along the river's edge and a forest of cedar and pine that extended west for miles.

From here she had an unobstructed view of the series of stately clapboard homes on the opposite side of the river, just below the apothecary, where many of the local ship captains lived with their families when they were not at sea. She had not actually seen Capt. Grant since he had brought her here, but she had seen his ship, the *Sheller*, anchored in the river or being unloaded at the end of Dock Street. By listening carefully to snippets of gossip when she had gone into the village with Phanaby, she had learned that he was a confirmed bachelor who called his ship his home, and that he sailed between here and a number of coastal cities as far north as Boston and as far south as Charleston.

She stopped for a moment and scanned the river, but since all the ships anchored there had dropped their sails, she could not be sure if the *Sheller* was among them. She did not know if Grant was part of her father's network, or if any of the other towns or villages on his route had become home to the fallen angels who had started new lives. She suspected he was simply one of many sea captains who carried her father's precious cargo simply for the money they earned.

Choking back the fear that her father's life and his ministry might soon end if he was wrongly convicted, she hurried along to the one place that gave her any sense of hope, as well as privacy. She finally rounded the bend and spotted the finger of land she now claimed as her own, and her smile stretched into an ear-to-ear grin when she approached the very place where Jane Canfield's flower garden had once flourished. She set down her heavy canvas bag and rotated her shoulder to ease out a kink before tackling today's work to get the earth ready to receive plants that would bloom with color again — at least she hoped. The garden itself had surrendered to weeds many years ago. Ruth had spent two hours here every morning for the past week, ripping out anything and everything that had taken root.

She stared at the rocks peeking through the broken earth and sighed. Although the soil was dark and moist with promise, it also contained a heavy crop of rocks that needed to be cleared before she could plant anything at all. Ruth assumed that the rocks must have bordered the garden at one time, but since many were scorched, it appeared that someone at another time had used them to provide a bed for an open fire.

Still, she was not going to let anything, including a little hard work, keep her from developing this garden into a private sanctuary where she could be alone with her thoughts and forget for a time the future of her father and the disturbing news that reporters were seeking to find her.

She leaned back on her haunches to rest her arms. According to Phanaby, the nearest family lived on a ranch a good four miles downriver. Ruth had caught a glimpse of their cattle grazing on wild salt grass, but she had never seen anyone tending to them, which meant that this little piece of land was hers and hers alone to enjoy for as long as she lived here in the village.

Completely at ease with her isolation, if not ecstatic, she removed her shawl to make it easier to work. She neatly folded it and set it on top of a patch of clover a good bit away from the garden and opened the canvas sack. She secured a pair of old gloves Phanaby had given her and put them on, happy to have them despite the fact they were too big for her. After glancing at the rocks one more time, she chose a small, iron garden pick as her first weapon of choice from the tools Phanaby had loaned to her.

The first rock she attempted to remove was so stubborn she gave up trying and tackled a smaller one, which gave up its hold on the earth but tore a small hole in the palm of one of her gloves in the process.

"Why?" she asked, gritting her teeth as she struggled to remove the next rock. "Why does everything I want to do have to be so hard? Can't you help me do this?" she grumbled, hoping God might just this once take mercy on her.

By the time she finished struggling seven rocks from the ground, she had also managed to berate God for every trouble He had sent her way lately, starting with the accusations against her father that had resulted in his arrest.

Disgusted with herself for losing whatever grace she had received during her morning prayers, she squinted as she wiped away a band of perspiration on her forehead. Now that the sun was much brighter, she realized she had forgotten her bonnet again. Blinking back tears of frustration that added more exhaustion to both her body and her spirit, she sniffled, but it was the strong smell of fire, far too close to dismiss, which had her quickly scrambling to her feet.

Heart racing, she whirled about, looking for the source of the fire. When she noticed the smoke swirling up from the chimney in the abandoned Canfield cabin, only yards away from her garden sanctuary, her heart sank down to the soles of her feet and stayed there.

Someone had moved into that vacant cabin.

An overwhelming sense of disappointment flooded her body, and her heart started to pound when she heard someone open the cabin door. Her disappointment flashed straight to annoyance, which lingered there for a moment. Clenching her fists, she squared her shoulders and tilted her chin up defiantly, yet she had no right to be annoyed, let alone claim an entire finger of land as her own.

When she spied the figure of a man approaching, however, she instinctively took a step back. He was too far away to be able to distinguish his features, but he appeared to be a very old man who was wearing well-worn denim coveralls and a yellowed shirt. Leaning heavily on a makeshift cane, his shoulders were rounded, if not hunched. Even though he stopped every few steps, as if he needed to garner up enough energy to take a few more, he exuded a level of annoyance, if not outright anger, that made her heart pound even harder.

EIGHT

Jake paused when he was halfway through the copse of young pine and cedar trees and feigned the need to stop to get enough energy to continue walking. He had been working so feverishly for the past few weeks, grabbing only a bit of sleep here and there, he almost did not mind using the cane he had fashioned by his own hand out of a twisted tree limb late last night.

Because he knew and trusted Capt. Grant, he had come here to Toms River. It didn't take long to learn from village gossip that a young woman had arrived only days after Grant delivered that wooden chest to Mrs. Garner and had moved in with the family — a woman he believed could very well be Ruth Livingstone.

Unfortunately, Jake was still too unsure of his own abilities as a reporter to completely trust his own instincts. He was too far away from her now to see if she matched the description his brother had compiled for him from a number of sources to know if he had made a crucial mistake and wasted precious time by waiting several days before trying to actually meet her.

Shadowed by the canopy of foliage overhead, he coughed and rounded his back a bit to give evidence of the ruse he'd devised for his temporary identity as Jake Spencer. He observed the wisp of a woman, who was standing near a pile of rocks he had seen her struggle from the ground this morning. He had been encouraged to see that she was petite in size, which seemed about right, although the dark blue gown she wore hung a bit from her frame, as if she had recently lost some weight. Her dark wavy hair was long and styled quite simply, however, just as he had expected it to be. Still, he was far from satisfied that this young woman was the one that every daily newspaper in New York City had sent their best reporters to find.

He resumed his painfully slow progress down the rocky path toward her. Step after careful step, ever mindful of the image he needed to project, he kept his gaze locked with hers while he mentally sorted through the information he had memorized about the elusive minister's daughter.

According to all accounts, she was a shy, soft-spoken, reserved young woman who had only started keeping house for her infamous father five or six years ago, replacing a long series of housekeepers who had helped the young widower raise his infant daughter. While he devoted his time to the needs of the city's fallen angels, she lived far from the controversy surrounding her father; indeed, from everything he had read, the minister had never allowed her to actively participate in his work at all.

Yet the more he closed the distance between the two of them, the more he worried that Capt. Grant might have sent him here on a fool's errand, designed solely to keep Jake from returning to work in the city. Even if this young woman, known locally as Widow Malloy, matched the description he had been given of Ruth Livingstone, he could not disregard the existence of the young child she claimed was hers, a claim he was not able to prove or disprove. The woman he was approaching looked very annoyed, if not defiant.

He was ready to turn back, admit he had made a costly mistake by coming here, and return to New York City on the morning tide to investigate there further, when she relaxed her stance and smiled sweetly at him.

"Now look at you," he murmured under his breath. Heartened and intrigued by her transformation into the shy young woman he expected to find, he also found the freckles on her cheekbones uncommonly appealing. Fully confident now that he had chosen the right ruse to penetrate whatever shield she chose to hide her real identity, he had to remind himself not to rush forward and instead hold steady to the persona he had adopted.

He kept his pace slow until he finally stepped out from the shadows into the full glare of the sun, only to see the woman undergo yet another transformation. Although she nervously twisted her hands together, her shoulders snapped back as if someone had reminded her that she had a backbone. Her tentative smile drooped into a frown of disappointment that almost instantly tightened into disapproval, giving him just a hint of the rather annoyed woman she had been only moments ago.

When her gaze finally lit with surprise, he immediately pressed his advantage. Leaning his full weight on the cane, he frowned. "I believe you're trespassing. Please leave," he said firmly, hoping his words sounded harsh enough to get her full attention, but not gruff enough to actually frighten her into leaving.

"Y-you're not old at all. Y-you're actually quite y-young," she stammered, as if she could not believe her own eyes.

"And you're still trespassing. Please leave," he repeated.

He watched her pale gray eyes darken with the same embarrassment that turned her cheeks bright pink. "I was told the Canfields abandoned this property years ago and that no one lived here."

He cocked a brow. "At best, you've been misinformed, which proves to be decidedly unfortunate today for me."

"And for me as well," she murmured so softly he almost missed hearing her.

"I expected the news that I'd rented the property for the next several months would spread rather quickly in a village that wasn't even large enough to warrant being called a town. I came here specifically to be alone while I finish recuperating. With some privacy — which I will not have if you venture back here again and which I most assuredly will not have if others follow you," he said and winced for effect. "Now if you'll excuse me, I need to get back to the cabin so I can rest, which is exactly what I would have been doing right now if you hadn't shown up here."

He paused, looked down at the rocks she had set into a pile, and shook his head. "I can't even begin to fathom why you'd be harvesting such ordinary rocks, but I'm quite certain you'll be able to find what you need elsewhere."

After drawing in a long breath, he turned around to walk back to the cabin. He took several slow steps, but she did not even try to argue that his assumption that she was looking for rocks was completely ridiculous. He was disappointed, more with his own inability to lure her into a prolonged conversation than he was with her for having far less backbone than she needed if she expected to outwit the many reporters looking for her.

Ruth held very, very still. It just was not fair that she would have to give up the one place she hoped to call her own. Not fair at all. Resentment that God would allow her private sanctuary to be taken away from her tugged yet again at her troubled spirit.

She quickly reassessed her situation and focused her gaze on the man who was struggling to get back to the cabin. He was not the elderly man she had first assumed him to be. In point of fact, he was probably only a few years older than she was. The sun highlighted his dark auburn hair, which he wore pulled back into a queue, and his eyes were a deep shade of hazel. He was not a particularly tall man, but next to her slight frame, even a short man would look quite tall. He had a deep cleft in his chin that added a bit of impishness to his features, but he was definitely in no physical condition to pose any threat to her well-being.

Her father had always enjoyed robust health, but she had nursed him through enough minor illnesses to know that he found his weakened state to be an embarrassment that often displayed itself in gruff words and complaints he later regretted and tried to assuage with a host of apologies.

Hopeful that the man who was walking so painfully away from her was no different and that she might be able to forge some sort of compromise that would allow them both the privacy they desired, she hurried forward and easily closed the short distance he had put between them. "I'm not certain what folks do wherever it is that you come from, but I wasn't harvesting rocks," she offered, following only a few paces behind him.

He ignored her and kept walking.

"No one harvests rocks. They harvest crops, of course, but I doubt anyone would ever consider rocks to be a crop. They're quite a nuisance, actually, and I had to work very hard just to remove a few of them this morning. See? I even tore one of my gloves," she offered and held out her hand, hoping he would turn around to see it.

Again, no response from him as he entered the shaded area beneath the trees where she had first seen him.

Frustrated, she refused to give up until she had prompted him to acknowledge the fact that she was walking right behind him, instead of acting like she had simply evaporated when he had dismissed her. "I was trying to clear the rocks from the soil so I could replant the garden that once grew here. I'm told Jane Canfield grew the prettiest flowers in the village."

"Well, she doesn't live here anymore. I do, and I'm quite certain I've no need for flowers," he grumbled, without bothering to stop and turn around so they would be able to have a normal, face-to-face conversation.

"Perhaps if you would stop, for just a moment, we might —" She swallowed the rest of her words and charged forward when the poor man stumbled and dropped his cane. "Here. Let me help you."

When his hand gripped her shoulder, she planted her feet in order to bear some of his weight without losing her own balance. Grimacing, he held onto her long enough to regain solid footing before he let go. "Thank you," he offered, although he kept his gaze averted, no doubt embarrassed that he'd needed to accept her help.

She took a step back after handing his cane back to him and nodded. "You're welcome. Perhaps . . . perhaps your decision to live here alone, without anyone to help you, was a mistake. I could help you," she offered, voicing the idea before she had quite thought it through herself.

He snorted. "The next time I stumble over my own two feet, I'd rather not have to worry about whether or not I'll snap you in two if I lean on you too hard. I'll manage on my own, thank you."

"You're probably right in that regard, but I could help you in other ways. Assuming we could come to some sort of arrangement that would let me tend to my garden, that is."

He cocked a brow. "I already told you. I don't need any flowers."

"Yes, you made that very clear," she said.

"I can also cook for myself, so if you're thinking that you might —"

"I wouldn't want to cook for you. I don't have the time," she insisted. "But I could bring you supplies from the village from time to time or take something into the village for you. Some mail, perhaps."

He let out a long sigh, but before he offered yet another objection, she continued. "You can barely manage to walk and —"

"Which is one of the consequences of falling off a roof and breaking your back, which I did several months ago. I assure you, lying abed, waiting to see if my back would heal well enough for me to even attempt to walk again was far worse," he said quietly. "Now that I can get around a bit, there's nothing I need more right now than a place where I can finish healing up with a bit of privacy, especially when my back decides to indulge in very painful spasms."

Her heart swelled, both with admiration for his courage to survive such a devastating injury and in hope they might find common ground. "One of the consequences of becoming a widow with no means of supporting a little one is having no choice but to move into a relative's home. And . . . and there's nothing I need more right now than a place where I can go for a few hours each morning for a bit of privacy," she replied.

He dropped his gaze.

For several painfully long moments she was afraid he would turn her down and send her away, but she was completely unprepared for the offer he finally made.

"Pile up the rocks you dig out, but leave them for me. I'll need some of them to repair the cabin hearth. There's a small shed behind the cabin. You can store your garden tools there and take or use anything else you might find in there. If I need something from the village, I'll leave a note for you in the shed. Otherwise I expect you to respect my privacy; in turn, I'll respect yours."

NINE

Ruth was more than halfway home before she realized she did not even know the name of the man now living in the abandoned cabin.

There was a bit of traffic up and down Main Street now, and she waited until several wagons passed by before she paused midway on the bridge and glanced downriver. Just beyond her garden on the narrow tip of land that jutted into the river, she could see smoke was still curling up from the top of the chimney that just barely poked over the treetops. The cabin itself, however, was completely hidden from view.

Ruth assumed the occupant was back inside and shook her head. "Poor man," she whispered, thankful that the heavy burdens that troubled her own life did not include a devastating injury like the one he had suffered.

"Poor man, middling or rich, to each a

natural body is sown, but to each, a spiritual body must be raised, for a home in Paradise awaits only the faithful."

Ruth looked up, recognized the man who was standing at the railing just a few yards away, and clapped her hand to her heart to keep it from leaping out of her chest. "Reverend Haines!"

He walked over to her, his eyes glistening. A good thirty years her senior, he was quite ordinary in looks, but he had been blessed with a deep, rich voice. "I'm so sorry, Ruth. I didn't mean to startle you. I was just sounding out an idea for a sermon. I thought you saw me standing here when you stopped."

She let out a long breath. "No, I didn't see you, which isn't your fault at all. I'm afraid this is the second time this morning that I've been too preoccupied to notice what's going on around me."

He smiled. "Since you were working again this morning in that garden you're trying to restore, I can only assume you met Jake Spencer at some point."

"You know about my garden?" she asked, and tucked Jake Spencer's name away for future reference.

Turning back to face the railing, he pointed downriver. "It's right over there.

Same spot as Jane Canfield's garden used to be."

"I suppose it's the talk of the village," she said, disappointment edging her words. She stared down at the water flowing beneath the bridge.

He chuckled. "No, not yet. It won't be long before folks take notice, though, unless those flowers you plant don't bloom until fall."

"How did you know that I — ?"

"I slip out here to the bridge early in the morning to think and pray a bit when I'm having trouble with my sermon, which is how I came to see you over there for the past few days. I'm usually gone by the time most folks even start their day and before you cross the bridge on your way home."

"But not today," she noted.

"Perhaps we're both a bit . . . unsettled," he offered.

When she looked over at him, she saw that he was leaning against the railing now and had dropped his gaze to stare at the waves below.

"My wife, Wealthy, passed six years ago tomorrow. As the date approaches, I'm afraid it's still a difficult time for me, even though I know with all my heart that she's safe and happy again now," he whispered.

Ruth was surprised by the pain that laced his words. Even this long after her death, he was still pining for his wife. She now understood why the childless widower had not remarried, although she could not explain why the women she had overheard gossiping about him did not know why their efforts to attract his attention had been in vain.

He cleared his throat and gazed at her. "Being strong of faith doesn't mean we don't grieve or question God's will. It just means we have to learn to trust Him more completely, which our faith helps us to do. I still struggle with trusting Him, just as everyone else does when their lives seem overburdened. Just as you must do. I know it's still difficult to accept your husband's recent passing and how hard it must be to be forced to accept the charity of relatives, but you still have your precious Lily to love and to hold and to remind you of the love you once shared with her father. God will help you. Trust in Him."

Trust in Him.

Those were the very last words her father had spoken to her in the final moments before she left with Capt. Grant. She missed him desperately. How she longed to hear the whisper of his voice when he said farewell each morning before he took to the streets. Or the sound of his boots when he cleared off the mud before he entered the house at the end of the day to share supper with her.

She fought the tears that threatened to spill down her cheeks by clenching her jaw and taking long, slow breaths of air, and her throat tightened with guilt. Deceiving others in the village about her true identity might be necessary, but deliberately withholding the truth from a minister, especially this very kind minister, was even more difficult.

Her conscience trembled, striking chords of need that tempted her to put her trust in him. But fear that she would somehow put her father's fate at risk forced her to keep her secret to herself. "Yes, yes I do have Lily and . . . and family to take us in. Your words are very comforting. I think perhaps," she added with sincerity, "you've found the heart of your message for this week's sermon after all, since trusting in God is quite often a challenge for any believer."

When Rev. Haines finally glanced over at her, his smile was back. "Perhaps I have. Thank you."

She cocked a brow.

"For listening to an old man's troubles

and reminding me to trust that He would guide me to the message He wanted me to share with the congregation this week," he explained, then offered his arm. "Come. I think it's time for both of us to get started on the rest of our day. Let me walk you partway home, at least. I promised Spinster Wyndam that I'd drop by for breakfast, and I don't want to be late."

She took his arm and they started across the bridge. "I don't think I've met her yet."

"She's been a bit sickly of late, but I have no doubt you'll meet her soon," he replied. "She's nearly eighty now. Lived all her life in the village, but still hasn't given up her favorite pastime, I'm afraid." He met her gaze of curiosity with a bit of a grimace. "She's a relentless matchmaker."

When Ruth stiffened, he patted her arm. "Don't worry. She's still too determined to make sure she introduces me to someone so I marry again to bother you, although that may change once she finally meets you. And in the meantime, you shouldn't worry about Mr. Spencer bothering you when you're working on your garden, either," he offered when they stopped at the end of the bridge.

She let go of his arm. "Oh?" she prompted, anxious to learn more about the man.

"He stopped by the parsonage yesterday to tell me that he wouldn't be attending services until he was more fully recovered. I'd like to think that he was sincere, but in truth, he was so adamant about how much he valued his privacy while he was recuperating, I think he was more interested in making certain I wouldn't drop by to invite him to join the congregation. He really doesn't seem to want any visitors at all."

"He does appear to be rather obsessed with his privacy," she seconded.

He raised a brow. "Then you've spoken with him."

She nodded and moistened her lips. "Just this morning. Briefly."

"I thought I spied you talking with someone, but you were just a bit too far away for me to know for certain. At least you now know that you won't have to worry about trying to find another place for your garden."

"But how would you know he agreed to let me — ?"

"I took the liberty of making certain he understood that you might need a bit of privacy yourself, and he should think long and hard before he tried to keep a poor young widow away from her garden."

"But why would you . . . I mean, I appreciate that you spoke up for me, but why would you do that?"

He grinned a bit sheepishly. "When I was first called to my ministry here many years ago, Jane Canfield always made certain there were flowers at Sunday services. I thought I might convince you to do the same."

"Of course . . . assuming I actually get to put some plants into the ground," she replied, but she felt guilty for not telling him that she planned to no longer be here when the plants actually had flowers in full bloom.

"Well, you don't have to worry about Mr. Spencer stopping you. Before he left the parsonage, he assured me that he wouldn't mind at all if you did your gardening there." He looked over her head for a moment and waved at someone on the other side of Main Street before glancing back at Ruth. "I'm sorry. I really do need to talk to Mr. Landrus now that he's spotted me. Would you mind awfully much if I left you here?"

"Not at all," she said.

While he crossed the street, she turned and clomped down the alley. "Jake Spencer, you're a miserable man. Just because you're in a bit of pain, that's no excuse for being so mean to me," she grumbled, frustrated

101

that she had practically begged him to let her return to her garden when he knew he had already promised Rev. Haines that she could.

When she remembered that he had only agreed to her request after she had promised to do errands for him, she stomped even faster. "You're more than miserable. You're a conniving, manipulating . . . ugh!" she cried, too annoyed to think clearly enough to find just the right words to describe him.

She slipped back into the storeroom and sat down on the bottom step of the staircase. "Poor man, indeed," she said, loosening her laces and tugging off her boots. "If I had any other place on this earth where I could find a piece of ground for a garden and some privacy, I wouldn't step one foot on that precious land in front of that cabin you rented. Not one." She grabbed her boots with one hand and the railing with another before she started up the stairs.

She had not climbed more than two steps before she had to slow her pace because the bottoms of her feet were so tender from the ill-fitting boots. She mounted two more steps, stopped abruptly, and groaned in frustration. She had left her garden tools in his shed, but to make matters even worse, she realized she had forgotten her shawl, which meant she had to go back and fetch it later.

"Mercy!" she exclaimed and grumbled her way up the rest of the steps. She eased the door at the top open and was barely in the hall before she caught the aroma of fried bacon. With her stomach growling, she stopped in her room only long enough to deposit the boots before hurrying down to the kitchen.

Phanaby met her in the hallway. "I thought I heard you come home," she said and handed Ruth several newspapers. "Amos Sloan sent these over special, just half an hour ago when the first ship at the docks was unloaded, because he was afraid once the news spread, he wouldn't be able to keep his wife from selling them at twice the price. Reverend Livingstone's trial is over, Ruth. It's finally over."

Trembling with joy and disbelief that the nightmare had finally ended, Ruth stared at the headline in the *Sun* for several long heartbeats and whispered it out loud: "Not guilty."

One by one, she scanned the headlines in the *Herald,* the *Transcript,* and the *Galaxy,* all of them dated several days ago, to make certain the verdict was the same in each newspaper before she remembered to breathe. Her heart fairly quivered with happiness, and with tears pouring down her cheeks, she finally looked up and met Phanaby's gaze.

Phanaby was crying now, too. "Reverend Livingstone's been acquitted! He's been acquitted! Now he can continue with his ministry so he can help other women like you," she managed and swiped at her tears. "Most folks won't be satisfied with this verdict, and they wouldn't understand why we are simply overjoyed," she cautioned, "but it's a blessing to be able to share this news with you here, in the privacy of our own home."

Ruth smiled through her tears and trembled with many emotions that wrapped her heart with a joy not even Phanaby or Elias could understand. They did not know that Rev. Livingstone was her beloved father.

Now his faith in God had been rewarded and he was free.

Now the whole world had to accept that he had been wrongly accused of a very horrific crime, and when she clipped these articles and added them to the ones she had cut out from the newspapers before, she would not have to fear there would be any more.

And now, one day very soon, she would finally be able to go home and reclaim the life she had left behind.

Praise God, she was going home!

TEN

Glancing down at the little girl she carried on one hip, Ruth smiled, noting that Lily had a wardrobe far finer than Ruth had ever owned. Lily looked like an angel this afternoon. Her pale blue frock was just a shade lighter than her eyes. The dainty embroidered daffodil that rested in the fabric right over her heart was nearly identical in color to the ringlets that framed her pudgy little cheeks, although most of her hair was hidden by a sweet little straw bonnet with butter yellow ribbons tied beneath her chin.

For once, the little imp was even acting like an angel while Ruth carried her up Water Street to complete a number of errands. Instead of constantly squirming and trying to climb down, Lily sat contentedly, chattering her usual gibberish while she played with the trim on the collar of Ruth's gown.

Ruth caught a glimpse of the two tiny

white scars on her wrist, and her smile deepened. Lily had not bitten her again, either, which was a relief since she did not know if she would ever have the courage to put Phanaby's advice into practice and bite Lily back.

When they reached Main Street, she set Lily down onto the planked sidewalk. "Hold still a moment," she urged and tugged at the hem of Lily's frock until it fell neatly again in gentle folds that reached the top of the toddler's shoes. "Now remember, you mustn't let go of my hand," she cautioned and folded her hand gently, but firmly, around Lily's tiny hand.

Lily looked up at her and smiled broadly enough to add a charming dimple to each cheek. "Lily good."

Ruth chuckled. "Yes, Lily is a good little girl," she replied, hoping this little charmer would remain on her best behavior until they got back home again. Ruth was careful to keep her strides short, and they made slow but steady progress together without Lily trying to yank free to toddle off on her own.

Unlike earlier in the day, Main Street was now noisy and bustling with activity at mid-morning. In between wagons loaded with swamp moss and cedar headed east toward

Dock Street, where their cargo would be loaded onto packet ships, she could see groups of shoppers hustling in and out of stores on either side of the street.

She nodded and waved to several women, along with their children, she had met at Sunday services and chuckled when Lily raised her free hand to wave, too. She was grateful none of the women stopped or crossed the street to chat, because she honestly could not remember any of their names.

When a farmer drove his cart so fast the wheels kicked up a cloud of dust, Ruth stopped and brushed herself off and watched with amusement while Lily imitated her actions. In all truth, ever since Phanaby had shown her the headlines in those newspapers a few hours ago, Ruth had been too overjoyed to mind much of anything, and she was actually looking forward to reading the entire articles after she put Lily down for her afternoon nap.

She did not tense when the stagecoach passed by, because she no longer had to worry that some traveler passing through the village might recognize her or that a reporter who was looking for her had just arrived. She did not mind stopping twice to re-tie the laces on Lily's shoes. She did not even cringe when she thought about running into Jake Spencer later when she went back to retrieve her shawl while Lily was napping.

For one very simple reason: The world around her was filled with joy that made her feel safe and secure again because her father had been acquitted. No one could possibly have any interest in her whereabouts now, and she knew it was only a matter of days before she would be going home.

"Home! Home!" Lily cried as she tugged and tugged on Ruth's hand, urging her to turn around. "Home!"

Unaware that she must have spoken some of her thoughts out loud, Ruth stopped in front of the butcher's shop and bent her knees to be at eye level with the little girl. "We're not going home yet. We have lots of errands to do, remember?" she said as she tucked an escaped curl back beneath the bonnet.

"Home," Lily whispered. "P'ease home."

The toddler's eyes darkened and pooled with tears, reminding Ruth of a summer sky that suddenly threatened rain. She wiped away the single tear that escaped and patted Lily's cheek. This little girl could not say more than a few intelligible words. If she could put words to the anguish that glistened in her eyes, Ruth had the distinct feeling she would tell Ruth that she wanted to go back to the only home she had ever known, too.

For the first time since she had taken charge of this little girl, Ruth also realized they shared another bond, a secret hidden from everyone else who lived here in the village. Both Ruth and Lily had lost their mothers at a very young age, and although Ruth did not remember the events surrounding her mother's death, she knew what it was like to be confused by the deep void in her life.

"We'll find you a new home soon, baby girl. I promise," Ruth whispered. Now that he was free again, she was certain her father would contact someone within his network of believers who would adopt Lily. She was sorely tempted to write to him and suggest the Garners, but she did not know how they would explain the fact that Ruth had abandoned the child to them.

More important, she had promised her father that she would not contact him under any circumstances, and she would not break that promise to him. Not now. Not when everything was unfolding exactly as he had told her it would.

"Patience, patience," she murmured,

hoisting the distressed child to her hip. "Let's see if Mrs. Sloan has any lemon sticks for you at the general store today, shall we?"

Rewarded with a smile, Ruth hugged the little girl close to her until a sharp nudge in the middle of her back caught her by such surprise she pitched forward. Instinctively, she wrapped her arms tightly around the toddler and took several small but frantic steps before she finally had her feet planted and Lily firmly on her hip again.

She swirled about, prepared to soundly berate whomever or whatever had bumped into her. Lily's squeals of delight at being tossed about, however, sweetened Ruth's annoyance before she even got a glimpse of the two elderly women standing directly in front of her. She did not recognize either of these women, but the look of shock on their faces was unmistakable.

Neither of the two plainly dressed women stood any taller than Ruth, but they carried enough girth between them to make it nearly impossible for anyone to pass by them without leaving the sidewalk and using the roadway.

The woman on the right, who wore the droopiest bonnet Ruth had ever seen, took the tattered umbrella hanging from one arm and poked her companion on the leg. "See what you did? You almost knocked over that fragile young thing and her baby."

"I did no such thing. You walked right into her," her companion replied and nudged her friend with her elbow before turning her attention to Ruth without bothering to push the spectacles hanging on the tip of her nose back into place. "I'm Widow Gertie Jones, and I hope you'll forgive my cousin for bumping you —"

"I'm Widow Lorelei Jones," her cousin blurted. "Our fathers were brothers. That's why we're cousins."

"We married brothers, too, which is why we have the same last name."

Lorelie glared at Gertie before looking back at Ruth again. "Which is neither here nor there at the moment, I suppose, but the fact of the matter is that I most surely did not walk into you and that sweet little piece of heaven you've got on your hip," she insisted. "My cousin did, and since she won't take responsibility for nearly knocking you off your feet and properly apologize, then I'll just have to do it for her, exactly like I've done for the past fifty-four years. She's terribly sorry, aren't you, Gertie," she said, without bothering to look at her cousin.

"I am sorry that you were so busy gossiping, you weren't paying a whit of attention to what you were doing, Lorelei. Otherwise you'd realize that you were the one who bumped into . . . What did you say your name was?" she asked, flitting her conversation away from her cousin and directing it to Ruth.

"She hasn't had the opportunity to tell us her name, Gertie, and I daresay the last thing the poor girl has on her mind right now is a proper introduction. And I wasn't gossiping at all. I was simply repeating what I read in the *Galaxy* about that minister who killed that poor degenerate soul and got away with it. It's a pity the good people of New York City couldn't find a jury willing to do its duty and send that man straight to the gallows instead of putting him back on the street so he can carve up another woman."

"I thought you said it was the *Sun,* but I could be mistaken. Not that it matters. All the newspapers said the same thing, more or less. Now, if you ask me —"

"Ruth. I'm Widow Ruth Malloy, and this is my daughter, Lily," Ruth blurted to keep both of them from saying anything else against her father.

Lily, for her part, seemed thoroughly

mesmerized by the whole encounter and sat quietly on Ruth's hip, with her head leaning against Ruth's shoulder and her gaze shifting from one woman to another as each spoke.

Two faces lit with recognition. Two pairs of eyes shimmered with pity, but it was Gertie who spoke first this time. "We'd heard you'd come to live with the Garners. We lost our husbands, too, but we were both quite a bit older than you are."

"I was forty-seven and Gertie was fifty-one. How old are you?"

"Twenty-two," she replied.

"We heard all about how your poor husband, Mark, died from that sudden illness and you had to close his stationery store in the city and how you lost everything and had to move here with your little baby to live with relatives you barely knew." Gertie held her spectacles farther up on her nose and clucked her lips. "You're a sweet baby, aren't you, Lily?"

Lorelei shook her head. "Matthew. Her husband's name wasn't Mark. It was Matthew."

"Actually, it was Martin," Ruth offered. "Now, if you'll excuse me, I have a few errands to run, and I need to get home in time to help with dinner." She turned and hurried off before either of the women started another convoluted conversation about who had bumped into her.

Ruth hurried into the butcher store, ordered the chicken Phanaby planned to roast tomorrow to celebrate news of Rev. Livingstone's acquittal, and went across the street to the general store. It took a moment for her eyes to adjust to the dimmer light inside the single-room establishment, and she walked past the two men sitting next to each other on stools, who were in the midst of a seemingly good-natured discussion.

Relieved that there were no other customers in the store, Ruth approached Mrs. Sloan, who was folding and refolding a single length of plaid fabric. After setting Lily down on the counter well beyond reach of anything, she put her hand on the child's lap to keep her from falling off. "When you're finished, would you please get these things for us?" she asked, laying the list Phanaby had made on the counter, along with a small canvas bag she had folded up in her pocket. "And I'd like a lemon stick for Lily, too," she added, which had Lily clapping and grinning from ear to ear. "Mine! Mine!"

Mrs. Sloan dropped the fabric onto the counter and pushed it toward Ruth. "I'm more than finished. In fact, you can have this piece for half price. I don't even want it in my shop. While you make up your mind, I'm going to get what you need and hide the scissors so Mr. Sloan won't be able to cut another length of fabric again," she snapped. She then yanked a lemon stick out of a glass jar, handed it to Lily, and charged away, scissors and list and canvas bag in hand.

Ruth fingered the fabric, considering whether there would be enough to make a pretty apron for Phanaby, while the conversation behind her heated up into an argument. Voices rose, making it impossible for her not to overhear the two men and to realize they were arguing about her father.

"He killed her! Sure as I'm sitting here, he killed her, but the jury didn't have the gumption to send that fiend to the gallows."

"He's a minister!"

A snort. "He's a man, just like you and me, 'cept we don't visit brothels late at night like he did. You can bet Reverend Haines wouldn't do any such thing."

A chuckle. "Reverend Haines wouldn't be too happy if he heard you even talkin' about placin' a bet."

Cringing, Ruth tapped her foot impatiently. Just when she wondered how much longer she could hold silent, Mrs. Sloan burst through the curtain carrying the canvas bag, which was now filled. "Everything Phanaby wanted is inside. You're taking the fabric, too?"

"I am. Thank you," Ruth replied, grateful that Mrs. Sloan's voice was loud enough to distract her from the men's conversation. Working quickly, she set Lily on her feet so she could finish her lemon stick before Ruth ended up with a gown that was as sticky as Lily's was becoming. She took Lily by her free hand, slid the handle of the bag over her wrist, and headed for the door.

Unfortunately, she had to walk even slower with the toddler to make certain she did not trip, and the men continued their argument without even acknowledging her or lowering their voices.

"They don't have a body, and until they find a body, I'll never believe he killed her."

"They'll find it, and when they do, there won't be a jury this side of heaven that won't convict him."

Confused by the turn of their argument, she hurried Lily along as fast as she dared.

"Did you read the same newspapers that I did? They're not even sure the girl's dead. She could be hiding out somewhere, and now that her father's been set free, she's bound to show up again."

"And there'll be a sketch of her on every newspaper the day she does. I hope she knows she's got a lot of explaining to do, especially if they find out she was hiding the evidence that would have convicted her father."

It was then Ruth realized they were talking about her.

Jake waited until midnight and slipped through the darkened village with only a meager sliver of moonlight to guide him. Once he reached the end of Dock Street, he climbed into a dinghy and rowed toward the ship anchored offshore.

The river was smooth tonight, with barely a wave, making his journey quick and easy. He boarded the ship, discussed the letter he had written to his brother with Capt. Grant, and returned to shore, fully satisfied that the man who had sent him here would deliver the letter as he had promised.

After returning the dinghy back where he had found it, he retraced his steps and worked his way back to the village. On a whim, he turned down the alley that ran behind several buildings at this end of Water Street and stopped when he reached the apothecary. All of the windows on the second floor, where the Widow Malloy lived with the family who had taken her in, were dark.

Somewhere behind one of those windows, the woman he had finally met today was sleeping. She was completely unaware that by this time tomorrow night, Clifford would already have acted on Jake's letter. Within days, he would send a reply that would either confirm that Martin Malloy had indeed operated a stationery story in the city before he died, leaving a widow and a young daughter who were now living with the Garners, or that Ruth Malloy was actually Ruth Livingstone.

He drew in a long breath, turned, and made his way back to his cabin, convinced that one way or another, his own future was also tied to the answers his brother would send back to him.

ELEVEN

"Don't touch that!"

Startled, Ruth dropped the miniature wooden chest back onto the dresser in the Garners' bedroom and whirled about.

Phanaby charged into the bedroom. "What do you think you're doing?" she snapped as she grabbed the wooden chest and held it close to her.

Cheeks burning, Ruth took several steps back from the dresser, perplexed by Phanaby's strident attitude. "I-I was just trying to dust your room before I put Lily to bed for her afternoon nap," she managed, although she was unable to keep some of the tears that had welled from trickling free.

Phanaby closed her eyes for a moment and drew several long breaths before meeting Ruth's teary gaze. "I'm sorry. I didn't mean to yell or frighten you," she said. "It's just that this chest holds a lot of sentimental meaning. I don't want anything to happen to it," she whispered as she placed it gently back on top of the dresser.

Mindful of Phanaby's treasured vase, which Lily had broken, Ruth swiped at her tears. "I understand. I'm sorry. I had no idea —"

"No, please. I'm the one who should apologize. I-I overreacted," Phanaby insisted and pressed a hand to her forehead. "I've been nursing a headache all day, but that's no excuse for the way I talked to you. Forgive me." She took hold of Ruth's hand.

Ruth managed a smile and squeezed Phanaby's hand. "Forgiven."

"Thank you. On top of taking care of Lily, you already do far too much around here as it is. Perhaps it might be best if you left cleaning our room to me," Phanaby urged.

"Of course. Speaking of Lily, I should probably get her settled down for her nap. A nap would probably help with your headache, too."

"You may be right. Come," Phanaby said as she urged Ruth out of the room. "I'd like to get a kiss from that little one before you put her to bed."

A short time later, Ruth laid Lily down in the bottom of the trundle bed and tucked a light blanket around her. "Sleep tight," she whispered and pressed a kiss to Lily's forehead.

Lily scrambled out from beneath the blanket and popped onto all fours before Ruth had taken a single step to leave. "Lily play!"

"Lily sleep," Ruth said gently, but firmly. "You can play when you wake up."

Rocking back and forth, Lily burst into exaggerated tears that Ruth had learned to recognize as a sign that the child was simply overtired. Rather than trying to reason with the single-minded toddler, she sat down on the edge of the bottom mattress, laid Lily down again, and covered her with the blanket. "That's a good babe," she whispered, and hummed softly, rubbing the small of her back until the toddler stopped crying and drifted off to asleep.

At moments like this, when Lily was lying asleep next to her, so tiny and innocent and so very vulnerable, the desire to protect her and keep her safe was so strong and overwhelming, Ruth wondered how she was going to give this precious baby away for perfect strangers to raise.

With her own eyes beginning to droop and her head nodding forward, Ruth wanted nothing more than to crawl onto her own mattress, just above Lily's, fall asleep, and stay there until she had gotten word from her father that it was safe to come home.

Instead, she shook off her weariness and tiptoed out of the room, hoping she would find the energy to finally start working on the apron she wanted to make for Phanaby.

Phanaby was waiting for her in the hallway but held silent until Ruth had eased the bedroom door shut again. "Here. Take off the one you're wearing and put this one on," she whispered, holding a large white apron like the one Elias always wore when he was working downstairs in his shop.

Ruth hesitated for a moment before she untied the apron she was wearing. "I'll try not to stain this one as badly," she said as she exchanged aprons with the woman.

Chuckling, Phanaby rolled the soiled apron into a ball. "I'll set this one to soak, but I wouldn't worry overmuch about getting any stains on that one. Elias's customers rarely spill anything on him, they don't usually throw anything at him, and they never scream at him, either," she teased.

Ruth had the apron strings nearly tied together, but instantly dropped her hands back to her side. "H-his customers?" she sputtered. "Are you trying to tell me that I'm supposed to go downstairs and —"

"I was hoping you would, so I could get a

bit of a nap myself so I don't snap at you or anyone else today. If you'd rather not . . ."

"No. I'll do it, but I-I'm just not certain that I'll be able to —"

"Don't work yourself into a stew," Phanaby cautioned, walking around Ruth and tying the apron strings snugly at her waist. "It's been three days since you came home all flustered and upset by what those old men at the general store were arguing about. You can't stop people from gossiping about Reverend Livingstone's trial or that poor daughter of his who's gone missing, any more than you can convince men that they're twice as guilty of spreading gossip as women are. You can't keep yourself up here forever, either, and don't try to tell me you're not hiding out. You haven't even gone back to your garden, which means the shawl you left behind is probably ruined. And you did promise Elias that you'd help out a bit when he needed you, as I recall."

"I did promise to help, but I was thinking I could tidy up the storeroom. I never thought he'd want me to help him with customers."

Phanaby took her by the elbow and guided her down the hallway to the staircase. "Elias just got in a large shipment of patent medicines. He needs to check each crate to

124

make certain none of the bottles or jars cracked or broke open before he stacks the crates in the storeroom. He can't do that very easily if he has to run back and forth between the storeroom and the shop. Don't worry about Lily. I'll keep an ear out for her while you're downstairs."

Ruth took a long breath and started down the staircase.

"Ruth?"

She held onto the railing and looked back over her shoulder.

"Remember, you aren't the only one whose heart is aching because of the terrible things reporters write in those newspaper articles about Reverend Livingstone," Phanaby offered, her gaze troubled.

"I'll try," Ruth whispered, but her heart was not just aching. Her heart was truly breaking because she could not speak out to defend him or tell anyone here that she was proud to be his daughter.

An hour after she had taken Mr. Garner's place in the apothecary, Ruth had given two customers the remedies that had been prepared and set aside for them, dusted the display in the front window, and wiped down the entire length of the counter.

When she heard the front door open, she

125

looked up into the mirror and stiffened when she recognized the man who entered the apothecary. She dropped her gaze for a moment, then turned around after she forced her lips into a smile.

The middle-aged man was wearing the same patched overalls and plaid shirt he had been wearing several days ago when she had seen him arguing with another man in the general store, and he shuffled over to the counter. "You must be that new widow lady moved to the village. I heard you were living here," he said, making it rather obvious that he had been so busy arguing with his friend that he had not taken notice of her. "Where's Elias?" he asked.

"Mr. Garner is working in the storeroom," she replied. "Would you like me to fetch him for you?"

He did not bother to answer her; instead, he leaned over the counter and pointed to one of the two brown parcels lying there. "Name's Toby. Jedediah Toby, just like it says right there. No need to fetch him," he said as he reached over and grabbed the parcel. "I'll settle up with Elias at the end of the month." He tucked the parcel inside his pocket.

"I'll be sure to tell him," she offered, anxious to get back to her work.

126

Mr. Toby, however, seemed rather content to stay and chat. "Heard you come here all the way from New York City with your baby."

"Yes, I did."

"Suppose you read all about that minister long before his trial, then." He leaned closer, his gaze sparkling with curiosity. "Is it true he actually went into them brothels and visited with those harlots in their bedrooms, just like he did the night he killed that woman? The newspapers said —"

"I'm afraid I wouldn't know anything about that. I was too distressed and I didn't have any free time to read any newspapers. I was struggling to provide for my daughter after my dear, sweet husband died so suddenly." She brought her apron to her face to dab at her eyes before he noted the flash of annoyance that made her cheeks burn.

"Why, look who's here, Lorelei! It's that sweet young woman we bumped into on the sidewalk the other day."

" 'We' didn't bump into her, Gertie. You did, but it certainly is convenient for us that I spied you in here through the window, Mr. Toby," her cousin replied as they approached the counter. "Since you didn't show up at the cottage to fix that broken window like you promised, Mrs. Jensen helped us to find someone else. He did a fine job of repairing her kitchen steps, so you needn't bother. We've hired him instead."

Ruth stared at the two women who had slipped into the shop so quietly, she had not even heard them. Apparently, neither had Mr. Toby, who spun around so fast he nearly lost his balance. She flushed with relief that someone had interrupted the difficult conversation she had been having with the man, even if that someone turned out to be the Jones cousins. Since the focus of their interest had shifted to Mr. Toby, she almost did not care that she had no escape from their banter, although she sent up a silent prayer that Elias would hear them and intervene.

The man sidestepped the counter and started for the door, walking in a wide arc to get around the two women. "I've been feelin' poorly. . . ."

"From all we've heard, you've been plopping yourself down at the general store instead of working," Gertie argued, her spectacles hanging precariously from the tip of her nose. "And the next time we need something fixed, we won't be bothering you. We'll be asking Jake Spencer to help us again."

Lorelei huffed so hard the brim on her

sorry bonnet flopped up and down. "He won't take a single coin from us, either. He knows how hard it is for widows like us to get by, unlike some other folks who take advantage."

Mr. Toby didn't respond. He just shuffled past them and hurried out the door.

As the women approached the counter, bantering back and forth with each other about their handsome new handyman and his easygoing nature, Ruth had a hard time believing the man they were talking about was the gruff, cranky, ill man she had met several days ago. "Good afternoon, ladies. Did . . . did I hear you say the man who helped you was Jake Spencer?" she asked.

Gertie sighed and a faint blush stained her sunken cheeks. "Lovely man. Lovelier smile. Makes me wish I were just a few years younger. I'd invite Mr. Spencer to supper tomorrow night if you hadn't put up such a fuss. I still might do just that."

Lorelei waved at her cousin's arm, giving her a playful reprimand. "You'll do no such thing. Even a child could see that Mr. Spencer is sufferin' quite a bit with that back of his that's still healin'. Since he already promised to repaint Mrs. Walker's shutters tomorrow morning, I doubt he'll be up to walking into the village twice in one day," she quipped, without answering Ruth's question any more directly than her cousin had done.

Simultaneously, they paused and looked at Ruth. "Do you know him, too?" they asked in unison, as if they finally realized she was still standing there.

"Yes, I believe we've met," she replied, curious to know why the man she had encountered, who had been so preoccupied with his privacy that he had accused her of trespassing, had apparently been leaving his cabin to go into the village to work. How could he possibly have done any work as a handyman at all when he was hardly able to walk and needed to lean on a cane just to keep his balance?

Unless Jake Spencer was not the man he had appeared to be.

The very thought sent chills coursing up and down the length of her backbone as possibilities clashed against one another in her mind. Perhaps he had just been having a particularly difficult time of it the morning they met. On the other hand, he may have exaggerated the state of his health and demanded privacy because he had something in that cabin he did not want anyone else to see.

Or he could be a reporter who had somehow tracked her here, which made little sense since he had practically tossed her off the property he had rented and had only reluctantly agreed to allow her to return.

Ruth realized now that she had made a mistake by hiding upstairs for the past three days. But she had no time to waste on fear or self-indulgent pity or paranoia. She could panic and assume the worse — that the man had come here looking for her — in which case she would have to pack, take Lily, and disappear this very night. Or she could remain calm and rational, dismiss Jake Spencer as a minor annoyance, and return to the everyday rhythm of her life here for just another day or two until her father sent word that his plans for their future were finally in place.

She chose the latter course of action, and almost immediately a plan took shape in her mind.

TWELVE

"Finally!"

Jake quickly turned off the sandy trail and disappeared into the thick of the forest the moment he spied the young Widow Ruth Malloy crossing the bridge at the head of the river. From his hidden vantage point, he waited until she turned down the path that led to the garden she had ignored for the past three days before tucking the crook of the cane over his arm. He then hurried back to his cabin, surprised that she was returning in late afternoon rather than at the break of day as had been her custom.

And that she was not alone.

Keeping the shore of the river in view, he worked his way through scrub pines, stands of fragrant cedar trees that towered over him, and wild mountain laurel that had burst into bloom just yesterday. He was nearly out of breath by the time he reached the cabin and rushed inside.

Caught off guard and unprepared, he gathered up a few of the newspapers lying on top of the stack on the floor near the hearth. He grabbed the single straight chair sitting by the front window and carried everything outside. He set the chair into place facing the river, exactly where he had planned to put it tomorrow morning, hung his cane on the back of the chair, and plopped down into the seat.

With his heart pounding with anticipation, he had a newspaper in his hands and had started reading just in time to hear her voice as she approached the bend in the path behind him.

"It's not much farther. There. Now take my hand and hold tight. Once we get there, you'll be able to play, just like I promised."

Several moments later, he heard a flurry of small footsteps followed by heavier ones. "Come back here. Lily, no! You mustn't run off. Lily!"

He nearly choked on the chuckle he was trying to swallow when a tiny pair of hands smashed the newspaper he was holding into his chest, and a pair of big blue eyes twinkling with a bushel of mischief stared up at him. Ribbons taut at the base of her throat kept the bonnet the little girl was wearing from falling to the ground, and late afternoon sun shined brightly on the mass of blond hair that curled around her face.

"Play," she squealed and tore off a corner of the newspaper when he tried to keep her from grabbing the newspaper away from him. His cane slipped off the chair and fell to the ground without distracting her.

Engaged in a tug of war with the impulsive little girl, he decided she was definitely not as delicate or fragile as her name implied. He stiffened, waiting for her mother to intervene, but Lily proceeded to tug at his hands with impunity. "Play! Lily play!"

He snorted. "Have you no control over your child? Or did you bring her here to subject me to her tantrum?"

His question brought Ruth to the child's side, but she made no effort to stop Lily or pull her away. "She's not having a tantrum. She's simply excited. I assure you, if you knew Lily as well as I do, you'd know the difference," she explained. Her smile was as sweet as her voice, and she simply stood there as if she were completely oblivious to his distress or her child's ill-behavior.

"I have no desire to know her at all, but I was hoping for a bit of peace this afternoon to enjoy my newspaper."

"In the middle of my garden?" She turned a bit and waved her hand in frustration, which simmered in the depths of her eyes. "You haven't got enough room outside? Or inside your cabin? You had to sit here?"

He glanced down at the ground, shrugged, and tried not to look smug. "This bit of ragged soil hardly constitutes a garden. You haven't returned to work on it, which implied you'd given up on the idea of planting anything here at all, even though I carried away those rocks you dug out, exactly as I promised I'd do," he argued, glancing down for a moment at the toddler, who was still tugging on his hands. He wondered how a child so small could be that strong.

He looked back up at the woman who claimed to be her mother, just in time to see the subtle curl of her lips. Clearly, she would have tossed one of the rocks at him if she'd had the chance. He lowered his hands, prepared to handle the child himself at this point, when a sharp pain in his thumb shot straight up his arm.

Instinctively, he dropped the newspaper, lowered his gaze, saw that Lily had her little mouth locked on his thumb, and pulled his throbbing hand away, all in the space of a single heartbeat. "Madam! Please! Now will you control this . . . this little —"

"Lily! No biting!" Ruth yanked Lily away and up into her arms while struggling to keep the screaming child from scrambling down again.

He did not think he had ever seen a woman's face change from pure sweetness to absolute horror in a blink of an eye, but he was absolutely certain he had never heard a child's scream as shrill as the one that exploded from that little girl's mouth. "I'm fine. Just . . . just get her to be quiet. See? There's no harm done," he added.

When he lifted his hand up to get the child's attention, he noted with surprise that her eyes were crystal clear. There was not a single tear on her face, not anywhere, but her cheeks were flaming red.

Lily, however, ignored him, and Ruth did the same, choosing instead to walk the child over to a small patch of grass several yards away where she sat her down. Kneeling beside her, she bent her face so low and so close to Lily's, he was half afraid she was going to bite the child herself. She hesitated for a moment, then sat back on her haunches and waited until the child stopped screaming before saying a word. "You're a good little girl, Lily, but you cannot ever, ever bite anyone. Ever."

"Lily play!" the little girl cried and tried to scamper back to her feet, but her mother gently forced her to sit back down again.

"No. When you bite someone, you cannot play. You must sit here until I tell you to get up, and if you misbehave again, I'm going to take you straight home."

Surprisingly, the little girl stayed put as her mother walked back to him, pulling out several blades of grass and playing with them. "I'm so sorry. She hasn't bitten anyone for weeks, and I thought perhaps she'd gotten past that bad habit."

"Obviously not." He shook his hand, hoping he could shake away the throbbing pain in his thumb. He would have stood up to walk it off, but remaining seated gave him the advantage of being eye to eye with the petite woman.

Ruth cringed, but took his hand in hers to study the bite. "I know how much this hurts, but at least she didn't break the skin."

Unnerved by how soft her fingers felt against his own, he pulled his hand away. "I assume that's an observation based on personal experience."

She groaned. "I'm afraid it is," she admitted as a blush stole across her face and accented the wisp of freckles resting on the crest of her cheeks. Bending down, she picked up the tattered newspaper, smoothed the pages, and handed them back to him. "I'm sorry your newspaper is so rumpled, although I doubt there's much worth reading in the *Galaxy*. Or any of those other New York newspapers you've got lying there on the ground next to your chair."

"I wouldn't know. I haven't read them yet," he argued, excited at the prospect of discussing the latest news with her. Though he was anxious to see what her reaction would be when the topic of her father came up, for now he feigned indifference.

She glanced from the newspaper he was holding to the ones on the ground and shrugged. "They're dated several days ago. I've read them. There isn't more than an article in the whole lot of them that would constitute decent news."

He cocked a brow. "You're not fond of newspapers?"

Her gray eyes darkened. "I'm not fond of reading articles written by reporters who offer to unsuspecting readers whatever version of the truth will sell newspapers. Or whatever version will fill the coffers of editors who try to outdo one another by promoting scandals that show no regard for decency, let alone the truth."

Stung by her attack on the very profession he was fighting so hard to reclaim as his own, he countered her argument without stopping to choose his words more carefully. "Reporters and their editors are motivated by a thirst for the truth that can't be quenched by anything less, regardless of how the truth might impact the people involved. Truth also sells newspapers. That's why people read them. They know they can rely on the newspapers to tell them the truth," he asserted. Surprisingly, he found she was using the very same argument he had used in the past when arguing with his brother about the very same issues.

"Unfortunately, that's not always true. In fact, I think it's usually not true at all," she insisted and glanced over at the toddler. "It's a rare event when any of the newspapers or the reporters who work for them are called to task for the lies they perpetuate in the name of truth. Even then, it's too late, especially for the people who've been falsely maligned, their reputations destroyed, their families devastated, and their fortunes gone."

He squared his shoulders, captured her gaze, and held it. Surprised by the depth of emotion staring back at him, he pressed her, hoping to make her refer directly to Reverend Livingstone's recent acquittal without bringing it up himself. "You obviously feel very strongly about the matter, yet I wonder if there's a single example you might care to offer to prove —"

"I have any number of examples I could give you," she quipped, then paused, as if sorting them in her mind. "Several years ago, there was a reporter for the *Galaxy*. I can't say I quite remember his name, but he wrote a series of articles that inspired half the city to donate to a poor elderly widow who had been duped out of her inheritance by a passel of cunning thieves."

Jake's pulse thudded hard as he searched her gaze, but he saw no hint of guile or any sign she knew that he was the reporter she was talking about.

"Do you remember that?"

He shrugged. "Vaguely," he replied, even though every word he had ever written about Victoria Carlington was indelibly printed on his conscience.

"By the time a more competent reporter for another newspaper had investigated the woman's background," she offered after taking another peek over at her daughter, "it was too late. The woman had left the city and disappeared with thousands of dollars, along with the alleged thieves who turned out to be her own nephews."

He had to swallow twice to get rid of the rock of emotion lodged in his throat. "You seem to have quite a remarkable ability to

140

recall something that happened so long ago."

"I remember it well because I was one of the readers who had been moved to send a sizable contribution to her and encouraged others to do the same, although I've learned my lesson and won't ever do something so foolish again. The only positive thing to come out of the entire affair is that the reporter ran off to a place where I can only hope he's not trusted again to report on anything that ends up in print." She then turned and ran after her daughter, who was toddling straight toward the river.

He gripped the side of his chair and forced himself to stay seated, until he saw the woman trip and fall to her knees. When he saw that Lily had already reached the water's edge and showed no intention of stopping, he bolted from the chair and ran past Ruth into the river. By the time he got to the toddler, waves of cold river water were lapping at the middle of her tummy, and she was laughing and smacking the water with her hands.

When he swooped her up from behind and planted her safely on his shoulders, she squealed in protest and yanked on his hair. "Bath! Lily bath!"

Gritting his teeth, he clomped back to the

shoreline and saw the expression of disbelief on Ruth's face. He realized then he had moved far too quickly for a man recuperating from a broken back. Waves broke over the tops of his boots when he stopped abruptly and grimaced, hoping he conveyed a look of extreme pain.

Ruth rushed into the water and tried to get her daughter, but dropped her hands. "I can't reach her. Could you please take her to shore and lift her down for me?"

He shook his head, which made Lily squeal again and tug another lock of his hair. "I can't. My back . . . just locked up again. I can't take another step or even lift my arms over my head. Try again."

She glared at him and charged away, mumbling under her breath. "You didn't seem to have any trouble walking back and forth into the village for the past few days, and you didn't have any trouble making repairs for any number of other women, and now you can't carry a little child a few more simple steps or lift her down from your shoulders?" She hoisted up the chair he had been sitting on, carried it back with her, and sat it into the water next to him.

"Th-that's my only chair," he argued.

"And that's my only daughter," she snapped and put her hand on his shoulder

142

to keep her balance while she climbed onto the seat.

Lily let go of his hair and reached for Ruth, and he had to fight to keep his balance. "Bath?" Lily asked.

Ruth lifted her into her arms, leaned on him again to get down, and cuddled the little girl close. "Yes, you can have a bath, but not in the river. You can have a bath when we get home," she crooned as she carried Lily back to shore. When she kept walking without so much as a backward glance, he saw the current slide the chair into the water and called, "Haven't you forgotten something?"

She looked over her shoulder and smiled. "I'm quite sure you can get another chair. Now that I think of it, I've heard you're probably talented enough to make one, but I can't stop to help you because I have more important things to worry about than your chair."

"What about me?" he argued.

When she turned about, he could see she was shivering just as much as Lily and even more than he was. He felt a tug of guilt he tried hard to ignore.

"What about you?" she asked.

"Don't you have a bit of concern that you're leaving me here, unable to move or reach my cane?"

She sighed. "Tell me why I should, and I'll consider it."

"In the first place," he argued, "I was the one who saved your daughter. And in the second place, since you seem completely insensitive to the fact that I'm still recuperating and still suffering from back spasms that render me a cripple more days than not, perhaps you might want to talk to Mr. Garner when you get home. He'll tell you it's true. You might also ask him to send over another remedy since the one he gave me two days ago isn't working anymore, although the fact that I just charged into the water before your daughter drowned because you were too busy spouting off about something you regret doing a number of years ago —"

"I'm coming. I'm coming," she grumbled, "but don't think for a moment that I won't ask him, because I will."

She was still mumbling something about how inconvenient it was to help him as she picked up his cane and made her way back to him. But he was so interested in how fascinating she was and how attractive she looked, despite the fact that her gown was soaked, her hair was windblown, and she

had a whining toddler in her arms, he
scarcely heard a word she said.

THIRTEEN

After her restlessness woke Lily up for the second time, Ruth rubbed the child's back to help her fall back to sleep and gazed out the bedroom window at the moonlit sky. Instead of counting the stars to help her fall asleep, too, she tallied up the full cost of her rash decision to visit her garden this afternoon while hoping to catch Jake Spencer off guard: One basket filled with damp, sandy clothing that needed to be laundered; a forgotten shawl; two pairs of soggy boots that would need several days of nonstop sunshine to dry out completely; and some tears to be mended. But these inconveniences were nothing compared to the possible loss of Lily.

She moved her hand in a lazy arc around the small of Lily's back while the little one sucked on her two fingers. Knowing how much Lily loved her bath, she should never have assumed it would be safe to take Lily anywhere close to the river's edge. She should not have assumed that an eighteen-month-old child would be content to sit indefinitely, playing with nothing more than a few blades of grass, either.

After whispering a prayer of gratitude that Lily had survived her traipse into the river with nothing more than a few chills that a mug of warm, sweetened milk had chased away, she added a promise that she would be more vigilant when it came to watching the child who was under her protection.

When she heard Lily's breathing gentle, she stopped rubbing her back, glanced down at her, and shook her head. Less than two months ago, she would never have imagined how difficult or all-consuming it would be to care for a child this age. If she had her way, she would grow an extra pair of arms and legs to keep pace with Lily, along with pairs of eyes on the sides and in the back of her head, just to keep watch over her.

Chuckling at how ridiculous she would look, she rolled to her side. After she fluffed up her pillow, she curled up and closed her eyes, but visions of the poor man she had left standing in the river, scarcely able to hold onto his cane, reminded her that she was guilty of making assumptions about him, too.

After Mr. Garner confirmed that he had indeed given Jake Spencer a remedy to help ease the spasms in his back, he also explained that these spasms would come and go, intermittently, for some time. They would ease as his back healed, but he would likely be plagued by problems with his back for the rest of his life.

She groaned and rolled to her other side. She wished she had known that before she had spoken to the Jones cousins and assumed the man had deliberately misled her when they first met because he'd had some sort of ulterior motive. "It's the pressure of the trial," she murmured, although she knew she was partly to blame, too.

Because of the scandal and notoriety about her father's trial — which the newspapers had inflamed and had only worsened with his acquittal — she could not and did not completely trust anyone here in the village. As fond as she had become of the Garners, she dared not tell them she had been lying to them from the day they met and admit that she was not a former prostitute but the daughter of the minister they secretly helped with his ministry to the city's fallen angels.

She had not come to know the members

of the small congregation here very well, but she respected and admired Rev. Haines. Yet she had lied to all of them, too, because it was just too dangerous to trust them with the truth — for Lily's sake as well as her own.

The only one she could really trust was her father, but the longer it took for him to send any word to her, the easier it was for doubts to creep into her heart that she would ever see him again.

Loneliness and disappointment overwhelmed her spirit. "Oh, Father, help me . . . help me to trust in you," she prayed.

In the midst of her prayer, Lily crawled up from her bed onto Ruth's. Snuggling close, she lay her head against Ruth's chest and wrapped her little arms around Ruth's waist. "Lily home," she murmured before falling back to sleep.

Battling tears, Ruth held the little one tight within her embrace and knew Lily had not been asking for Ruth to take her home again. She was telling Ruth, with every flutter of her little heart that was beating next to Ruth's, that she was home when she was right here, safe and secure in Ruth's arms.

Ruth rose the next morning with a renewed sense of hope, even joy.

When Phanaby left right after breakfast to take a pot of soup to a woman who had just given birth to her fourth child, taking Lily along with her to play with the older children, Ruth used her free time and Phanaby's generosity to good advantage. After she made two butter cakes, she used up the scraps of bread in the larder to make a huge bowl of bread pudding thick with cinnamon and plump raisins before she filled six thick slices of bread with ham left from yesterday's supper.

Humming softly, she went downstairs while the cakes were cooling, noted the disorder in the storeroom as she walked through, and entered the apothecary.

"You're especially happy today," Mr. Garner noted, without losing his rhythm as he worked a large pestle against the bottom of the mortar.

"I'll be even happier if you let me straighten up your storeroom while Lily is napping this afternoon."

He chuckled. "In point of fact, I think that's an excellent idea."

Her eyes widened. "You do?"

"Unless you'd rather work out here while I tackle the storeroom. My customers seem to like you, especially the Jones cousins. I expect them to stop by this afternoon to pick up the remedy I discussed with them the other day."

She grinned. "No, thank you. I think I prefer the storeroom. Did you have an opportunity to make another remedy for Mr. Spencer yet? I could take it out to him sometime this morning before Mrs. Garner comes back with Lily."

"It's over there," he said, nodding toward the shelves on the far wall. "Dark blue bottle. Right between the two brown ones . . . That's the one," he said when she lifted a narrow blue bottle from the shelf. "Tell him to mix a teaspoonful with a tumblerful of weak tea and drink it straight down each morning, but warn him that it can make him very sleepy. And while you're there, you might as well tell him that I'll probably need another week or so before I'm ready for him to start the work I discussed with him the other day."

She furrowed her brow. "Work?"

Mr. Garner set the pestle down to wipe his brow. "He's going to replace some of those rickety shelves in the storeroom with new ones he's also going to paint."

"Which is why you need the room straightened up a bit," she offered.

"True enough," he said and resumed his work. "Is that the smell of butter cake you

151

brought in with you?"

"You'll find out at dinner," she teased and started to retrace her steps.

"Ruth?"

She stopped and looked over at him expectantly. "Yes?"

He rested the pestle against the side of the mortar and toyed with one end of his mustache before he locked his gaze with hers. "Mrs. Garner and I have been talking, and well . . . you haven't been here but a matter of weeks and we, that is . . . we wanted you to know that we think you're becoming a fine young woman, and we feel blessed that Reverend Livingstone sent you and Lily here to live with us."

Her throat constricted. "I-I feel blessed, too," she said. Although she was looking forward to being reunited with her father, she would never forget the many kindnesses she had received from this humble man and his wife. "And I'm quite sure that Lily would agree with me, if she knew how to say the words," she said with a smile. "Not everyone would be as patient with her as you and your wife have been, and I thank you for that."

He waved off her compliment and resumed his work. "If you don't leave soon, Lily will be back, and you won't find it easy to leave her behind if she finds out you're going back to her 'big bath,' " he teased.

"Then I'll hurry along. You'll tell Phanaby that I'll be back before dinner?"

When he nodded, she slipped through the curtain and hurried back up the staircase. Fifteen minutes later, she was humming her way up Water Street with a basket containing one of the butter cakes, half of the bread pudding, and all of the ham-stuffed bread in one hand and the remedy from the apothecary in the other.

She soon rounded the bend and passed by her garden, then walked through the copse of trees and approached the cabin itself for the first time since he had moved into it. Since she had not seen any smoke curling up from the chimney, she assumed he was not in any condition to start a fire, but she was surprised to see that inside shutters on both of the windows facing the river were tightly closed.

She was but a few steps away from the door when a large brown bird of some sort came flying low to the ground from around the corner of the cabin. The bird landed right in front of her, looked at her, and made several sounds she could only describe as similar to a kitten purring. With her heart pounding, she took a few steps back, but the bird simply closed the distance between them.

She swooshed her basket in front of her. "Shoo, bird. Shoo!" she cried, grateful the bird was more scared than she was and flew off. She was still trembling a bit when she knocked on the cabin door. When he did not answer, she knocked again. After her third attempt, she cocked her head. He had not been able to walk himself out of the water yesterday afternoon, which meant he simply had to be at home. Unless he was still too angry with her to answer the door, he was either feeling too poorly to get out of bed or feeling embarrassed by his weakened state.

In any case, he would hardly be able to resist the food she had brought. She knocked on the door one last time. "I've brought your medicine from the apothecary," she called and gave him the instructions that Mr. Garner had given to her. She paused and set the basket down in front of the door. "I'm also leaving a few things I made for you to eat because . . . because I'm sorry I left you the way I did. Very sorry," she murmured, then turned and walked away.

It was not until she had walked back to her garden that she realized she may have erred and he was not home at all. She had made a mistake to leave the basket of food sitting outside. With all the wildlife around, including the bird that had nearly attacked her, the food she had made for him might not be there by the time he got home.

Sighing, she retraced her steps, only to find the bird strutting in front of the cabin door, clucking like a mad hen; the basket she had left had disappeared. She backed away cautiously, one quick step at a time, until she was out of the bird's view. Once she reached her garden, she never looked back and hurried home. Although she was disappointed not to have been able to give Jake her apology face-to-face, she was hopeful that the treats she had left would convince him she was sincere.

With time to spare before Phanaby would be home with Lily, she hurried down to the general store to see if more recent copies of the city newspapers had arrived. When she saw that no one was sitting on the stools in front of the warming stove, reading newspapers or gossiping, she sighed with relief and went directly to the counter, where Mrs. Sloan greeted her with a scowl.

"I could have sold these newspapers twice over and at triple the price," she snapped, making it clear she resented missing the extra profit, and handed Ruth a package wrapped in plain brown paper. "I had to wrap them up so folks who came here earlier demanding copies of their own wouldn't see I kept any aside — not that some folks in this village show any appreciation for what I do for them."

"I'll be mindful and tell Mr. Garner of your . . . kindness to him," Ruth replied before hastily leaving the store. Though tempted to stop to get a glimpse of the headlines, she walked around to the back door of the Garners' home and slipped upstairs to avoid being delayed by any customers who might be in the apothecary. She checked the second floor quickly, but Phanaby and Lily had yet to return. Thrilled to have the opportunity to read the newspapers in private, she laid the packet of papers on top of her bed.

Her fingers shook and her heart raced with anticipation as she untied the parcel and peeled away the brown wrapper. Lying on top, the headline in the *Sun* was printed in dark, bold type: *Final Justice for One While the People Demand Justice for Another.* She quickly dropped her gaze and read aloud the first line in the article below: " 'In a remarkable twist of fate that is certain to be welcomed by our readers, death has unexpectedly claimed the life of Rev. Gersham Livingstone, providing justice for the late Rosalie Peale that the jury in his recent trial was unwilling to render.' "

Scarcely able to breathe, Ruth clapped her hand over her mouth. Surely this article was either a dreadful mistake or some kind of cruel, twisted hoax.

Heart trembling, she shoved the paper aside to read the next. The headline in the *Transcript* was much shorter, but the words *A Murderer's Just Reward* chilled her to the bone. Blinking back tears, she quickly read through the short article below:

Rev. Gersham Livingstone, recently acquitted of murdering a poor unfortunate in this city, is dead. Apparently the Creator has a greater sense of justice than the jury of twelve citizens who judged the evidence against him. George Madison, the late minister's lawyer, along with several authorities summoned to Livingstone's home, discovered his client's body in bed early yesterday morning, after failing to gain access for the past three days. Dr. Ezra Wheaton, who performed an autopsy at the residence, confirmed the late minister apparently succumbed to a disease of the heart, no doubt aggravated by the stress of his controversial ministry as well as his recent trial.

"No! Please, God, no!" she whispered.

Close to a state of absolute panic, she pushed that paper aside, only to see a similar headline in the *Galaxy*. A horribly distressing sketch of her father, lying dead in his bed, captured her gaze. She blinked back tears to clear her vision and covered his image with her fingertips to study the rest of the sketch.

The details in the background were not only accurate but painfully familiar to her: the quilt on his bed, that she herself had made for him; the pear-shaped sconces on the wall; the two Bibles sitting on the table next to his bed, one of which had belonged to her mother. These were details that only someone who had been into her father's bedchamber would know. Grief pierced her heart.

"No. Please, God, no . . ." she repeated over and over, rocking back and forth and weeping uncontrollably because she had no hope left that the newspaper accounts were not true.

Her beloved father was dead.

FOURTEEN

Jake slid the inside window shutter open just a notch and saw the dark figure of the man who had knocked at his cabin door and startled him out of a deep sleep. After he climbed out of bed, he stopped to light a pair of candles on the mantel over the hearth where dying embers were still glowing.

"You have an answer for me?" he asked once the man entered and he latched the door tight again.

Capt. Grant glanced at the table in the corner of the room covered with newspapers and handed over a letter. "It's good to see you again, too," he quipped and extended his hand.

Jake cringed and shook the older man's hand. "I'm sorry, sir. I'm afraid I'm still half asleep," he offered weakly. "I saw you sail in earlier today and got copies of the city newspapers you unloaded, but when you didn't come by right after dark, I just assumed that Clifford still hadn't given you a response for me yet. How are you, sir?"

"Fair to middlin' for an old man, but I'd be a whole sight better if I could sit a spell."

Jake pulled over the chair that Ruth had dragged into the river and set it in front of the fire. "I'm afraid this'll have to do, sir," he said and added a few thick logs to the fire to chase the chill from the room. "Is there anything else I can get for you?"

Grant eased into the chair, lifted his feet, and rested them on the crumbling hearth. "I just need to dry out these old boots of mine. Next time, I'll row the dinghy across the river instead of traipsing all the way over here, assuming there is a next time. Go ahead. Read your letter. I'm as anxious as you are to hear what Clifford wrote."

Jake walked over to the mantel and broke the wax seal on the letter. "I should have expected that he'd be closemouthed about it to you," he said as he unfolded the single piece of paper.

The sea captain snorted. "In point of fact, he had a great deal to say."

Jake met his gaze and held it. "He actually talked to you about what he expects me to do?"

Another snort. "No, he was more interested in making it clear that he did not look kindly on the fact that I helped you travel a bit over the past few years. But I had a few words of my own to say to him he didn't want to hear, either."

"I'm sorry. If I had any other way to keep in contact with him other than through you —"

"I don't have any trouble speaking my piece with any man, least of all your brother, regardless of how old he is. Read the letter. Then we'll talk."

Jake nodded. He saw that the letter was dated the same day as the newspapers that had just arrived. He skimmed the opening remarks, which made it demandingly clear his brother expected him to continue with his assignment, even though Reverend Livingstone had died as a result of heart failure. "He wants me to stay and finish," Jake said.

Capt. Grant shook his head. "After what I read in each of the other newspapers, I rather expected he would. Livingstone's sudden demise has only inflamed public curiosity about his daughter's whereabouts. There's a growing consensus among the city officials I spoke to that she's still alive. There's even stronger speculation among the press that she took evidence that would have convinced the jury to convict her father."

"I read the newspapers, too," Jake reminded him. He turned his attention back to his brother's letter, but then quickly crumpled the letter in disgust.

"Bad news?"

Jake huffed. "Since both the *Sun* and the *Transcript* have added two additional reporters to find Livingstone's daughter, Clifford is assigning another reporter, Robert Farrell, to the story, which means he'll probably be coming here. He'll be traveling by stagecoach, following whatever leads he develops."

"This Farrell. Do you know him?"

"Not personally," Jake admitted, "but I understand he's young, ambitious, cocky, and totally devoid of principles."

"That doesn't surprise me. Clifford's desperate for Ruth's story. Did he say how soon Farrell would be arriving?"

Jake nodded. "Likely within days."

"You can't let him or any other reporter find her first," Capt. Grant insisted. The concern in his voice was far more of an incentive for Jake to succeed than Clifford's harsh directive. "Other than making it clear that he has little faith in you, did Clifford find anything out about Martin Malloy?"

162

"I didn't read that far," Jake replied. He uncrumpled the letter and finished reading:

I can report unequivocally that Martin Malloy did not operate a stationery store on Broadway or anywhere else in the city. Nor can I find any evidence that the man ever resided here, if he existed at all. I trust that this information will be helpful in your search for Ruth Livingstone, although your letter did not detail what her connection to this man might be.

Jake paused to share this information with Capt. Grant, then asked, "What do you think that means?"

"I think your brother is capable enough that you can trust his findings in this matter."

"I agree, but I was wondering what you think about Widow Malloy."

"I think it's fairly obvious that she's fabricated an imaginary husband who had an imaginary store, which means she's fabricated both her status and her name. That doesn't necessarily mean that she's the woman you're looking for, though, does it?"

Jake shook his head. "No, but from the description Clifford gave me, I think it's likely that she is, in truth, Ruth Livingstone. She must have been devastated to read of her father's death today," he murmured, surprised by his desire to protect a woman he barely knew.

"How well did you know Reverend Livingstone?" Jake asked, in part to distract himself from feelings about Ruth that were entirely unprofessional and totally inconsistent with his goal as a reporter.

The captain stared into the growing fire for several long moments. "Well enough to know that he loved his daughter very much. He would have gone to great lengths to protect her if he were still alive. If you think this woman is actually Ruth Livingstone, I'd say you have a bit of a problem," he suggested as he shifted his feet a bit closer to the fire.

"Problem?"

"The child. Lily. How do you explain her?" he asked, voicing the same concerns that nagged at Jake.

"She can't be Ruth's natural child," he replied. "I've never discovered any hint, either spoken or in print, that she bore a child. Her father's ministry was highly controversial long before he was accused of murder, and his detractors would have gleefully used the fact that he had a granddaughter who had been born out of wedlock against him."

"Quite so."

Jake raked his hand through his hair and sighed. "Then who is she? Who are her parents? And why did they allow Reverend Livingstone to send her off with Ruth? I know he had a large number of supporters at one time, but it's hard to imagine that any of them would sacrifice their own child for any cause, especially a man charged with murder."

"But he made the arrangements with me for Widow Malloy and her little girl to sail to Toms River a good week before he'd been charged with any crime," Capt. Grant argued as he stood to his feet. "You raise all good questions, and I have no doubt you'll find answers that I trust you will consider wisely. Have you determined what role the Garners play in all this?"

"Not yet," Jake admitted. He suspected the answers he needed were in that wooden chest Grant had delivered to Mrs. Garner. At this point, however, he realized he was pinning all of his hopes to redeem himself on the contents of that chest — contents that might very well be disappointing, if not totally useless after all. No, he would be far better served to focus his efforts on learning

165

as much as he could from Ruth herself, efforts all the more urgent with Farrell's imminent arrival.

Capt. Grant yawned and shook his head. "The older I get, the sooner dawn seems to come. It's time for me to head back to my ship. You know how to get in touch with me," he said and then headed for the door.

"I'll walk back with you," Jake offered.

A raised brow.

"Just to the bridge," he added and blew out the candles. He hurried ahead of his visitor, unlatched the door, and opened it. "Along the way, perhaps you can give me some advice."

Grant stepped outside. "About?"

"What do you know about turkeys?"

"They make mighty fine eating. Other than that, very little. Why?"

Jake shut the door and looked around. "You didn't by any chance encounter one when you approached the cabin, did you?"

The captain chuckled and started walking away. "Got yourself a pest, have you?"

"Apparently. The stupid bird just started following me around the other day and it swoops at anyone who approaches the cabin."

"So shoot it, clean it, cook it on a spit, and eat it."

Jake snorted. "I'm tempted, but I don't have a gun."

"Then I suppose you're stuck with it, but I wouldn't worry. It won't bite you," he said with a hearty chuckle.

"That's some consolation," Jake said. He figured having that dumb turkey following him around was going to be far less of a problem than meeting up with the little imp he rescued from the river. She had nearly ruined his efforts to convince her mother he was too disabled to pose any threat to her at all.

They parted ways at the end of the path, and on the way back to his cabin, Jake stopped to glance over at the rear of the apothecary. Like the other buildings in the village, the windows were dark. But unlike the rest of the people who were abed, he suspected that Ruth Livingstone was sleeping fitfully, if at all.

Although he had lost his father when he was only eight, he still remembered the crushing grief and confusion that had stayed with him for a very long time, especially at night when he felt totally and utterly alone. He did not know how Ruth Livingstone would grieve for her father when she could not openly acknowledge their relationship, but he did know the one place where she could go to grieve in private: her garden.

And regardless of how much he empathized with her situation, he could not afford to let sympathy keep him from completing the assignment he had been given.

Not when Farrell might very well be on the next stage that pulled into the village.

FIFTEEN

"Mr. Garner needs to speak to you. He's in the sitting room," Phanaby said, lifting Lily out of Ruth's arms. "I'll keep this little angel busy with me in the kitchen while I fix breakfast."

More curious than alarmed, Ruth followed Phanaby down the hallway and found Elias standing in front of the hearth. His glum expression matched her mood, still fragile since her father's death two weeks ago. "You wanted to see me?"

He nodded and motioned for her to take a seat on the settee.

She shook her head. "I'm fine standing. What is it?"

He cleared his throat. "With Dr. Woodward sick in bed with a fever, I was called out to Burkalow's in the middle of the night last night. One of the guests at the inn was suffering from a stomach disorder."

"I thought I heard you leave," she replied.

He dropped his gaze for a moment. "The guest is a reporter from the *Galaxy*, Robert Farrell. Apparently, he arrived on the stage late yesterday afternoon. He's looking for Ruth Livingstone, although I daresay he'd be quite interested in anyone connected to Reverend Livingstone and his ministry."

Ruth felt the blood drain from her face and bunched her skirts with her hands to keep them from shaking. Taking small, deliberate steps, she managed to get to the settee and take a seat before her legs gave way. Although Elias had no idea that she was, indeed, Ruth Livingstone, his need to protect her as one of Rev. Livingstone's Prodigal Daughters would serve her just as well.

"I talked to the man at rather great length when I delivered the remedy," Elias offered quickly. "He told me he spent a few hours in the village yesterday talking to a few people before taking ill, but he made it clear to me that he's far more interested now in continuing on his journey once he recovers than he is in staying here. I really don't think he poses any great danger to you or to Lily."

Ruth blinked back tears. After learning of her beloved father's death, she had spent every waking hour of every day living in a constant state of emotional and spiritual turmoil, unable to stop the endless flow of tears, unable to find peace, even unable to pray. Now, with a reporter in the village, fear overwhelmed her grief.

"Wh-what do you think I should do?" she asked, half afraid to hear his answer.

He shrugged. "Actually, nothing. I just wanted you to know —"

She nearly choked. "Nothing?"

He nodded. "At least for now. You haven't been out at all these last few weeks, and I'm not suggesting you should venture out unnecessarily now, at least not until he leaves. But I don't think there's any need to panic. Folks have gotten used to seeing you work in the apothecary now and again, so I think you should continue to do that, although today might be a good day to tackle straightening up that storeroom instead of helping me with customers."

"But what if this Mr. Farrell comes into the apothecary for more of the remedy you gave him last night?"

"There's no need to worry about that. I told him I'd deliver more to him at the inn. In fact, I've already prepared it and intend to walk it over later this afternoon. The remedy itself is fairly potent, so the man should be more inclined to sleep than anything else." He paused and shook his head. "Trust me, Ruth. Even if he is up to wandering about the village today, he's far more interested in finding Ruth Livingstone than anything else."

She exhaled slowly and reined in the temptation to tell Elias, as well as Phanaby, that she was the woman Mr. Farrell was looking for. She'd felt God urging her to remain silent up to this point, and protecting sweet Lily — and the Garners — was now her priority.

He smiled gently. "You do trust me, don't you? You know I won't let anything happen to you or to Lily, don't you?"

She managed to return his smile. "Yes, of course I do," she whispered, even as her heart trembled.

Fueled by uncertainty, fear, and a growing anger toward her father for leaving her, Ruth had Elias's storeroom looking cleaner than it had probably been in years.

At the sound of footsteps, she turned and saw Phanaby standing at the bottom of the staircase, holding Lily's hand. Noting the bonnets they were wearing, she managed a bit of a smile. "Are you going out?"

Lily broke free and toddled over to her.

"Come," she cried and tugged at Ruth's skirts.

"The storeroom can wait. Do come with us," Phanaby urged as she walked toward her. "A few of the ladies are cleaning the church today to get ready for tomorrow's services, and they never turn away an extra pair of hands."

Ruth rested the broom handle against the edge of a shelf and lifted Lily up for a kiss before setting her back down again. Surprised by Phanaby's suggestion, she frowned. "Do you really think it's a good idea for me to go out today?"

"I doubt that reporter is up and out of his sickbed, let alone at the church."

Ruth moistened her lips and tasted the dust she had stirred up in the storeroom. "I think it would be best I finish up here, but if you'd rather not take Lily with you, I can keep her here with me."

Phanaby glanced at all the litter on the floor and shook her head. "If I don't take her with me, she'll traipse through everything you sweep up and it'll take you twice as long to finish."

"So true," Ruth admitted, then scrunched down and planted another kiss on Lily's forehead. "By the time you come back, I'll be all done and we can make cookies together. Would you like that?"

Grinning, Lily clapped her hands, and she did not complain when Phanaby took her hand and led her toward the back door.

Grateful that Phanaby did not argue the point and insist that she accompany them, Ruth turned and picked up the broom again.

"Ruth?"

She turned and saw Phanaby standing at the back door.

"Sooner or later, you're going to have to go out again, Ruth. You haven't even gone back to your garden."

"Yes, I know, it's just . . ."

"You'll need your shawl for services tomorrow," she prompted. "Perhaps you can slip out to your garden tomorrow morning since you left it there."

"I'll try," Ruth offered, annoyed that she still had not retrieved the shawl she had left behind weeks ago.

"Just be sure to be back in time for services. It's the last time we'll have them for a few months since Reverend Haines is leaving to ride circuit on Monday. Which reminds me: I'll need to stop at the general store to get something I need for the picnic."

"Picnic?"

Phanaby smiled. "We always have a picnic

174

dinner after services to wish him Godspeed. I mentioned that to you the other day, but it appears as if you've forgotten."

Ruth sighed. "Yes, I'm afraid I did," she replied, uncertain that she should attend services.

"I wouldn't worry about that reporter being there, either," Phanaby said as if reading Ruth's thoughts. "Based on what Elias told me, the man will be eating nothing but clear broth for the next few days. And, Ruth, you're not the only one grieving Reverend Livingstone's passing," she added gently. "We respected and admired him, too."

Ruth dropped her gaze and gulped hard until the tears that threatened to spill down her cheeks slipped back to refill the well of grief that seemed endless. "I-I know. I'm . . . I'm sorry, it's just that it's so hard to think that . . . that I was the very last one he was able to help and that no one here, other than you or Mr. Garner, seems to understand what a good man he was, even though he was proven innocent," she whispered, repeating the words she had first used to explain why she had been so devastated by the death of a man she could not claim as her father.

"Not everyone in the village believes what the newspapers print, and we shouldn't give up hope. Someone as special as he was will step forward to lead Prodigal Daughters and continue Reverend Livingstone's ministry," Phanaby said.

Ruth sniffled twice. The articles in the press that fueled a public clamor demanding to know where she was — and whether or not she was hiding evidence that would have convicted her father — had only gotten worse since his death. She could hardly imagine that the organization he had founded would survive at all, let alone attract the interest of another minister willing to lead it.

When Ruth looked up, Phanaby was nodding while trying to keep Lily from reaching up to open the back door. "Well, then, I think we'd better be off. Since you didn't eat much at breakfast again, I set up a plate with some jellied bread for you and left it out, just in case you decided not to come with us. Just be sure to eat it all before Mr. Garner finds it," she said before she opened the door and hurried the two of them off.

Ruth had nearly half the floor swept clean when she heard the door to the apothecary open, followed by hurried footsteps and loud voices that competed for attention. Before she could even wonder what all the commotion was about, Mr. Garner poked his head through the curtain. "There's been a bit of an accident in front of the general store and two men have apparently gotten hurt. With Dr. Woodward sick himself, I think I should at least see if there's something I can suggest that will help them," he said. "I don't expect anyone this afternoon, but could you just listen for the door? I shouldn't be long."

"Go," she urged, curious as to what kind of accident had occurred.

He nodded his thanks, and she heard him gathering up a few of his remedies before the front door slammed closed.

Except for the gentle swoosh of her broom, she was surrounded, once again, by nothing but silence, and for the very first time that she could recall, she was all alone in this humble dwelling. She paused, struck still by the realization that she was now completely and utterly alone in this world. No one in this village, not one single breathing human being, really knew who she was or why she had come here.

Having a reporter here in the village was a vivid reminder that she needed to make a decision. She could step forward now and reclaim her name, despite the difficulty she'd face trying to prove she had nothing of interest to the authorities or the press. If she did just that, however, how would she explain Lily? Even if she decided to leave the child with the Garners, some reporter would eventually find her and uncover the fact that Rosalie Peale had been Lily's mother. Could she risk having Lily forever tainted by her mother's sin? Worse, would the authorities take the child away from her, since she had no rightful claim to her?

Or should Ruth remain silent and keep the identity she had claimed when she left New York City, to protect the child as well as herself?

"I'll hold my peace, for now," she whispered, but groaned when she heard the apothecary door open. She shoved the broom into the corner and planted a smile on her lips she knew was too tight even before she parted the curtain to greet the customer waiting for her. After stepping into the apothecary, she took one look at the stranger who had entered the shop and braced her hands on the counter for support.

Dressed in a finely cut suit of clothes that labeled him from the city, the man had a pallid complexion. He appeared to be young, perhaps only a few years older than she was, which surprised her. When he walked toward her very slowly, as if weak or in some sort of discomfort, she realized she was staring at her worst fear in human form. "Mr. Farrell?" she murmured, praying she would be able to hear him confirm his identity over the wild thumping of her heart.

He paused in front of the counter. "Indeed, I am. Did we perhaps meet yesterday before I took ill?"

She swallowed hard. "No, we didn't, but Mr. Garner mentioned he had been called out during the night to tend to a visitor to our village."

He groaned, then gripped his stomach with one of his hands. "I suppose I've been living in the city for so long that I'd forgotten how easy it is to spot a stranger in a village this small. I'm afraid I couldn't wait any longer for more of that remedy to be delivered. It helps me to sleep through the pain, which is still quite unbearable. Is Mr. Garner here?"

"I'm sorry. He's been called out for an emergency; otherwise he would have taken this to you by now," she offered as she turned and found the remedy Mr. Garner had prepared. She set the dark brown bottle on the counter in front of the man. "I hope you're feeling better soon," she offered, without adding that she hoped he would be on Monday's stage when it left.

He laid several coins on the counter and picked up the bottle. "The sooner I get this stomach of mine back to rights, the happier I'll be and the quicker I can continue on my journey," he assured her. He hesitated for a moment before he pulled a small paper out of his vest pocket, unfolded it, and held it out for her to see. "As you no doubt heard, I'm a reporter for the *Galaxy* newspaper, and I'm looking for this woman. Her name is Ruth Livingstone, although she's probably using another name. Perhaps you've heard of her. Her father was recently acquitted in a rather infamous trial —"

"I know who she is," Ruth managed while staring at the sketch he held in his hands.

"Have you seen her or anyone who resembles her?"

Ruth tried to keep her heart from leaping out of her chest. No wonder the man had made no progress by talking to the villagers. The woman in the sketch looked nothing like her at all, which she considered fortunate since the woman had a large hooked nose, a decidedly weak chin, and a very abundant bosom. "No. No, I'm sorry. I'm afraid not."

He refolded the sketch and slid the paper back into his vest pocket. "There's no need to be sorry. No one else I've talked to in the village has seen her, either, which isn't surprising. I believe she's actually living a good twenty miles south of here. Thank you for this," he said, holding up the remedy, before he turned and promptly left without giving her a second glance.

With her knees about to buckle from the strain of their encounter, Ruth held onto the counter for dear life until he was outside. Bowing her head, she drew deep gulps of air. After a good five minutes, her heart finally resumed a normal rhythm, only to start racing again when she heard the door open. She looked up and nearly groaned again when a man she had no desire to see, at least at this precise moment, walked into the apothecary.

Sixteen

Jake crossed the room and approached the counter that Ruth was holding onto as if it were a lifeline. Her face was uncommonly pale, and she looked at him as if he were the last person she wanted to see.

His need to pursue his professional goal, however, overrode his concern for her, particularly since he had learned that Robert Farrell had arrived by stagecoach late yesterday afternoon. "You haven't been to your garden for a good while, and I thought perhaps it was too chilly in the morning to return because you didn't have your shawl," he offered and laid it on the counter. "I'm sorry. It seems to have gotten snagged on some bushes when the wind blew it around before I found it."

"I can repair it. Thank you for bringing it back to me," she said.

"You're welcome. Are you feeling unwell? Is that why you haven't been tending your garden?"

A blush stained her cheeks. "I've been feeling rather peaked lately, but I'm just a bit overtired today. Mr. Farrell, that reporter, just left. Did . . . did you see him?"

"Reporter?"

"A Mr. Farrell. From New York City," she explained. "He's suffering from some sort of stomach ailment and needed more remedy. I'm surprised you didn't pass him on your way here."

He shrugged, surprised himself to learn that Farrell was out and about. From what he heard earlier this morning, the man was in his sickbed at Burkalow's. "No, I didn't see him, although I've heard about him. He's caused quite a stir in the village."

She curled her lips. "Indeed. Knowing your fondness for newspapers, I'm surprised you didn't seek him out to speak to him."

He stiffened briefly. "I'm too busy working, trying to earn enough to make my own keep, to spend time gossiping with anyone," he replied.

"You're working again?" she asked.

"Thanks to the remedy you were kind enough to bring me," he replied and held out the canvas bag she had used to carry everything to the cabin a few weeks ago. "I'm sorry I wasn't able to get to the door

183

before you left. The food was delicious and much appreciated. You needn't have gone to all that trouble."

She blushed and took the bag from his hand. "Indeed, it was little enough to do after the way I acted."

He raised a brow. "And how was that?" he asked, hoping to force her to make her apology more specific.

The blush on her cheeks deepened to the color of overripe strawberries. "I'm sorry that I wasn't kinder to you. Or more understanding. Once I got home and Mr. Garner told me more about your condition, I realized I had misjudged you. I apologize, and I apologize for Lily, too, for biting you," she added.

He smiled. "Apology accepted. I trust your daughter has recovered from her plunge into the river."

"She's quite well, thank you," she murmured, obviously embarrassed by her daughter's behavior.

"Is Mr. Garner about?"

She shook her head. "He had to leave for a few moments. If you need more of the remedy, I could tell him —"

"Actually, I was hoping to speak to him about starting that work we discussed."

"If you're referring to replacing the shelves

in the storeroom, he said he was going to postpone doing that for another week or two. If you need to wait for him —"

"No," he said quickly and arched his back a bit. "I need to finish up some painting for Spinster Wyndam before this back of mine tightens up for good. She's letting me spend the night in her barn tonight so I won't have to walk back and forth. I don't want my back acting up and risk missing services tomorrow. Just tell him I'll talk to him about it then or at the picnic afterward. Will you be at the picnic with Lily?"

She moistened her lips and looked down. "I suppose I will, unless . . . yes, I suppose I will."

"Until tomorrow, then," he promised before taking his leave.

Heartened by the prospect of seeing her again, he hurried down the side of the apothecary toward the bridge to return to his cabin. He'd forgotten to bring the trousers he planned to wear to services tomorrow. Approaching Main Street, he was half tempted to stop at Burkalow's just ahead to confront Farrell, but decided to wait until dark when he might be better able to slip up to the man's room unnoticed.

Half an hour later, after stopping to help a farmer reload some of the hay that had fallen from his wagon, Jake finally reached his cabin and charged inside, anxious to get back to Spinster Wyndam's and finish his work for the day.

"Living a bit rustic these days, aren't you, Asher? The accommodations at Burkalow's are much more suitable to my taste."

Jake stared at the well-dressed young man sitting on the lone chair in the room and snarled, "You must be Robert Farrell. Do you make it a habit of entering a man's home without permission?"

He shrugged. "Your brother sends his regards, though I would venture to add that he's growing rather impatient with your lack of progress in locating Ruth Livingstone," he said, ignoring Jake's question.

"Obviously," Jake snapped. "Otherwise he wouldn't have sent you here."

Farrell stood up and dusted off his trousers, as if the chair he had been sitting on was uncommonly dirty. "He *sent* me out to find Ruth Livingstone, which is exactly what I plan to do once I've got this stomach ailment of mine cured."

Jake narrowed his gaze. "And just exactly how do you plan to find her?" he demanded, uncertain how much Clifford had shared with the man about what Jake had learned here in Toms River.

"By following a lead I developed, and by using this," Farrell said, walking over, albeit a bit painfully, and handing Jake a sketch. "Take a good look. Once you do, I think you'll have to agree that the pretty young widow living with the Garners bears no resemblance at all to Ruth Livingstone."

Infuriated that Clifford had told Farrell about his work here and his suspicion that Widow Ruth Malloy and Ruth Livingstone were one and the same woman, Jake quickly studied the sketch. He held back a grin that threatened to undermine his determination to get this young man out of Toms River as quickly as possible. If Farrell was relying on the sketch of this homely woman to identify Ruth Livingstone, Jake had little, if anything to fear from the man.

"Well?"

"You're right. There's no resemblance at all. Where did you get the sketch?"

Farrell's smile was so smug, Jake was tempted to give the man a good swipe in the face. "From a source. A very reliable source, which you no doubt overlooked since you've been on an extended *holiday* for the past two years, hoping your last attempt at reporting, which ended in disaster, would be forgotten. You're obviously wasting your time here," he added.

"Perhaps," Jake admitted, deliberately fueling the man's arrogance, and handed the sketch back to him.

"I'm certain your brother will find that bit of news interesting, to say the least."

Jake stiffened. "I keep my brother well-informed, as he does me."

"Which is yet another reason why he sent me here."

"To speak to me?" Jake asked, growing angrier by the minute with his brother for not trusting him to do his job.

"Your brother asked me to relay a message to you."

Jake balled his hands into fists.

"Your agreement with your brother has been amended — that is, he's also turned the assignment to find Ruth Livingstone over to me. To quote him precisely, 'Get the job done before Farrell does.' I trust you know exactly what that means in terms of —"

"Get out," Jake demanded and pointed to the door. "And when you see my brother again, tell him that I will not discuss any agreements we have with each other with anyone else, especially a hireling. Which is precisely what you are."

Farrell shrugged and made his way toward the door. "I'll stop to see you again on my way back to New York City. If the lead I have is as good as I suspect it is, that won't be but a matter of a week or two. By then, perhaps you'll have thought of a proper excuse to give your brother for failing to find Ruth Livingstone — something I'll have managed to do by then."

"You forget your place, Farrell. Or need I remind you that I am your employer since I am still half owner of the *Galaxy?*"

"Not for long," he said and slipped out the door, leaving Jake wondering if the cocky young reporter was right. If he failed to get the story about Ruth Livingstone that Clifford demanded before Farrell did, he would end up losing his investment in the *Galaxy,* as well as any hope of redeeming himself and reclaiming his career.

The stakes now were higher than ever before, leaving Jake no choice but to set aside his concerns for Ruth Livingstone and concentrate on his own. Or face the very real possibility that he would fail his brother again . . . as well as himself.

SEVENTEEN

Walk faster. Faster. Faster!

Ruth scurried down the sandy path she knew so well very early the next morning. She did not need more than the faint light of dawn to find her way. She did not feel the chill of the damp air on her face or detect the scent of cedar needles and salt air. She did not taste the silent river of tears that pooled in the corners of her lips or see the wispy ribbon of gold sky on the cusp of the horizon.

Numb to all but the desperate need to reach the privacy of her garden this morning while the cabin was empty, she pressed a fist against her mouth, rounded the bend, and ran the last dozen yards to the mound of earth yet to hold a single plant. The unspeakable pain of losing her beloved father, which had twisted her stomach into knots, finally wrenched free, overwhelmed her fears about having her true identity discovered, and forced the very last breath from her lungs.

Unable to take another step, she dropped to her knees, squeezed her eyes shut, and wrapped her hands around her waist. She rocked back and forth, releasing the anguish that had taken root in her very soul. The steady hum of deep-throated groans matched the slow, heavy thud of her heart, then quickened with her pulse.

Her whimpers grew more insistent and she parted her lips, unleashing cries that deepened into sobs that came straight from the deepest corners of her heart. "Father. Father." The sobs made her heart beat even faster as she struggled to breathe, yet releasing her sorrow also exposed an anger — an anger so sharp and so piercing and so new to her spirit that she was incapable of taming it.

In fact, she embraced it.

"Why, Father? Why did you make me leave you in the first place? Why? And why did you leave me forever now? Why!" she cried and pounded at her thighs until her fists were stinging and her voice was raw.

With her chest heaving, she twisted her skirts and redirected her anger at the Father she was supposed to trust above anyone else in this world. She looked up at the heavens, where stars rested now on a bed of gray velvet, and swiped at her tearstained cheeks. "You . . . you did this. You called him Home. Why, oh, why?" she whimpered, over and over, until her anger was spent, her voice was hoarse, and both her body and her spirit were drained to the point of exhaustion.

Ruth pulled her knees up to her chest, wrapped her arms around them, and lay down her head. Drawing one slow breath at a time, she had no strength left to think beyond the wonder that her broken heart was able to beat at all.

Silent moment after silent moment, she sat there alone, completely and quietly unaware of the world. When she felt the warmth of the sun on her head, she loosened her shawl. Above her, the sun rested in pale glory just above the tree line on the barrier island to the east. Closer still, along the southern shore of the river, she was surprised to see a good dozen shorebirds standing in a single straight line facing the sun, while others arrived silently in twos and threes to join them.

She did not know much about these shorebirds beyond the fact that they were seabirds of some kind. While some were heavy-bodied, brown and white gulls with thick beaks, others were slender, wearing a coat of dark black feathers above snow-white breasts. She had seen them and heard them many times before, squawking and screeching in competition for food, but she had never once seen gulls standing in a single row facing the horizon. They were completely silent, as if paying homage to their Creator and trusting He would bless them with another day of warm sun and the endless bounty of the river.

Humbled by the idea that the seabirds recognized the power and glory of the very God she had worshiped all her life, while she doubted Him and failed to trust in Him, she bowed her head. "Forgive me for being so very angry with you and with my father," she began. "I-I can't promise I won't ever be that angry again, because I probably will, but I'll try harder. I really will," she vowed, too ashamed to whisper anything more than a humble request for Robert Farrell to leave tomorrow on the morning stage.

Though anxious to get back in time to dress for services today, Ruth was still reticent about going out and about in the village with the reporter still present. She got to her feet and started brushing off her skirts when she suddenly had the feeling that someone was watching her. She turned around to face the cabin and froze when she realized that it was not someone, but some thing that was watching her.

Holding very still, she stared at the brown bird that had attacked her the other day. It was standing only a few yards away, and it was most definitely watching her. When she had told Mr. Garner about her incident with the bird, he had told her it was probably a wild turkey. Because of its coloring and size, he said it was most likely a harmless young hen, since hatchlings would be much smaller at this time of year.

Even so, she had no desire to have the bird swoop at her again and took tiny sidesteps to reach the path. "Nice turkey hen. Don't worry. I'm leaving now," she whispered, relieved when the turkey made no effort to move.

When she finally reached the path, she even walked backward for a few steps. Satisfied she was not in any danger, she turned around but kept her pace slow and steady. She pulled her shawl a little tighter and looked back over her shoulder when she reached the bend in the path and blinked hard.

The hen was strutting along the path following her!

"Stupid turkey," she grumbled when she

realized her gown was snagged on a bramble bush. Frustrated, she stopped to untangle her skirts. Seeing that the bird had stopped, too, she worked quickly to get free. When she started walking down the path again, she increased her pace, confident she could walk faster than a simple turkey.

When she looked back one last time and saw that the bird was keeping pace with her, she whirled around and stomped her foot. "Fair warning," she cautioned harshly.

The bird stopped and cocked its head.

"I can be a very angry woman. Now, I'm going to my home, and I suggest you go to yours. If you don't, if you swoop up and try to peck me, I'll swat you down, which I'm tempted to do anyway since you're probably the critter responsible for all the snags in my shawl."

The bird ruffled its feathers.

"Fine. Have it your way, but if you make me swat at you and you just happen to break your neck when you hit the ground, I'm taking your carcass straight to Phanaby to cook you up for dinner. And I'm going to enjoy every bite. Now go. Scoot! Away!"

The bird stared back at her, but didn't budge.

"Mercy! You're as despicable as . . . as that newspaper reporter here who's trying to ruin my life," she snapped, and then turned around and marched to the end of the path at the south side of the bridge before the bird finally disappeared into the brush.

"I wish I could make Robert Farrell and every other reporter searching for me disappear as easily," she grumbled, then hurried back toward the village.

Jake waited until long after Ruth disappeared from view before he shuttered the cabin window in the loft and climbed back down the ladder.

Drenched with guilt for intruding on the poor woman's privacy, he dismissed the urge to start a quick fire for one compelling reason: He could not afford to risk having her see smoke swirling from the chimney and realize he had been at home while she had been at her garden.

Jake grabbed a fresh pair of denim trousers and put them on. He'd had no intention of leaving Miss Wyndam's barn just after dark last night and returning to his cabin again, but had accidentally spilled paint on the trousers he was to wear to services.

After brushing his hair, he poured fresh water into a basin so he could shave. He picked up the shaving brush, swept it through the water, and worked up a good lather of soap before he used the sliver of a mirror he had set on the mantel to make sure he slathered over his entire beard.

One tiny stroke of his single-edge razor on the cleft of his chin left a gash, and he could see his hands were shaking too hard to even attempt the task. He cast the razor aside. The way his life was unfolding, he would end up with more nicks on his face than he had managed to inflict the first time he put razor to beard.

Settling for a bit of stubble on his face instead, he wiped his face and held a cloth to his chin, hoping the bleeding would soon stop. He turned away from the image staring back at him in the mirror, but he could not stop the echo of that woman's sobs, which had driven him from his bed to open the shutter on the loft window.

He had heard such deep, guttural grief only twice before. Once when he listened to his mother weep after his father's death, and once several months ago when the family who had hired him to repair their roof had buried their two-year-old twin sons. And he knew now, beyond any doubt, that Ruth was deeply grieving the loss of a loved one: her father.

Farrell's claim that Jake was foolishly risking his future as a reporter by staying here, however, overwhelmed the sound of her gut-wrenching sobs that echoed in his mind, and he stiffened. As important as it was to confirm her identity, he had never intended to eavesdrop or to intrude on the grieving woman's privacy. Farrell, on the other hand, would have relished the opportunity. Jake was equally certain that Farrell would have no qualms about sensationalizing what should remain a very private moment, all in the name of truth, however hurtful that might be for her.

"Truth," he murmured, recalling the conversation he'd had with Ruth, bantering about the public's insatiable thirst for scandal and an individual's right to privacy.

He pulled the cloth away from his chin to distract him from thoughts that were confusing him and looked back into the mirror. The cut was no longer oozing, but he had smeared blood on the end of his chin. After dipping the end of the cloth into the basin of water, he wiped away the blood very carefully so as not to open the wound.

When he recalled Farrell's voice echoing his brother's ultimatum, he bristled. Clifford was a responsible, though rather ruthless, businessman, but he was still Jake's brother. Perhaps he was a bit too driven to make the *Galaxy* the top-selling newspaper in New York City to suit Jake's more reticent personality, but he was one of the most admired newspapermen in the city. Now that he had sent Farrell out to find Ruth Livingstone, Jake knew he had to focus on finding that wooden chest Capt. Grant spoke of, to determine if the contents had any relevance at all to his assignment.

When Ruth's voice echoed in his mind, demanding equal attention, he swallowed hard. She had reopened wounds he had struggled too long to heal when she mentioned the series he had written about Victoria Carlington. He would be a good reporter again, even a great one like his brother, and he was definitely not going to disappear into anonymity like Ruth had hoped his punishment would be.

"Maybe Farrell was right about one thing. I probably stayed away too long," he admitted and walked over to the cabinet in the corner to see if he could find something to eat for breakfast that did not require a fire to heat it. In the process of moving a tin of stale crackers aside, he knocked over the blue bottle containing the remedy from Mr. Garner and sent it crashing to the dirt floor.

He jumped back, but still ended up with a large, wet stain on his trousers. "At this rate,

I'll be left with nothing but my nightshirt to wear to services," he complained, then stomped across the room to change into his last pair of clean trousers.

At least he did not have to worry about what to say if Spinster Wyndam mentioned at church that he had gone home last night. Ruth would never believe that he had not heard her crying.

Gazing out toward Ruth's garden patch, he suspected that more than a few of the older folks, who did not sleep soundly anymore, or parents of young children, who were often up during the night, may have heard the sound of a woman sobbing. Because Ruth had been raised in the city, she probably did not know how easily sounds echoed over the river. His one hope was that Farrell would have been so dosed with Mr. Garner's remedy that he had slept soundly without hearing anything at all.

Still, he figured he could not keep the villagers from gossiping about what they might have heard during the night, though he believed he had the perfect excuse to explain why he had not heard anything at all.

Despite what Farrell or Clifford might think of him, Jake knew that the very fact that he cared about Ruth's feelings did not

mean he was not a good reporter.
Just a kind one.

EIGHTEEN

Rev. Haines stood in front of the packed meetinghouse and concluded the Sunday service with a final, personal message. "Although I'm leaving tomorrow for several weeks, you will never be far from my thoughts. I will continue to pray that your deep faith in almighty God will remain constant, that your hope in Him will conquer your fears, and that your love for our Savior will sustain you, comfort you, and bring you joy," he offered, repeating the theme of today's sermon. "Pray for me, too, that I may bring this message of faith, hope, and love to those who live beyond our village. Praise God."

"Praise God!"

The members of the congregation had answered enthusiastically in a single voice, but Ruth had managed only a whisper. Her faith felt too tenuous, her hope nearly gone. Still, she took a moment, as the congregation rose to leave, to remain sitting. Although she was grateful the reporter had not come to services this morning, she said a quick prayer, asking God's help to at least keep Farrell away from the picnic.

Phanaby had told Ruth she'd heard her cries echoing across the river earlier this morning, and she wondered how many others may have heard as well. She did not need to look into a mirror to know that the hour she had spent pressing cold, tea-soaked cloths to her face had not done much good. Most of the redness in her face had dissipated before leaving the house, but she could feel the puffiness around her eyes. Every time she blinked, it felt as if she had tiny grains of sand caught beneath her eyelids.

Someone, if not everyone, was bound to notice how poorly she looked, and if they had heard the same sobbing sounds as Phanaby, they might suspect she was the woman who had been crying at dawn. Her only consolation was in knowing that Jake Spencer had spent last night at Spinster Wyndam's rather than at the cabin.

The congregation was slow to clear outside, and Ruth adjusted Lily's sleeping form to a more comfortable position in her arms, willing her to sleep as long as possible.

Unlike the small but elegant church where her father had preached every Sunday, this meetinghouse was very plain, even austere. Instead of arched windows of colorful stained glass, the windows here held ordinary clear glass. Roughhewn benches, rather than polished pews, provided seating.

The size of the congregation, in all truth, was about the same, since her father had not been invited to preach to the larger, more affluent congregations in the city. The manner of dress here, however, was much less formal, and members of this congregation considered freshly laundered clothes to be their Sunday best, which suited Ruth's meager wardrobe just fine.

The only decoration came from two large vases on either side of the pulpit that held bouquets of early roses in a variety of colors that included white, pale yellow, shocking pink, and deep crimson. They added the only hint of beauty, which explained why Rev. Haines had encouraged her to grow flowers in her garden for him.

At the time, Ruth had been certain she would be gone by the time the flowers she had yet to plant would be in bloom. Now she found it hard not to resent the fact that she would remain here because she had no other place to go, a child to protect, and an identity to keep secret.

Sighing, she shifted Lily a bit to ease the tingling in her arms. She was a bit small for her age, according to Phanaby. But when she was asleep in Ruth's arms, she was dead weight and Ruth grew impatient to leave. Finally, when the line of people in the main aisle started moving again, she followed Phanaby with no small measure of relief.

When they finally reached the front door, Ruth and Phanaby walked outside while Elias remained to help several other men who were carrying benches outside to the plot of land beyond the cemetery on the north side of the building.

Phanaby took her free hand. "You look much better now. It'll do you good to mingle with folks awhile today. And I have it on good authority that Mr. Farrell has no plans to attend the picnic today, either."

Ruth's heart skipped a hopeful beat. "Really? How did you — ?"

"Mrs. Burkalow told me," she whispered. "Now try to relax and enjoy yourself today. Just remember: Time heals our hurts very slowly, but it does heal them. Hold on to that hope. That was part of Reverend Haines's message today, wasn't it?"

Ruth moistened her lips and raised her gaze to meet Phanaby's. "Yes, it was," she admitted, although she had little hope left that God was truly looking out for her best interests.

Phanaby waited a moment until a parade of men marched out of the building with the benches. "Then hold on to that hope. Hold on to that little one, too. She needs you so very much," she murmured, tracing the contours of Lily's face. "You go ahead now and join the others while I help set out the rest of the food."

When Lily stirred and started opening her eyes, Ruth rocked from side to side, hoping she might lull her back to sleep. "I'll be glad to help."

"Nonsense. Lily looks like she's waking up. Take her to play with the other children. Talk to some of the other young mothers," Phanaby insisted and hurried off.

Left to her own devices, Ruth was half tempted to slip away unnoticed and take Lily home, but she knew that Phanaby would be disappointed in her. She scanned the grounds between the meetinghouse and the picnic area and quickly made up her mind. Rather than walk along the path that led through the cemetery to reach the crowd of people gathered on the other side, she decided to take the longer route by walking the perimeter of the property along Lawrence Street, which was bordered by shade trees just beginning to wear a new season of foliage.

She had only taken a few steps before she stopped so abruptly, she had to put her hand to Lily's back to keep the child from pitching forward. She turned and stared at the two men standing in the alley across the street, arguing with each other, and realized she recognized them. Although they were well out of sight of the rest of the gathering across the way, she had a clear view of the men from this vantage point.

She had only met Robert Farrell once yesterday, but his face and form had been indelibly imprinted in her mind's eye, if only for self-preservation. She had spent much more time with Jake Spencer, but she had never seen him as agitated as he was now. She watched in fearful fascination as Jake jabbed his finger into the other man's chest. She could not hear what he was saying, but she did not miss the angry set to his features or the arrogant grin on Farrell's face when he shoved Jake's hand away.

As they continued to interact, their anger eventually dissipated, much to her relief. As they talked together more calmly now, she had the distinct impression they actually knew each other.

They know each other.

Her blood froze, and she urged Lily even closer when she saw the two men shake hands and part ways, each disappearing at the far end of the alley. How Jake Spencer and Robert Farrell knew each other or what they were discussing was troublesome. Knowing now that Jake had lied to her yesterday when he claimed he did not know the reporter and had not even met him was far more hurtful and disturbing, setting off all sorts of alarm bells that left Ruth trembling.

She tried to make sense of what she had just seen. Why had Jake lied to her? And why had she assumed he was nothing more than he appeared to be — an ordinary man trying to recover from a dreadful injury?

She paused to shift Lily back up a bit and shook her head. Maybe she was simply overreacting, or maybe she was misinterpreting what she had seen. Had Farrell and Jake simply run into each other, whereupon Farrell said something that angered Jake? If that were true, what were they doing in that alley?

Sighing, she continued on her way since she did not have any answers to her many questions, but her trust in Jake Spencer had been sorely eroded. She faulted herself for letting down her defenses and vowed to be much more careful in the future, especially when she was at her garden.

When Lily finally woke up and tried to squirm down, Ruth relished the distraction and set the toddler on her feet. She tried to keep hold of Lily's hand, but Lily promptly yanked free. "I suppose it wouldn't hurt to give you a little freedom," she said, hoping she had not put their mutual freedom at risk through her interaction with Jake Spencer.

Suddenly Lily charged in front of her, headed for the roadway to the right. Ruth swooped her up and set her back down again in the soft grasses on her left. "No, Lily," she said firmly and blocked the child when she tried running back to the roadway again. To her relief, Lily toddled ahead in the grass as Ruth watched her carefully, ready to intervene again. Wearing a lavender frock and matching bonnet that Phanaby had chosen this morning, the little girl looked absolutely adorable, but the color itself gave Ruth pause.

According to what she had read in the newspapers, Rosalie Peale had been well-known for wearing the lavender gowns that had become her trademark. Lily's wardrobe, which was finer in both quality and extent than Ruth's, proved that her mother had earned well, too.

Rather than judge the poor murdered woman for the sinful life she had chosen for herself, or the child she had loved well enough to provide such an elaborate wardrobe, Ruth focused her attention on Lily. She paused to watch, in awe, as Lily started twirling round and round, her arms open wide. When she started to lose her balance, Ruth edged behind her to keep her from falling. She sat Lily down on the ground when she saw that the child's eyes were getting a bit glazed and quickly sat down beside her. "I think you need to rest a bit," she crooned.

Lily promptly lay back and tugged on Ruth's arm, and Ruth realized she used those very words when putting Lily down for her afternoon nap. Chuckling, she lay down beside the little one. "Just for a moment, then we have to join everyone for our picnic dinner," she suggested, and realized she was probably making a spectacle of herself by lying in the grass with Lily.

Ruth glanced over at the crowd of people enjoying the picnic and smiled. Folks were too busy chatting or filling their plates with food to notice much of anything else. Looking up, with the brim of her bonnet blocking the glare of the overhead sun, she pointed to a small group of clouds corralled between two branches. "Those are pretty white clouds, Lily. See?"

Lily pointed upward. " 'Loud," she repeated, looked around, squinted, and pointed to her left. " 'Loud."

"That's yellow. That's the sun, and you can only see a tiny part of it," she said gently. "The sun is really much bigger than those little clouds, and it's very bright so we mustn't look directly at it."

"Big!" Lily cried and opened her arms wide. "Lily big!"

"Yes, you're getting to be a very big girl, and a dear one," Ruth murmured, surprised at how quickly Lily was slipping past all her defenses, nurturing feelings as instinctive and natural as if Lily had been her own child.

"Mercy! Are you both hurt?"

Startled, Ruth turned her head in the opposite direction and saw a curtain of gray flowered skirts. She raised her gaze and saw the face of an elderly woman she had yet to meet. Unfortunately, she did recognize the man standing next to her, leaning on his cane, and assumed his companion was most likely Spinster Wyndam.

"We're both fine," Ruth insisted and

scrambled to her feet. She urged Lily to stand up again and brushed off the bits of grass and dirt clinging to the toddler's frock before attending to her own skirts. "We just stopped to play a bit," she explained.

The elderly woman, who had a pale brown freckle that dimpled one of her cheeks, was by far the homeliest woman Ruth had ever met. But she gazed at her with kind eyes that also twinkled with a bit of mischief. She nudged Jake with her elbow and looked up at him. "And here I was hoping you could rescue this lovely young woman and her precious little girl. We ladies do love a strong, handsome protector, you know," she ventured before returning her gaze to Ruth.

Ruth tried not to cringe, wondering if Jake would be her protector or her nemesis.

"Mr. Spencer pointed you and your daughter out to me while you were walking over to join everyone," the elderly woman said. "But the next time I looked, there you were, lying on the ground, and I insisted that he bring me along to make certain you were both all right. I'm afraid it never occurred to either one of us that you might have taken a moment to play. But that's not important now. After all I've heard about you, I so wanted to meet you, Ruth. I'm

Spinster Wyndam. Gloria Alexandra Wyndam."

Ruth caught Lily around the waist and hoisted her up to rest on her hip. "I'm pleased to meet you," she said, although she had hoped to avoid the inveterate matchmaker, especially since it seemed obvious the woman had set her sights on pairing up Ruth with Jake. "Mr. Spencer," she said to acknowledge him and noticed his cheeks were a bit flushed. A remnant from his earlier argument? Or embarrassment at Spinster Wyndam's obvious intentions?

She glanced down at Lily and furrowed her brow. Now that the child was closer to eye level with the newcomers, she seemed too mesmerized by the freckle on Spinster Wyndam's cheek to do more than sit quietly and stare at the woman. Completely ignoring Jake Spencer, Ruth continued the conversation with the woman. "I trust that you were pleased with the painting work Mr. Spencer did for you yesterday."

Spinster Wyndam smiled. "Indeed I am, although I was rather disappointed that he had to return home instead of staying overnight in the barn. I barely slept all night for worrying about him walking all the way home with his poor back bothering him after all the work he did for me."

Ruth felt the blood drain from her face, horrified to think he had been inside the cabin when she had been at her garden this morning to hear her crying, or worse — that he had actually gotten out of bed, gone outside, and seen her so distressed. "You were home last night," she managed, wondering if he had reported what he must have seen and heard early this morning to Farrell, which might have sparked their argument in some way.

"Unfortunately, I had little choice," he offered, garnering Ruth's attention again. "I spilled paint on the trousers I'd brought with me to wear to services today and had to get another pair. Since I didn't want to risk aggravating my back, I thought it best not to walk all the way back again."

Ruth's heart started to pound, and she had to lock her knees together to keep her legs from buckling.

"I'm afraid I took a double dose of that remedy from Mr. Garner as soon as I got back to the cabin."

Her head snapped up. "You did?"

He moved his cane closer. "My back started to seize up again, and I knew I had to do something because I didn't want to disappoint Spinster Wyndam," he offered. "I managed to get the medication and put a blanket on the floor because I knew I couldn't make it up the ladder to the sleeping loft. By then, I couldn't even crawl over to the door to the cabin and latch it tight."

He paused and started to chuckle. "I sleep very, very soundly with a single dose, just like Mr. Garner said I would, but after twice as much, I'm afraid I'd still be sleeping if that dumb turkey that's been hanging around the cabin hadn't slipped inside and started poking at me."

Her heart leaped with relief. "No!"

"Yes, it did, dear," the spinster said with a grin. "See? He's got a good gash, right there on his chin. Even so, he still managed to come back to escort me to services, just as he promised, although he was a tad late," the spinster added with a frown. "We scarcely made it inside before the services started, but I thought he completely abandoned me afterward. Fortunately, he came back from running some sort of errand just in time to help me meet you, although I can't fathom how he can be off and about with that bothersome back of his."

"Indeed," Ruth murmured, noting the flush on his cheeks had deepened.

Jake cleared his throat, and she saw his knuckles whiten as he leaned more heavily on his cane. "If truth be told, I slipped out to go back and get a bit more of the remedy. My back is rather unpredictable, and I didn't want to have to leave the picnic early."

Another lie. How many more lies would he tell her?

He cleared his throat. "That said, I don't suppose I could convince either of you ladies to keep the sorry tale of that turkey nipping me to yourselves so folks would just think I nicked myself shaving," he said meekly, glancing from one woman to the other.

Spinster Wyndam shrugged. "I suppose I could, but only if you agree to come to supper this week at my house with Ruth."

He nodded, albeit reluctantly.

"You'll come, won't you, Ruth?" the woman asked.

"I-I don't think so," Ruth said, anxious to distance herself from this man and the woman's efforts to match them together. "Lily takes up much of my time, and with the housework and helping Mr. Garner in the apothecary, I really don't think I should impose by asking them to watch Lily while I —"

"Then bring her with you," the elderly woman insisted.

Ruth cringed. "No, really, I couldn't. Her table manners are still so poor, and she

216

tends to be a bit cranky by the end of the day. Thank you, but no. I really shouldn't."

"Then I'll just speak to Phanaby myself and ask her to watch Lily for you. I'm quite certain she would want you to have a bit of free time for yourself. And don't argue with me. I'm your elder. Now come along, Ruth. A number of us have a few special gifts to give you to welcome you to our village, and we're anxious to see how you like them."

NINETEEN

Much to Ruth's complete consternation, Robert Farrell did not leave on Monday or even the following day. He finally boarded the stagecoach at the very last possible moment on Wednesday morning, just before the stage pulled out at seven o'clock, splashing southwest along ruts filled with water from the heavy rain the night before.

Ruth, however, was more horrified than overjoyed since Elias and Phanaby were also on board. En route for a two-day visit with friends who lived in Forked River, they had Lily tucked on the seat between them, a basket filled with breakfast, and Ruth's prayers that they would survive traveling with their little companion without incident.

Ruth kept pace with the stagecoach, waving to her new family inside and trying not to panic before it finally pulled ahead. By the time she had decided she needed to tell the Garners about seeing Jake and Farrell together, the couple had announced their trip, insisting on taking Lily along. Noting their excitement, she decided to wait to tell them, fearing they'd delay their trip otherwise. She did not trust anyone more than the Garners to protect Lily, and she tried not to let her fears get the best of her, ruining the total freedom, endless peace, and absolute solitude she would enjoy for the next two days.

Her intent was to gather the bushel of gifts from the women in the congregation and carry them out to her garden, along with her own picnic breakfast. She'd also promised Phanaby she'd deliver a pail of food to Jake Spencer.

The air was still moist with the recent rain, rich with earthy scents she had never detected while living in the city. She hustled down Main Street and nodded politely to several passersby she had seen at Sunday services, as well as Mr. Toby, who was sitting outside the general store on the other side of the street, waiting for it to open.

When she spied several people talking together outside of Burkalow's Tavern two squares ahead and realized two of those people were the Jones cousins, she left the walkway and started across the street to reach an alley that would take her to the

219

bridge without being seen. Otherwise she would lose half her morning listening to the two cousins bantering back and forth without saying much at all.

She had no desire to meet up with Spinster Wyndam, either. Unfortunately, the inveterate matchmaker had been able to convince Phanaby while at the picnic that having Ruth to supper with Jake Spencer was a good idea. But she had every hope that Phanaby would support Ruth's decision not to go once Ruth told her about Jake lying to her about not knowing Robert Farrell.

Ruth reached the alley without incident, but hesitated to continue because the alley was so muddy. Still, to preserve her time of solitude, she decided to navigate around the thick puddles of mud and lakes of rainwater. She was only partway down the alley, however, when she heard something following her.

She looked back over her shoulder and saw a young man she had never seen before, who was astride a scrawny, slow-moving mule. She was confident she could stay far enough ahead that neither the man nor his mule posed any threat to her — until she noticed the reins in the man's hands were slack, his shoulders were sagging, and his eyes were closed.

In all truth, he looked like he had fallen asleep!

"He's either crazy or he knows he can completely trust that aged mule — something I'm not prepared to do," she grumbled. Tightening her shawl around her shoulders, she maneuvered around several large puddles as fast as she could but had to slow down to stretch her legs over the deep ruts in the roadway that surrounded rainwater that had yet to drain away.

She glanced over her shoulder again, noted the mule was much too close, and sighed with relief when she noticed a wide patch of dry ground just ahead, bordering the alleyway where she could get out of harm's way. She managed to reach it yet realized too late that the lighter color she assumed to be dry ground was in reality a large, flat boulder.

The smooth surface was dry, but her slippers were just damp enough that she slid forward. She struggled and finally found good balance when a wave of cold water washed over her feet. "Ugh!" With her teeth clenched, she whirled about and nearly lost her footing in the process.

She glared at the gangly young man sitting on the mule directly in front of her, not caring a whit that her cry of distress had startled him awake.

Blushing, he tugged at the reins. "Whoa, Shortcake. Whoa, you dumb critter. I said whoa!"

The mule brayed a protest but eventually obeyed. As soon as the animal stopped, the man hopped off its back, dragging the filthy coarse blanket he had been using into the mud, and ran back a few steps to reach her. "I'm so sorry, ma'am. Shortcake didn't mean no harm," he croaked, his voice slipping between childhood and manhood.

His face was as crimson as some of the roses that had decorated the meetinghouse on Sunday, and the blush spread to his ears as well. Dressed in coveralls that had more patches than cloth, he was extremely thin and looked as if he had not eaten a full meal for a good long while.

He snatched the hat off his head, unleashing a cowlick as thick as some of the cattails growing along the river's edge, and twisted it nervously in one hand while holding the end of the reins in the other. "You hurt any?"

She clenched her teeth and took a quick peek over her shoulder to inspect her skirts before she offered him a scowl. "Other than having the hem of my skirts drenched with muddy water, along with my slippers? No, I'm not hurt, although it isn't fair to put any blame on the mule. You're the one who fell asleep, not . . . Shortcake," she snapped, once she remembered the name of the mule.

When his eyes filled with unmanly tears that he swiped away with his shoulder, guilt nudged at her conscience, and she wished her reprimand had been less sharp. "I don't suppose that it was entirely your fault," she offered. "When I saw that you'd fallen asleep, I should have called out to wake you up, instead of ignoring the fact."

"Ma'am?" he murmured, as if he could not believe he had heard her correctly.

She looked down at her skirts and shrugged. "I expected to launder my gown after working in my garden today, so I suppose that having my skirts dirty before I get started instead of afterward doesn't really matter."

His lips turned up to form a tentative smile. "Yes, ma'am. Thank you, ma'am. But didn't . . . didn't your feet get wet some, too?"

She shifted from one foot to the other. For propriety's sake, she dared not lift her skirts to show him her slippers. "I have a pair of work boots I probably should have worn today in the first place," she said. "I'll just make a stop at home and change into them and set my slippers in the sun to dry out. Now, if you'll excuse me, I really must be on my way. I have a good walk ahead of me. Just don't fall asleep again, at least while you're riding Shortcake."

"Ma'am?"

She looked back at him. "Yes?"

"You're a real kind lady, and you're right. It weren't Shortcake's fault. It was mine," he said quickly, his face reddening when his voice cracked again. "I'd surely like to make it up to you, if I could."

She waved off his concern. "Thank you, but I'll be —"

"You said you had to walk a ways. I could let you ride Shortcake. She's old, but she's steady, at least when she's got a good rider on her back."

Ruth's eyes widened. "No, I couldn't . . . I mean, I shouldn't . . . I wouldn't want to keep you from wherever it is you were going," she gushed, unwilling to entertain even the notion of sitting on that mule when she had never been astride an animal a day in her life.

"My name's Ned. Ned Clarke," he said, extended his hand, but quickly withdrew it, which was probably best because it was so dirty. "I'm headin' to Double Trouble. Capt.

Grant told my pa that Mr. Ford down at the mill is hirin' there, but I can still do that after I help you."

"Did you say Capt. Grant?" Ruth blurted, surprised the sea captain knew enough about the area to be aware of any available jobs.

"Yes, ma'am. I did. The captain is a real nice man. My pa told me he helped Mr. Power find work a few months back, too. Capt. Grant even said when I get a little older I could have a job with him on the *Sheller,* but I can't leave my pa here all by hisself."

Ruth tucked away the hope that Capt. Grant might someday be as helpful to her and quickly introduced herself. "I thank you for your offer, but I've got quite a bit to carry out to my garden on the other side of the river, so it really wouldn't do for me to ride —"

"Shortcake can carry your stuff for you! She's good at that," he argued, his eyes bright with hope.

Ruth narrowed her gaze. "Really?" she asked, tempted to think she might not have to lug that heavy bushel all the way out to her garden.

His head bobbed up and down. "She carts all the charcoal my pa makes out in the pinelands to the docks here in the village. That's where we met the captain, but my pa's been pretty sick for the past few months, which is why I'm tryin' to find work."

"Follow me," she urged.

Two hours later, Ruth was sitting in Dr. Woodward's office waiting for the doctor to finish tending to Ned's badly sprained wrist. Shortcake was at the livery, where Mr. Ayers was providing the mule with feed, which Ned would eventually pay for out of the wages he would earn after starting to work there as soon as his wrist healed.

Most of the contents of Ruth's bushel basket had survived the accident that had injured the boy, except for the new gardening gloves Phanaby had given her. The only living thing that escaped without any injury or loss was that stupid turkey hen! If it had not fluttered out of the bushes in front of Shortcake, frightening the poor mule half to death, Ned would not have been hurt and her bushel basket would not have landed upside down on the ground, nearly ruining her gifts.

She had very definite plans for that animal once she found it, and those plans included a big pot, lots of boiling water, and a tasty dinner for the Garners when they got home.

When she heard the grandfather clock in the other room announce the hour with eleven strikes, she tried to look on the bright side. The day was still young. The sun was still shining. She also had more than a day and a half left to enjoy to herself before she again faced her uncertain future — a future that had seemed a little more uncertain, considering Farrell was traveling today with the Garners and Lily.

Still, the morning had not been a total loss. After talking to Ned, she had a glimmer of hope now that Capt. Grant might prove to be sympathetic to her plight if she really needed his help.

TWENTY

Time was running out.

Although Farrell had left on the morning stage, Jake knew the man would be back. The only question that remained unanswered was how soon that would be. He did not know what, if anything, the reporter would learn from the Garners while they traveled together to Forked River, but he knew the middle-aged couple well enough now to be certain they would continue to protect Ruth and Lily from the man who posed such a threat to them.

In point of fact, Jake was much more concerned about his relationship with Ruth. She had been cool, if not distant with him at the church picnic, and she had not returned to her garden since then, which made it abundantly clear that he had lost much-needed ground in his attempt to earn her confidence. With the Garners out of town, as well as Lily, he could ill-afford to waste this opportunity to regain Ruth's trust.

Snorting his frustration, Jake climbed the ladder to the sleeping loft for the last time to see if Ruth was on her way here. When he caught sight of her clomping down the path just beyond the bend, his mind raced with one overwhelming thought: time for the drama to begin!

He slammed the window shutter closed, charged across the loft, and practically slid down the ladder, earning a huge splinter in the palm of his hand for his hastiness. As soon as his feet hit the dirt floor, he ran to the cabin door, unlatched it, and cracked it open before he lay down, flat on his back, at the bottom of the ladder. With his heart pounding, he shut his eyes and took several long, deep breaths to ease the band of anticipation that tightened around his chest. Mentally, he imagined Ruth slowly rounding the bend, her face flushed.

Soon he heard her footsteps approaching the cabin, and he wondered if that pesky turkey was standing guard, as usual.

"Mr. Spencer? Are you home? It's me. Ruth Malloy. I've brought some food for you," she said and uttered an exclamation of surprise when the door slowly creaked open from the pressure of her knock. "Mr.

Spencer?"

A short pause. A rustle of skirts.

"Mr. Spencer!"

"I'm not dead. Just . . . incapacitated." He gritted his teeth and moved his arms just enough to prove his point.

A little color erased the pallor on her face, but she pulled the covered pail she was holding with both hands closer to her. "Is it your back again?"

He closed his eyes for a moment for effect and stared at the open rafters overhead when he opened them again. "Yesterday, today, and probably every day I have left to spend in this world," he grumbled. "Yes, it's my back. I had the foolish notion that I should try to fix the leaks in the roof during the rainstorm last night, which I actually managed to do. Unfortunately, I was heading back down the ladder a few hours ago after making certain the repairs were still working when my back seized up."

A sharp intake of breath. "You fell!"

"Only halfway," he said, meeting her gaze again. Her eyes were open wide, simmering with genuine concern that he quickly tried to ease. "I didn't expect that the aftereffects of the spasm would have kept me lying here this long, but I don't think I did any more damage to my back."

She took a cautious step closer. "Are you certain? I can fetch Dr. Woodward for you."

He shook his head. "No doctor. But if you could help me, I think I could manage to sit up, at least."

Ruth moistened her lips and approached him slowly. "Tell me what to do."

He tapped one of his shoulders. "If you could just use your hands to push me up a bit, I'll have the momentum I need."

With a reluctant nod, she knelt down behind him and did as he asked. He was scarcely sitting up when she quickly rose and backed away.

Gritting his teeth, he slowly leaned back against the ladder. "I wouldn't argue if you offered to get some more of that remedy from Mr. Garner. I think I used up the last of it."

"He's not home. He closed the apothecary and took Mrs. Garner and Lily to Forked River today, and I don't expect them back until late tomorrow afternoon." She paused. "Are you certain there isn't a bit of the remedy left?"

He sighed. "Maybe some. You can find it in that cupboard over there," he suggested and pointed to the cabinet in the back corner, which meant she would have to walk directly past him to get to it. "It's in the

231

dark blue bottle —"

"I know what it looks like. I help Mr. Garner in the apothecary from time to time, as you might recall."

When her eyes glanced between him and the cabinet and she moistened her lips, he thought it fairly obvious that she was weighing propriety against necessity. "I doubt anyone would judge you for coming inside to help me, but perhaps it would be best if you just left whatever it is you've got for me in that pail and leave it by the door," he offered quickly, all too familiar with the villagers here who would distort almost anything to have something new to gossip about, especially if it concerned the attractive young widow.

Would she choose to protect her reputation and go? Or would she choose to help him and stay? He asked himself those questions each time his heart pounded another beat while he waited for her to make up her mind. What he didn't realize was that his entire future depended on what she decided to do.

Ruth stood in the doorway and took several deep breaths while she battled yet another twist to the day she had planned for herself. As concerned as she was about the man sitting on the floor, and as disillusioned as she was about his character, the man obviously needed her help.

Though moved by a sense of duty, as well as her conscience, she could not forget how he had lied to her. With her guard up, she got right to work, planning to leave as quickly as she could before she confronted him with what she now knew: He was a liar and a man she no longer trusted.

After putting the pail down on the floor, she took the chair sitting near the hearth and propped it in front of the door to keep it from closing and draped her shawl across the back of the chair. She untied the ribbons on her bonnet, set it onto the seat of the chair, picked up the pail, and walked toward him. "I think it's better if I keep the door open, which would make it clear there's nothing improper going on here," she suggested, worried her words sounded a little more strident than she intended.

She set the pail on the table next to the newspapers he had spread out there before she turned around and faced him.

"That's probably a good idea," he agreed, "as long as that pest of a turkey hen doesn't decide to take advantage of the opportunity to come inside, too."

She cringed, just thinking about what

would happen if that critter came inside. "I hadn't thought of that," she admitted.

"I tried to get rid of it when I first moved into the cabin, but I gave up. I'm afraid I've even been leaving a few grains for it to eat now and again. I hope it didn't bother you overmuch."

She shrugged, unimpressed by his attempt to make her think he was a caring man and annoyed that he had no idea she had caught him in not one lie but two. "Not so much when I tried to get to the door, but earlier . . . that's a different story."

While she set out the contents of the pail on the table, she told him about meeting Ned and quickly explained how the turkey had swooped down and startled Shortcake when it landed in front of the mule.

"My bushel basket ended upside down and poor Ned wound up with a badly sprained wrist when he fell trying to calm down the mule," she said as she set out the last of the food.

He had a rather odd look on his face, and she frowned. "I'm sorry. I didn't think to ask if you'd like to have something to eat. Mrs. Garner thought you'd enjoy some fresh bread, and she sent a crock of apple butter and the extra chicken left from dinner yesterday. I suppose I could fix a plate

for you or find something else in the cabinet
—"

"Just check the medication," he whispered. "Please. I don't dare attempt to get up from this floor until I have a dose of it."

She swallowed hard and kept her gaze averted when she walked by the man on her way to the cabinet. Since the door on the cabinet was missing, she had a clear view of the meager supplies sitting on the shelves and quickly found the blue bottle.

She unplugged the cork and looked inside. "You were right. It's completely empty," she said. "You'll have to wait for Mr. Garner to return for more, but I'll check the apothecary when I get back. He may have made some up for you in advance."

She noticed he was shivering a bit and realized the hours he had spent lying on the dirt floor probably had chilled him.

Without bothering to ask, she walked straight to the hearth. He only had a few spindly branches of kindling, but the three logs sitting there would keep a small fire burning for him for a few hours, assuming she could find something to help them catch.

Anxious to leave and finding herself more and more annoyed with the man, Ruth decided not to waste any time searching outside for more kindling and walked back to the table. She grabbed a few of the newspapers lying on top and rather enjoyed crumpling them up. She found the tinderbox sitting on the mantel and knelt down, ready to set the newspapers on fire when he startled her.

"Stop! Wh-what are you doing?" he yelled, sounding as if he thought she was about to set the cabin ablaze.

She looked over at him, saw the horrified look on his face, and frowned. "You're shivering with cold. Before you take a good chill and end up with lung fever, I decided to start a fire."

"That much is obvious, but there must be kindling you can use instead of my newspapers."

She cocked a brow. "You don't have any kindling, and I'd prefer not to go outside to get any when there are perfectly good newspapers sitting right here that I can use instead," she insisted, then saw that his gaze of disapproval did not soften.

She shrugged. "Have it your way. I'll go outside for the kindling, but if I have an encounter with that hen and have any trouble with it or it pecks at my shawl, I'm going to leave and you can sit there on the cold, damp floor until —"

"Use the newspapers if you must, but make certain to take the ones on the bottom of the pile. I've already read those," he suggested.

"But these are already crumpled up," she argued. Visions of him talking to Farrell in that alley on Sunday flashed in her mind's eye, and she lost hold of her temper. "Fine. I'll set these aside and use some of the others, although I daresay you must have heard all the latest news from Mr. Farrell when you talked to him on Sunday. In fact, you looked as if you were quite well-acquainted, despite your claims otherwise."

To her supreme satisfaction, Jake actually paled.

"You saw us together?"

"As a matter of fact, I did, which raises the question of why you lied to me about not knowing him. Not once, but twice," she said, before she turned away and concentrated on getting the fire started. For the first time since she had met him, he seemed to be at a loss for words, and she filled the vacuum, once the logs caught, by getting a few utensils and a banged-up tin plate that looked clean from the cabinet and carrying them back to the table.

"I'm sorry," he murmured.

She ignored him, slathered a spoonful of

237

apple butter onto several slices of bread, and laid them on the plate next to two pieces of fried chicken.

"I said I was sorry," he repeated, a bit louder.

Frowning, she glanced at him. "Are you sorry you lied, or sorry that you were caught in your lies?"

He cleared his throat. "I'm sorry I lied to you, and I'd like to explain —"

"Actually, you don't owe me an explanation," she insisted. She suddenly became aware, for the first time, of all the lies she had told to him. "No, you don't owe me anything."

Dismissing her lies as necessary, if not crucial, to keep Lily safe, she also rejected the notion she was being a total hypocrite and dropped her gaze. "All I really expect from you is exactly what you promised me when you told me I could keep tending my garden on your property. My privacy. Nothing more," she said and set the utensils on the plate next to the food she had prepared for him. "Otherwise I'll simply have to find somewhere else to plant my garden or give up the idea completely."

TWENTY-ONE

If Jake had any hope left of completing his assignment and reclaiming his career, as well as his brother's forgiveness and support, avoiding Ruth by meeting her demand for privacy was out of the question.

He drew a deep breath, locked his gaze with hers, and prayed he was not about to make the biggest mistake of his life. "If it's only privacy you want from now on, consider your request granted, although I must admit that I'm extremely disappointed in you." When her eyes widened with surprise, he pressed his point. "I might add disillusioned, as well, but I'm quite certain you're not interested in hearing why, so if you wouldn't mind, just leave the food on the table and make sure the door is closed tight when you leave. I won't bother you again. You have my word."

She gasped, and her cheeks flamed. "Y-you're disappointed in m-me? And dis-

disillusioned?" she sputtered, balling her hands into fists. "I'm not the one who lied."

He shrugged, annoyed at the disadvantage of sitting on the floor when he was trying to win any advantage he could. "Granted," he said calmly. "At least I'm not guilty of rash judgment or a closed mind. I leave it to you to lay claim to those rather unfortunate qualities."

Her eyes darkened to thunderclouds of disbelief. "My mind is always open. I'd be willing to listen to any reasonable explanation you might have for lying, assuming I could trust that explanation not to be another lie. But I know what I saw and I sincerely doubt there's anything you could say that would convince me I'm wrong."

"What exactly did you see?" he prompted, unable to fashion any explanation she might accept until he knew precisely what she had seen.

She relaxed her hands and placed her palms on the table, as if needing something solid to hold on to. "I was walking down Lawrence Street with Lily when I saw you in an alley down the way. You were arguing with Mr. Farrell, although the two of you seemed to end up leaving together as . . . as friends."

Grateful she had not seen Farrell leaving

his cabin Saturday afternoon, which would have been much more difficult to explain, Jake nodded. "That would have been on Sunday, just after services and right before the picnic started," he admitted, recalling the acrimonious conversation he'd had with Farrell, followed by how distant Ruth had been when he had escorted Spinster Wyndam over to meet her.

"When I asked you if you had seen the reporter, you told me you hadn't, which was obviously a lie."

He narrowed his gaze. "As I recall, you asked me that question on Saturday, when I stopped at the apothecary. At the time, I hadn't seen him or talked to him at any time or in any place in the village."

She blinked. "W-well, that's true, but you also said you didn't know him, when it was quite apparent that you and he were well acquainted when I saw you both together in the alley the next day. And when . . . when Spinster Wyndam mentioned you had abandoned her briefly after services, you said you'd gone back to get some remedy for your back —"

"Which I did," he interrupted. "That's when I ran into Farrell and argued with him."

"The alley isn't on your way back to your

cabin. It's quite out of your way since it sits on the opposite side of the river," she argued.

He sighed, as much for effect as to garner the strength to lie to a woman who by all rights would run screaming from this cabin if she knew he was a newspaper reporter who planned to reveal to the reading public her identity, her whereabouts, and what role she had played in her late father's recent legal difficulties. "The truth is that I didn't run into Farrell in the alley. He was following me."

"Following you? Why?"

He let out another sigh. "Farrell offered me a job."

"A job? What sort of job?"

"To use his words, he offered me an 'unusual opportunity to serve the public,' " he said, trusting Ruth would never have the opportunity to verify his version of what had transpired. Once she heard the tale he was about to spin, she would never talk to Farrell when he stopped back in the village en route to New York City, either. Yet, manipulating Ruth by lying to her stoked fears that he was becoming as unscrupulous as Farrell — a fear he nudged away with difficulty.

"Why would he do that?" she argued. "According to what you said, you weren't even acquainted."

"While staying at Burkalow's, he said he heard there was a newcomer who was doing odd jobs around the village. He got my name and searched me out. Apparently, he assumed I'd be interested in earning even more by keeping my ears open and reporting anything I heard about Ruth Livingstone to him when he returned in a few weeks. He also asked me to keep an eye on the stagecoach, checking travelers and such, to see if she passed through here."

She paled, losing the blush that had earlier stained her cheeks. "Wh-what did you tell him?"

He cringed. "Actually, I'm afraid I lost my temper and jabbed the man in the chest while I told him that I would not return the many kindnesses the villagers have shown to me by being a snitch or a gossipmonger," he explained, though he had actually been warning the man not to interfere with his work here in the village and to remember Jake's status as co-owner of the *Galaxy*. "When he told me he would simply find someone else who was 'less bothered by principles,' I pretended to have a change of heart to keep him from doing just that. Reverend Haines has the advance Farrell gave me. I trust he'll put it to good use, although he has no idea where the money came from if you have a mind to ask him when he returns. I didn't think it would serve any purpose to tell anyone at the picnic, including you and Spinster Wyndam, about Farrell's offer, other than to set off a round of unnecessary gossip. I hope I can trust you to keep what I've told you to yourself."

She nodded. "Of course. I-I'm sorry I . . . that is, I-I owe you an apology."

Jake felt their relationship tip in his favor, and yet he felt more relieved than vindicated. Maybe now he'd succeed in his task and fulfill his journalistic aspirations.

"You were right. I used rash judgment and I closed my mind to the possibility that you would have a reasonable explanation for what I had seen."

He nodded. "Apology accepted."

"What are you going to do when Farrell comes back? He'll expect you to —"

"He'll expect a report, which I'll gladly give him: I haven't seen anyone looking like the sketch he showed me of Ruth Livingstone. And no one here knows anything about Ruth Livingstone, other than what they read in the newspapers. That should satisfy the cad," he assured her.

"Cad indeed, although I probably shouldn't waste my breath gossiping about that unprincipled man."

"I know how much you avoid reading the newspapers, but you'd have an even lower opinion of him if you knew what he'd written in a recent article about Reverend Livingstone's daughter for the *Galaxy*." He hoped she would take this bait as easily as she had accepted his version of events. "As much as I am loath to admit it, you were right to think of some reporters as unscrupulous. I'm afraid Farrell fits that description rather well," he added, determined not to earn that same description for himself.

She stiffened her back and glanced at the crumpled newspapers lying on the table. "What article?"

"The one on the first page of Monday's *Galaxy,* which is probably unreadable, if it's one of the pages you crumpled. I wouldn't bother —"

"It's no bother," she insisted as she started smoothing out each of the balls of paper. "I'm rather curious to see what that man wrote."

He watched her carefully. He had been close enough to her several times now to get a rare glimpse into her soul, where he saw grief and confusion and uncertainty disturb an innocence and purity of heart that challenged all his assumptions about her. At this moment, however, as he watched her gray eyes shift from pale gray to dark orbs of determination, he struggled to gain control of his emotions where this woman was concerned. He only hoped he had not pushed her too far, but he needed to see her reaction to the latest news, which his brother had confirmed in his letter.

He knew the precise moment she found the paper with the article he wanted her to see. Her eyes widened, but he could not see how much they changed in color because of tears she repeatedly had to blink away while she attempted to read. When she finished and set the paper down, her hands were shaking and her face grown far too pale, and he hated the fact that he was responsible, in part, for her distress.

"I'm not certain why information like . . . like that had to appear in the newspaper when it should offend most people's sensibilities," she whispered. "This poor woman's . . . this poor woman's father was proven innocent and now rests in his grave. Mr. Farrell has no right to claim that the public has an interest in what a former friend of Reverend Livingstone has to say, or that the allegations made against his daughter, Ruth, have a single merit of truth to them." She turned her back to him.

"I happen to agree with you," he said firmly. In truth, he was convinced that in this particular instance, his brother as editor had stepped well beyond integrity by printing the information. "No decent man ever speaks out against a young woman like that, especially one who claimed to be a close friend of her father's. And for Farrell to report the man's claim that he had discovered she had been working at some unnamed brothel with her father's approval — when neither Rev. Livingstone nor his daughter is available to defend themselves — is the mark of a cad and an opportunist."

He paused, unable to tell if she was holding silent because she was trying to gather her wits or because she was trying to hold back tears. "Whether or not the story is true becomes irrelevant, because it cannot be verified, in which case the newspapers should never have reported it," he added. An ache grew in his gut as he questioned not only his brother's integrity for publishing it but also his own for calling it to her attention.

"I'm quite certain it's not irrelevant at all. Not to Ruth Livingstone," she murmured and walked out the door, unaware that she had left him wondering if he could finish the challenging task he had chosen to do for his brother by finding that wooden chest and verifying her identity . . . or if he should simply pack up his tools and disappear again.

All he knew for certain was that he had lost much more today than he had gained by getting her to trust him again.

TWENTY-TWO

Ruth felt absolutely nothing. Not anger. Not disappointment. She could not feel enough to know she was numb. She did not recall walking back from Jake's cabin or crossing the bridge to reach Main Street. She did not remember climbing the back staircase or changing out of her soiled clothes or starting a fire in the sitting room hearth, either.

But if she had not done any or all of those things, she would not be sitting on the floor of the sitting room, next to a steady fire, dressed in her nightclothes, and staring at three newspapers that were finally dry enough to read. Her heart did not race with dreaded anticipation or pound with fear. It simply beat to keep her alive, just as her mind simply rested in this precise moment, with no hurtful memories or ruined dreams.

Over the past two months, she had embraced every possible emotion and risen from the deep pit of grief and sorrow to the heights of pure joy, but she had never felt simply . . . nothing at all.

Not even the void where her heart or her emotions had once been.

It was as if her spirit had somehow slipped out of her body, leaving her soul troubled by a shattered faith and her human form only a shell that remained to merely function.

Sighing, she chose the *Sun* from the array of newspapers she had spread out to dry earlier that morning. Calmly and objectively, she read every article even remotely connected to her father and to herself. Most of them revisited previous articles. The two that did focus on her father's former friend's allegations, which the newspapers described as "stunning" and "shocking," also used words like "scurrilous" and "salacious" to describe her alleged character and behavior.

"Apparently the reporters for the *Sun* have a penchant for alliteration," she noted and slowly crumpled each page of the paper into a tight ball before placing all four of them very carefully into the fire. She watched the fire flare as it devoured the balls of paper and waited while the ashes fluttered into the embers like fallen butterflies.

She chose the *Transcript* next and repeated

the process to review the contents. She found a sketch of herself, identical to the one Robert Farrell had shown her, framed by one very long article and two shorter ones. She found some satisfaction knowing that Farrell would not find the sketch helpful in finding her and that the latest reports had her living somewhere in Philadelphia. The two short articles had nothing new to offer, except the news that Harrison Steward, her father's former friend, had left for an extended tour of the South. "Which he financed, no doubt, with his Judas money," she muttered before she turned her attention to the longest article. She read the last paragraph twice:

Thus, the Prodigal Daughters as an institution no longer exists. Its founder rests in his tomb, while his poor unfortunate victim lies cold in her grave, unable to cry out for total justice. This paper and all of its resources remain committed to be her voice until Ruth Livingstone has been found and the full truth has been revealed.

She folded the four-page newspaper again and again until it was the size of her fist, poked it beneath the bottom log, and watched the wad of paper burn until the ashes were fragile gray wisps that disappeared just like her father's lifework.

After picking up the *Galaxy,* she decided she had no desire to read Farrell's article again and let the fire destroy it, just like the others. Sitting quietly, she remained by the fire until only golden embers remained and nothing but silence surrounded her.

And in that stillness, bathed with soft light, her body fairly trembled as she once again felt her spirit grasp the tattered remnants of her faith. She closed her eyes, breathing slowly, breathing peacefully, evaluating her options now that she felt whole again.

She could choose to dwell on the past and let it haunt every moment of every day and be trapped in dark shadows. Or she could take another path, one that would require the courage to recognize the blessings she had been given and walk in the light that beckoned to her in the future.

She folded her hands in prayer and bowed her head. "Heavenly Father, I don't know where to begin," she murmured, but when she suddenly thought of last Sunday's sermon, she latched on to it. "Reverend Haines told us that with faith there is hope and where there is hope, there is love . . . which means I need to ask you to help me strengthen my faith in you. I give my worries, all my troubles to you, Lord." Ruth continued to pour her heart out until there was only room for His faith and His hope and His love to dwell within her.

By the time she finished, she expected to feel completely drained and exhausted. Surprisingly, she felt rejuvenated, and headed straight to her bedroom to keep one of her promises. When she returned, she was carrying the stack of articles she had cut from the newspapers.

She added a bit of kindling and a small log to the embers in the hearth. Once the fire was burning strongly again, she tossed in the clippings and waited until every word printed in those articles had joined the others buried in the ashes.

"I'm not living in shadows, and I'm not chasing them any longer. No more newspapers. I'm not reading them anymore. I'm not going to be afraid of what they might print about me or my father, either. I'm following the light. Only His light," she vowed.

Next, she went into the kitchen to find an oil lamp, which she set onto the kitchen table to light. She had not eaten a thing since breakfast, in part because she had sent her picnic dinner home with Ned, but mainly because she had been too upset after the time she had spent with Jake to feel like eating anything after she left his cabin.

She checked the larder. Even with the food gone that she had taken to the cabin, there was more than enough here for a snack and for all day tomorrow. She chuckled and shook her head. Phanaby had prepared enough food to feed half the village.

Without worrying what either Elias or Phanaby would think or having to be careful to set a good example for Lily, she polished off a platter filled with nothing but the food she loved most: raisin pie and thick slices of bread with lots of molasses on top.

She put the kitchen back to rights and decided she still was not tired. She got the apron she was making for Phanaby from her bedroom and took it into the living room, where the fire would keep her toasty warm and where Phanaby's sewing basket had the notions she would need. On second thought, she returned to the kitchen for the oil lamp before she settled down to work.

She sorted through the array of sewing tools stored inside the basket and snipped the frayed threads on the edges of the fabric before she started to hem them.

Once she started sewing the hem into place, her thoughts strayed and focused on

Jake Spencer until her needle got stuck in the fabric. She remedied the problem by forcing the needle through a piece of soap from the sewing basket and smiled when the needle glided through the fabric with ease.

Jake Spencer was a lot like that troublesome needle, she decided, and chuckled out loud. The comparison was a bit odd, but it fit her perceptions of him perfectly.

At first she had dismissed him as nothing more than a miserable recluse, who threatened the peace she had found working in her garden, along with the privacy she craved. She stopped for a moment, tied a knot in the thread before it got too short, rethreaded the needle, and resumed sewing. Now, however, she knew he was not miserable or reclusive by nature. He might be cranky now and again, but only when his back acted up.

In all truth, when he used the remedy from Mr. Garner, she might even agree with most of the others in the village that Jake Spencer could be quite a charming man, and she felt badly that Mr. Garner had not made any remedy for the man before leaving for Forked River. She felt even worse when she recalled how terribly she had misjudged him.

Jake was not uncommonly attractive, but she liked the way the sun caught the reddish highlights in his hair. The cleft in his chin made him look a bit roguish, too, when he did not have a nick in it.

"Ouch! Speaking of nicks," she grumbled, yanking back her finger and pressing her thumb against the small dot of blood where she had poked the needle into her flesh. "That's what I get for thinking he might be a prince of a man. Even if he did prove he isn't completely incorrigible by accepting my apology, I'm still not convinced we share all the same views about newspapers today."

Pausing, she checked her finger to make sure the bleeding had stopped and chose not to think about the nature of their discussion of the news. "Stay out of the shadows and follow His light," she whispered. "Just follow His light."

A loud, hard pounding downstairs on the back door came so unexpectedly, she nearly leaped out of her skin. Heart thumping, she recoiled against the back of her chair. For as long as she had been here, no one had ever come to the apothecary at this hour, when everyone in the household would normally be abed.

But most, if not everyone, in the village also knew that the Garners were out of town, and when Ruth opened the apothecary tomorrow, she would only dispense the medications he had prepared in advance. She could hardly imagine anyone would demand to buy them now, in the middle of the night.

The pounding started again, more urgent this time, and a man's voice rang out. "I've been looking and looking for you. I know you're in there. Open up!"

Trembling, Ruth set aside her sewing. Fear that Mr. Farrell had somehow snuck back into the village and waited until everyone was asleep and she was alone to come here grew stronger with every wild, erratic beat of her heart. Or had another reporter followed the same lead that had brought Farrell here?

"Regardless of who he is, the man's apparently not going to give up," she whispered, all too aware she had no one here to protect her, but more important, there was no one that could protect her from the fact that she was, in truth, Ruth Livingstone.

Her one and only consolation was that Elias and Phanaby were not here to discover that while she had welcomed their kindnesses to her and to Lily, she had been lying to them all along.

More pounding. More shouts. "Open.

This. Door! I know where you are and I'm not leaving until you let me in!"

Fearful that the insistent reporter would wake the entire village, she got to her feet. "I'm coming!" she shouted and headed toward the hallway. She stopped by her bedroom to get her shawl before she remembered she had left it behind again and so exchanged her robe for a heavier one instead.

She headed toward the door at the end of the hallway with her shoulders set and her head held high and her heart and soul wrapped around one thought: follow His light. When she opened the door and looked down, she saw a sliver of light coming through the window and the bottom of the door and sighed.

"The man brought a lantern?" she questioned, but used the meager light to guide her down the steps. "I'm coming," she shouted again when he kicked at the door. Once she was in the storeroom, she grabbed the broom and glanced out the window, but the glare of the lantern made it impossible to see anything beyond the shadow of the man standing there.

Broom at the ready, she unlatched the door and cracked it open, just enough to poke her head through. Temporarily blinded by the light, she caught a glimpse of a large, very tall, very broad-shouldered man before he shoved at the door and forced his way in, leaving the lantern sitting outside.

He stole every breath from her lungs when he lunged at her and grabbed her, effectively disarming her when he pinned her against him. "Now that I've found where you are, I'm never gonna let you go. Never."

TWENTY-THREE

The man overpowered Ruth so quickly and so completely, she had only one desperate thought: survival.

Strong arms wrapped around her upper body, pinning her arms at her sides and rendering her makeshift weapon useless. With her face pressed against his chest, she could not see anything at all. She had mere seconds before he crushed the life out of her, yet it seemed as if time had either stopped or was passing in slow motion.

Struggling to breathe, she could not draw in enough air to scream, even though his chest would absorb any sound she made if she did. She kicked him once, but since she was wearing bedroom slippers, she only ended up smashing her toes. With her heart pounding and sheer panic gripping her spirit, he gave her one more option when he lowered his head to kiss her.

His breath was so rank with spirits, her

stomach churned, and she reacted without a single hesitation when his mouth was a hairsbreadth away from her lips: She bit him as hard as she could.

"Darlin'!" he yelped and staggered back a few steps, dragging her with him. Though he hit his back on the shelves hard enough to send some of the baskets and medications stored there to the floor, he pulled her hard against him and tried to kiss her again.

She bit him twice as hard on his cheek.

Yelping and spewing expletives she had only heard once before from a seaman on Capt. Grant's ship, he relaxed his hold on her to cradle his face, and she squirmed free.

"Fiend!" she hissed and smacked at him with her broom.

He pushed off from the shelves, knocking one of the more rickety ones down, and staggered toward her with outstretched arms. "But darlin'!"

She backed up a few steps, flipped the broom from end to end, and aimed for his legs with the wooden handle. "You're addled, you fool! I'm . . . not . . . your . . . darlin'!" she hissed. She hit him again and again as she backed away from him, but he was unfazed and just kept coming.

The closer they moved to the light streaming in through the open doorway, the more she could discern his features. He obviously was not Robert Farrell, and she knew she had never seen this bear of a man anywhere in the village. When she reached the doorway, she was still hitting him, but she was almost ready to accept the idea he was too intoxicated to feel any pain at all.

When he suddenly pitched forward, she managed to leap out of the way. She landed on the bottom step, just in time to see him fall through the open doorway and land facedown on the ground outside. She peeked outside, saw his upper body lying next to the lantern, and grimaced. Since all the blood oozing out from beneath his face could not have come from the bites she had given him, she assumed the man must have broken his nose when he fell.

She snorted, smoothed the hair away from her face, and glared at his form. "If your feet weren't halfway inside blocking the door, I'd slam it shut and leave you right where you are, you addled simpleton. But if you broke your nose, you probably can't breathe. Not lying facedown in the dirt, which means I have to help you," she snapped.

She stopped just long enough to set her broom down and readjust her nightclothes. Once she had her robe tied tightly again, she picked up the broom and carried it outside with her, just in case he woke up and tried to grab her again.

She tried rolling him onto his back with one hand. "Pointless," she muttered. Stooping down, she tugged at one of his shoulders with all her strength, but the man was dead weight. She tried again and kept tugging until her face grew hot from the exertion and her arms were aching.

Finally, he started rolling over, but she heard the sound of multiple footsteps charging down the alley from Burkalow's Tavern before his back even hit the ground.

"What did you do? Bring an army with you?" she snapped and glanced at the doorway. Even if she had the strength, she did not have the time to drag him clear of the doorway so she could get back inside and latch the door closed before his friends arrived.

Running up the staircase and locking the door at the top of the steps made better sense, but if these men broke down the door, she would have no escape from them, short of jumping out a window. "Not an option," she hissed, noting the footsteps were getting dangerously close.

She stood next to him, blocking most of the light from the lantern, planted her feet, and brandished her broom with both hands to defend herself.

"We're coming, Widow Malloy! We're coming!"

Confused, she lowered the broom the moment the men came out of the shadows and into full view.

When the three very sober, very breathless men reached her, they braced to a halt and stared at the man lying at her feet. Ruth could not tell which of the three men was more surprised, because tears of relief blurred her vision.

When she could see clearly and her heartbeat slowed, she realized two of the men were gaping at her. She looked down at Mr. Burkalow, who was kneeling by the unconscious scoundrel who had assaulted her.

"It's him," he pronounced and got back to his feet.

Ruth stared at the fallen man and blinked her eyes several times in disbelief. From the way his nose was bent at an impossible angle, the man had most definitely broken it when he fell. But in addition to a bruise already forming on his forehead, his bottom lip was split open where she must have bitten him. He also had a circular wound on the flesh of one of his cheeks that bore the unmistakable pattern of teeth marks that would heal but leave a scar.

Instinctively, she flexed her wrist that bore a scar similar in shape, albeit much smaller, and groaned. Granted, she had bitten that horrid man out of desperation and fear. But she had bitten him nonetheless, and she wondered fleetingly if it was desperation or fear rather than sheer temper that had led Lily to bite.

When Mr. Toby took a step toward her, she flinched.

"You feelin' all right, Widow Malloy? That man hurt you any? I could fetch Doc Woodward for you."

"No, he . . . he didn't hurt me. He frightened me half to death, but I'm fine," she said.

"I'll go fetch the sheriff, then."

"No! I mean . . . there's no real harm done," she insisted, horrified to think the sheriff or any other official might get involved.

Mr. Ayers, the owner of the livery who had hired Ned earlier that afternoon, looked down at the man on the ground and shook his head. "Better fetch Dr. Woodward anyway. Widow Malloy might not need him, but this poor fella sure does. He'd be hurtin' real bad if he weren't sleepin'."

She snorted. "That 'poor fella' attacked

265

me!" She did not realize she was pointing the broom at Mr. Ayers until he raised his hands in surrender and took a very deliberate step back from her. "I'm sorry. I'm still a bit . . . flustered." She lowered her broom.

"There's no need for you to apologize," Mr. Burkalow argued, but he did not approach her, either. "I had a sense this man was goin' to find another bucket to drown his sorrows in when he left the tavern after I refused to serve him another drop. Never suspected he'd end up findin' a whole bucket of trouble here, though I suspect he wouldn't have either, even if he hadn't been addled."

"Do you know him?" she asked, dismissing any blame to put on Mr. Burkalow's shoulders at the moment.

"His name's Maxwell Flynn. Never knew him to stir up this kind of trouble before. He lives about five miles out in the pinelands, but comes into the village now and again, lookin' for his Abigail," Mr. Toby offered.

She cocked her brow. "Abigail?" she asked and assumed Abigail was the woman Mr. Flynn had referred to as "darlin'."

"That's his wife. She died a few years back, but when he's consumed more spirits than he should, he sometimes gets confused,

I suppose," Mr. Burkalow explained, nodded to the other two men, and motioned for them to help get Mr. Flynn on his feet.

"He'll be right upset when he wakes up and learns he attacked you," Mr. Ayers said as he braced one side of the unconscious man with his shoulder.

Mr. Toby braced the other side. "I came runnin' as soon as I heard a man hollerin' and poundin' on somebody's door. Met up with these two fine gentlemen at the corner."

"I wish we'd gotten here sooner," Mr. Burkalow offered meekly, picking up the lantern. When he glanced at Mr. Flynn's face, she thought she detected a bit of a smile, but dismissed it as nothing more than embarrassment. "Young Maxwell here can't speak for himself right now, but I expect he wishes we got here a whole lot sooner, too. We'll wait while you lock up again," he suggested, "but since Elias is away, if anyone else comes knockin' again, don't open that door. Whatever it is you think they need from the apothecary isn't somethin' they can't wait to get until morning."

"Yes, thank you. Thank you all for helping me," she said before slipping back inside. Once she had the door latched closed, the light from the lantern disappeared, and she

267

heard the men dragging Mr. Flynn away.

Leaning back against the door, she hugged the broom to her chest and sighed. She did not relish the idea that Mr. Burkalow or the other two men thought she had been foolish to open the door this late at night when she was all alone. But she rather liked the glimpse of admiration in those men's eyes that she had been able to defend herself. She was rather proud of herself, too, now that the whole sorry incident was over.

After she set the broom in the corner, she grabbed the railing and realized her arms were aching from her encounter with Maxwell Flynn. Then she looked down and realized she had just spent a good bit of time standing outside with three men in the middle of the night discussing why she had rendered a man unconscious, all while she was wearing nothing but a nightdress and robe.

She groaned and shook her head. The gossipmongers would find great entertainment at her expense. "But at least I don't need to worry that some newspaper will have a sketch of me beating that man with a broom in their next edition. All I have to contend with are a few wagging tongues, and those I can ignore."

She took four more stairs, misjudged the

last one, and stubbed her toes. Tears sprang to her eyes as pain shot up her leg. She wriggled her toes to make certain she had not broken any of them before continuing, and realized for the first time how close she had come to being dreadfully hurt by Maxwell Flynn.

But with each step she climbed, she unleashed the deep resentments still churning beneath the faith she was trying so hard to rebuild. "I wouldn't have even gone outside tonight if I hadn't been worried that it was Farrell or some other newspaper reporter pounding at the door. I could have stayed inside where I would have been safe," she snapped.

Two more steps and her resentment focused squarely on the person responsible for putting her in this situation in the first place. The only person she had loved all her life, the person she grieved for now because she would never see him again in this world, and the person whose name she would never carry again: her father.

"I wouldn't be worried about reporters at all if you hadn't dedicated every waking moment to minister to those . . . those women and forced me to come here. You knew how much I wanted to stay with you. You knew how hard it would be for me to learn how to take care of Lily, but Lily was more important to you than I was," she whispered. "What about me? Why wasn't I important to you, too?" She sat down on the top step.

Surrounded by darkness and weakened by her frightening encounter tonight, she wept for every heartbreak and disappointment that she had been too afraid to voice, as a child or as a young woman. The long, lonely hours she had spent growing up, waiting for her father to come home, only to have him leave again right after dinner and supper. The disappointment of having him forget her birthday, or be so late for an outing they had to cancel it. The series of housekeepers he had hired to care for her physical needs, though they had neither the time nor the inclination to see how very lonely she was.

She leaned against the frame of the open doorway and did not wipe away the tears that covered her cheeks. She was too drained physically to stand up. She was too drained emotionally to pray. But when she wondered why God had put her on a path that had held so much heartache in the past and offered nothing more in the days ahead, she felt His presence.

And for now, that was all she needed in order to face another day when she was strong enough to trust in Him again and truly follow His light.

Twenty-Four

"In all truth, I prefer Darlin' Deputy. Which do you like best? Darlin' Deputy, Night Witch, or Broom Lady?" Gertie Jones asked, ignoring her cousin who stood next to her at the apothecary counter. She looked at Ruth with a hopeful expression on her face.

Lorelei sniffed. "Broom Lady is the best of the lot, if you ask me."

"I wasn't asking you. I was asking Ruth. It's her nickname, after all."

"I hardly think Ruth is interested in a nickname when she has a perfectly lovely name already. But you stated your opinion, and now I'm stating mine: Darlin' Deputy sounds a bit tawdry."

"Broom Lady makes her sound standoff-ish —"

"Exactly my point. If any man, or woman, for that matter, thinks they can take advantage of her —"

"Broom Lady!" Ruth blurted, exasperated. Still, she managed to smile. "Is there something I can get for you this morning, ladies?" she prompted.

"Not today," Gertie replied with a triumphant sparkle in her eyes.

"We just stopped by to reassure ourselves that you weren't hurt by that awful man," Lorelei offered. Standing on tiptoe, she leaned over the counter as far as she could and stared at Ruth from the top of her head to her slippers and back again. Gertie did the same.

Ruth froze in place. She knew her face did not have any marks or scratches, and she was relieved neither woman could see through the sleeves covering her arms. Otherwise they would have seen the angry bruises that skipped from elbow to shoulder on both of her arms, which ached every time she moved them. They could not see her stiff neck, either, but she could definitely feel it.

"You look fine," they said in unison and dropped back to the soles of their feet.

Gertie put a small basket she had been carrying on top of the counter and grinned. "We brought you something, too."

"I thought I smelled something good," Ruth offered.

273

"That's just the molasses cookies we put in there so people wouldn't know what we really brought," Lorelei replied. "Go ahead. Take a peek."

Ruth lifted the checkered napkin covering the basket and looked inside. Sure enough, she saw half a dozen molasses cookies, but they were sitting next to something else. When she removed the cloth, she realized it was a pipe of some kind, only slightly longer than her hand.

Lorelei waved her hand anxiously. "No, don't lift it out. Cover it up again. Somebody could walk in and see it."

Ruth rewrapped the pipe, placing the napkin over the top of the basket again. "Is that a pipe?" she asked, although she was not entirely certain she wanted to hear the answer.

Gertie nodded. "We each have one under our pillow for protection, and we wanted you to have one, too."

"It's made of iron. That's why it's so heavy," Lorelei said. "After the way you defended yourself last night, any man with a lick of sense will know not to bother the Broom Lady, but you never know what a man will do when he's as addled as Maxwell Flynn must have been last night. Keep that piece of pipe handy, just in case you can't get to your broom in time."

"It might even fit in your reticule," Gertie suggested.

"Thank you. I think it might," Ruth replied with a small smile.

After she stored the basket behind the counter, she looked from one woman to the other and moistened her lips. As much as she hated gossip and tried to avoid it, even before her life had been turned upside down and inside out, she had to expect customers would invariably bring it into the apothecary, especially today. Curious to learn how Mr. Flynn was faring, she asked the two cousins about him.

Gertie chuckled. "From what we heard, once Dr. Woodward patched him up and he sobered up, Mr. Flynn stopped at the general store and then the bank on his way out of town."

"He frightened poor Spinster Wyndam before he left, too. Told me so herself," Lorelei added.

"I expect she'll be by shortly. She told us she had a few errands to finish first," Gertie said and nudged her cousin with her elbow. "Come along. We have just enough time before we have dinner to stop and thank Mr. Ayers and Mr. Burkalow for helping our dear Broom Lady," she announced, and the two cousins took their leave without saying another word.

While Ruth was happy to see them go, she was concerned about her plans to have supper at Spinster Wyndam's home tonight. At Phanaby's insistence, she had reluctantly accepted the woman's invitation at the church picnic, but at the time she had not known that Elias and Phanaby would be away and returning later today. Since they had taken care of Lily for the past two days, she did not want to impose by asking them to watch Lily while she went out for supper. Besides, she was growing more and more anxious for them to return, if only to find out if traveling with Robert Farrell had posed any problems and raised any concerns that might affect her remaining here with them.

Until she reminded herself of her promise to remain always in His light.

She could not decide if the fact that Jake Spencer would probably not be there, with his back bothering him again, made the invitation more or less appealing. She felt bad that Elias had not left any remedy she could take to the cabin for him and wondered if she should get word to Spinster Wyndam, suggesting she postpone their plans since it would be pointless to have a matchmaking supper for Ruth alone.

Not that she was interested in matchmaking at all. After the way she behaved at the cabin yesterday, she would not be surprised if Jake did not want anything to do with her. Even if he did, she was in no position to marry any man. Not now with a child and a tenuous future. Perhaps not ever, unless the press ended the public's fascination with her whereabouts once and for all.

She was, however, quite certain she would much prefer having a quiet supper at home with the Garners. In addition to hearing about their trip, she also wanted to explain her misadventure last night before they heard any of the rumors circulating around the village. But mostly, she wanted to have time with Lily.

"I miss that little one," she murmured. She was surprised by how empty she felt after not being with Lily for an entire day and night since she had been feeling so burdened lately by all the care a child her age required.

Yet for the next four hours she had little time to think of anyone or anything else other than the virtual parade of women who marched in and out of the apothecary bearing more gifts for her. Some of the women she knew from the congregation; others she had seen in the village at one time or another, but now she had names to put to their faces.

By the time she was ready to close the apothecary for the day, she had a shelf behind the counter that was filled with quite an assortment of "weapons" to keep at hand to defend herself just in case she could not get to her broom, along with well-meaning advice not to answer the door so late at night.

She went into the storeroom to get a basket to store her gifts, looked around, and sighed. One of the rickety shelves Mr. Garner was going to have Jake Spencer replace was lying on the floor, along with everything that had been stored there, leaving the room once again in disarray.

She picked up her gifts and set them into the basket she found. In addition to the piece of iron pipe from the Jones cousins, she had a hatpin from Mrs. Sloan at the general store that was similar to the one the woman claimed she kept behind the counter, and a horseshoe only large enough to fit a pony, which Mrs. Avery had gotten from the livery when her husband was not looking. She also had a corkscrew from Mrs. Burkalow, who had borrowed it from her husband's tavern, a wooden spoon with the handle sharpened to a point from Mrs. Toby, and a host of other implements.

She snatched one of the molasses cookies from the other basket and ate it slowly, wondering why Spinster Wyndam had not stopped by the apothecary since both Gertie and Lorelei had said she would. After she finished the cookie, she set the basket of gifts on the floor and walked around the counter. She was halfway to the front door to latch it closed for the day when she saw Spinster Wyndam through the display window. She was holding a rather large box. When their gazes met, the woman waved to Ruth with her cane to indicate she wanted Ruth to come outside.

So Ruth stepped outside and greeted her with a smile.

"Thank you for saving me some steps," Spinster Wyndam said. "I need all the energy I've got left to get the table set for our supper, but first I have two things to give to you. One could have waited until you came for supper, but the other one you probably need now." She took a paper from her pocket and handed it to Ruth. "Don't fret. It's nothing terribly awful. Just read it. You'll see."

Although Ruth was disappointed that supper with the elderly spinster could not be avoided, she unfolded the paper and read the message on the paper quickly:

Dearest Ruth,
    We are extending our holiday by one day and will explain when we return. All is fine, and Lily is quite well.

With affection,
Phanaby Garner

Ruth's eyes widened. "They're staying another day," she said. She was curious about the circumstances that would prompt Elias not to be at the apothecary for three straight days. Even though Phanaby insisted everything was "fine," Ruth grew worried that something had gone wrong, something caused by traveling with Robert Farrell or connected to her in some way. Still, Ruth knew Phanaby well enough to be fairly certain that she would have warned her if real trouble was brewing. Curious to know how Phanaby had managed to get this note to her, she asked Spinster Wyndam directly while she refolded the note and put it into her apron pocket.

The elderly woman chuckled. "Allan Yost was in Forked River visiting his grandmother. You may not have met him, since he rarely comes into the village. Phanaby gave her note to him, and he brought it back early this morning and gave it to his neighbor Isaac Martin, who brought it with him when he carted a wagon of sphagnum moss to the docks. From there . . ." She waved her hand. "Anyway, I ended up with it and brought it to you, along with this," she said as she handed a large but very light box into Ruth's hands. "You can open it later. I reminded Mr. Spencer just a while ago that supper's at six, and now I'm reminding you. Don't be late," she cautioned and walked off, leaving Ruth standing there.

She went back into the apothecary and latched the door before carrying the box over to the counter and opening it. She stared at the gift and nearly laughed out loud, convinced Spinster Wyndam had given her the most unique weapon of all. While obviously not new, the straw bonnet had four white quill feathers with shafts that could poke someone's eyes out if she was not careful. She carried the box with her bonnet, along with the basket of her other gifts, upstairs and stored them next to her trundle bed before she hurried to change for supper.

Ruth got lost trying to find Spinster Wyndam's cottage, which was nestled between two stately clapboard homes on the north side of the river, where she had never ventured before tonight.

It was well after six when she finally arrived and knocked at the door. She had gone back to Main Street to get better directions, and her cheeks were still burning as much from her extended walk as from embarrassment.

She raised her hand again to knock, but lowered her arm when she heard the click of the woman's cane as it hit the floor. She heard not one but two latches release before the door swung open, and she braced for a reprimand for being so tardy.

Instead, Spinster Wyndam greeted her with kindness and stepped aside to let her enter. "Got lost, did you?"

"Yes, I'm sorry." Ruth walked into a small sitting room, where a low fire was burning in the hearth. Oddly, sheets yellowed with age were draped over two chairs and a settee, as well as every other piece of furniture in the room.

"I don't care much for cleaning house anymore. Covering everything up means I don't have to dust," her hostess explained.

When Ruth removed her bonnet and handed it to her, her arms ached, just like they had when she put it on, but the smile on the woman's face was well worth the stares she had gotten walking here because of this particular bonnet.

"I used to wear that bonnet in my younger days, but I added a few new quill feathers for you just this morning," the elderly woman explained before she tossed the bonnet into the air.

Ruth's eyes widened even more when she saw the bonnet sail through the room and land on top of one of the chairs. Still reeling from this strange display, she followed the woman to the kitchen. She was surprised to see three places set, but chairs sat in front of only two, while Jake Spencer stood at the far end of the table carving what appeared to be either a very large chicken or a rather small turkey.

But the closer she got to the table, the more she realized the roasted bird was definitely too big to be a chicken. Ruth suddenly knew exactly where Spinster Wyndam had gotten those quill feathers for the bonnet — from something Jake Spencer had killed for their supper.

Twenty-Five

Jake had rehearsed the explanation he would give to Ruth for his nearly complete recovery, but he could not remember a word of it when she walked into the kitchen and stared at him.

Even with her mouth agape and her eyes simmering with curiosity, if not shock, she looked as if she had survived last night's incident quite well. She had a rosy blush on her cheeks, while her ivory complexion was flawless, and he could not see any evidence she had sustained any injury at all. She was not limping and walked as gracefully as she ever had, except when she wore those clunky boots.

She was barely a few feet away from him, yet still failed to acknowledge him. He assumed she was simply wondering how he had managed to come for supper tonight when yesterday he had been almost completely immobilized. Anxious to calm any remaining fear she might have about trusting him, he followed her gaze and realized she was looking at something else entirely.

When she finally looked directly at him, her eyes had darkened to the color of slate and he nearly flinched. It was not curiosity staring at him now but condemnation, along with horror, which left him perplexed. "Y-you cooked it?" she stammered.

Spinster Wyndam chuckled. "Of course not. I cooked it. He's just carving it. Men carve so much better than we women do. I never did have a man to do it for me, which is why I like to invite one over for supper once in a while. Now, let that poor man help us to our seats so he can finish slicing up that goose."

He set the knife down and helped the elderly woman take her seat first. When he pulled out the chair opposite their hostess, which is where he had draped Ruth's shawl, she ignored him. Indeed, she continued to gape at the centerpiece of the elaborate meal Spinster Wyndam had set out on the table.

Finally, Ruth literally plopped into her seat. "It's a goose. It's not a turkey," she murmured.

"Goodness no," the spinster quipped.

Grinning, Jake returned to his task and

started to slice the last of the breast meat. "You don't favor turkey?" he teased.

"I-I do, but I thought . . . I mean . . . When I saw that roasted bird sitting there, I thought . . ." She paused, glanced at the look of bewilderment on Spinster Wyndam's face, and looked to him for help.

"Ruth and I have a mutual pest," he began. By the time there was nothing left of the goose but a carcass, he had finished telling the tale of the territorial turkey who had taken up residence at his cabin. Spinster Wyndam was dabbing away tears of laughter, and Ruth's eyes had gentled to pale gray again as her lips formed a smile instead of a frown.

"I've threatened to cook that turkey hen more than once, but when I saw it sitting there on the table, I couldn't imagine eating the little pest," Ruth explained.

"You thought those feathers on your bonnet were turkey feathers? Silly goose," their hostess said. When she realized the pun she had made, she laughed out loud before she finished explaining that a number of other women had given Ruth a few gifts today, too.

Leaning hard on his cane, Jake made slow but steady progress toward his place at the end of the table, hoping to make the excuse

286

he knew he had to offer sooner or later sound more plausible. "May I ask the occasion that inspired all those gifts?" he asked, hopeful that today was her birthday, a fact he could easily get his brother to confirm. It would be a critical key to solidifying his deep conviction that Ruth Livingstone and Ruth Malloy were the same woman.

He stood at his place at the table and waited for Ruth to answer him.

Ruth's smile froze for a moment. "I-I suppose I could tell you," she replied, but Spinster Wyndam spoke up.

"You may ask, but neither one of us is going to give you an answer. There are precious few secrets we women get to keep, and this is one of them."

Ruth's complexion paled to the color of fresh snow.

"Besides," the spinster continued, "if we keep chatting, our supper will get cold. Pass that platter of meat to Mr. Spencer, will you, Ruth?"

Ruth picked up the platter with both hands, turned in her seat, and held it out to him. When she saw that he was still standing and there was no chair for him, she set it down on the table and furrowed her brow. "You're not going to sit down?"

"I'd like to sit and join you, but I'm afraid

I can't," he explained and dropped his gaze because he was also afraid she would see through his lie.

Spinster Wyndam patted his arm with the tip of her cane. "When I saw him earlier this afternoon, he told me about the mishap he had yesterday and that he couldn't possibly come for supper because he'd aggravate his back if he sat down. I told him I didn't mind at all if he ate his dinner standing up, and I assured him you wouldn't, either."

Ruth's eyes glistened like pools of silver.

"It's not so bad," Jake said. "By this morning I found I could walk or stand without much pain, but I doubt I'll ever stand straight again if I sit down tonight." He took several slices of the meat and put them onto his plate. "I stopped at the apothecary on the way here, but it was closed. I was hoping Mr. Garner had returned and could make up some remedy for me, but —"

"But I told him the Garners delayed their return until tomorrow," their hostess interjected. "I do hope Elias left some remedy for Mr. Spencer so he doesn't have to wait until tomorrow to get some relief."

Ruth moistened her lips. "I'm sorry. If he left any for you, I couldn't find it. I looked last night when I got home."

He shrugged and slid the handle of his cane on the end of the table so it would hang there. "I can wait until tomorrow for the remedy, but I'd rather not wait any longer to enjoy this fine supper."

Spinster Wyndam smiled and began briefly lifting the lids off the serving dishes that left little room on the table for anything other than their place settings. She announced each dish, perhaps to clarify any more misperceptions. "Fried oysters, straight from the kitchen at Burkalow's Tavern. I can't even bother with all the mess it takes to make them. Pickled beets. Corn cakes. And finally, my favorite: carrots glazed with butter and honey."

Jake's mouth watered, his stomach growled, but his mind raced in anticipation of walking Ruth home after supper. He just could not decide whether to feign a fall in front of the apothecary to get her to invite him inside or to ask to see the shelving he had been hired to replace. Either way, he hoped to get an opportunity to look for that wooden chest tonight.

Two hours later, he and Ruth were walking down Main Street.

At twilight, the heart of the village was slowing down. Burkalow's Tavern at the far end and a smaller tavern near the docks, which only seamen and rougher elements frequented, were the only establishments open at this hour. The roadway itself was deserted as well.

Overhead, the sky was clear yet not dark enough to detect a single star. The air was laced with just a hint of a breeze that carried the light lavender scent she wore — a scent he had not detected above the smells in the kitchen during supper.

Jake looked down at the young woman holding his arm, and his pulse started to race. He could easily see himself, in another time and in another place, becoming enamored of this very intriguing, rather attractive woman.

Fortunately, his mind took control of those dangerous thoughts and quickly yanked him back to reality. He was not here as a man anxious to court her, despite Spinster Wyndam's intentions. He was here as a reporter to investigate whatever it was she was hiding. And even if all his efforts in that regard were for naught, she would never forgive him for violating every ethical code of professional conduct in the process, including lying to her repeatedly, most especially yesterday at the cabin.

When his brother's voice echoed in his

mind, challenging him not to be a fool again, he slipped back into the persona that would justify his methods and focused on his one and only goal: his professional redemption.

He glanced at the rather silly bonnet she was wearing, took another slow step, and chuckled. "Did you really think that I slaughtered that turkey so Spinster Wyndam could have a few feathers for your bonnet and roast it for our supper?"

She pulled the ends of her shawl together with one hand and slightly increased the pressure on his arm with the other, which unleashed feelings that triggered alarm bells in his mind. "I'm afraid I did."

He shook his head. "You never noticed the feathers were white, rather than brown?"

"Not really." She looked up at him and grinned shyly. "It really is a silly looking bonnet, isn't it?"

He chuckled again. "Yes, it is, but if you didn't like it, why did you wear it?"

She dropped her gaze and shrugged. "I knew how much pleasure she had in giving it to me. Since I was going to her home, I didn't want to disappoint her, so I wore it anyway."

Pausing for a moment, he drew in a long breath and moved his cane to hit closer to his feet before he started them up again. "Are you going to be as thoughtful with the other gifts you received, or did they suit you more?" he asked, hoping he might tempt her to explain what they were and get her to admit the reason for the gift giving today was her birthday.

"No one will likely ever see the other gifts, or at least I hope they won't," she said. She caught his eye and smiled. "The very best gift I received was getting my shawl back. I'm not certain how you managed to repair and clean it, but I know it took a great deal of time and effort. Thank you." She dropped her gaze. "I should think it would be too much to hope that you managed to walk down Main Street this afternoon without hearing what they're calling me now."

He cringed, although he found it amusing that a woman who valued her privacy was now so well known. "I believe the prevailing favorite is 'Broom Lady'."

She tightened the pressure of her fingers on his arm, and he stopped abruptly and leaned hard on his cane to allow his brain time to refocus on the task at hand.

After letting go of his arm, she turned toward him. "Are you all right?"

"Fine," he said, wondering why Ruth Livingstone had not been a spoiled, bad-tempered, plain woman instead of a considerate, alluring woman with such gorgeous eyes. "It's just a twinge. It'll pass in a moment or two."

She sighed. "I wish I could say the same for all the gossip about what happened last night."

He clenched his jaw and tightened his hold on his cane until his knuckles whitened. Images of what could have happened to her fueled the urge to track down that scoundrel himself. Before he could regain his composure, however, Ruth suddenly charged down the alley, yanking feathers out of her bonnet as she ran toward a man who was sitting on the ground by the back door to the apothecary.

"Aggravating woman. She's got less sense than that turkey!" Jake hissed, but forced himself to follow her very slowly. He did not know if the man was the scoundrel who had attacked her last night or if he was one of the reporters from the *Sun* or the *Transcript* who might have traced her here. Regardless, he was ready to break into a sprint and intervene if that man made a single threatening move toward her, and worry about explaining his miraculous recovery later when she was safe.

He was, however, more inclined to strangle

this woman for putting herself in harm's way by running straight toward danger and leaving him well behind her.

TWENTY-SIX

Maxwell Flynn had come back, and he was waiting for her!

Spurred by frightening images of the damage Jake Spencer would do to his back if he protected her now as instinctively as he had done when he saved Lily from drowning in the river, Ruth broke into a run. She managed to put a sizeable distance between them and had a feather gripped in each hand by the time her unwelcome caller had gotten to his feet.

The moment Flynn raised his hands in surrender, she slowed her steps and caught her breath. With her heart pounding, she stopped completely when she was just beyond arm's reach of the man who had attacked her last night.

"I mean you no harm, Widow Malloy. I only stopped by to apologize," he offered and took a step back.

She narrowed her gaze and looked at him

intently. Unlike last night, he was steady on his feet, and his words were not slurred from consuming too many spirits. He looked as if he had been in a tavern brawl and had lost to the other hooligan. His nose was swollen and mottled by a large purple bruise like the one that surrounded the bite mark on his cheek. His bottom lip was caked with blood, and she felt more pity than remorse.

Since he did not look or sound as if he posed any threat to her, she lowered her aching arms and nodded for him to do the same. "I accept your apology. Now please leave," she said, anxious to have him gone before Jake, slowly making his way toward them, arrived and felt the need to prove himself the better man.

"You don't have to worry none about me comin' back and botherin' you again," Mr. Flynn promised and cleared his throat. "I've turned over the deed to my land to Mr. Miller down to the bank so he can sell it for me. I'm leavin' at first light for good, but I wanted to give this to you before I do. That's why I was sitting here waitin' for you," he explained. He put his hand in his pocket and handed her a tiny package. "I made this for my Abigail and gave it to her for the last birthday she ever had. She was twenty-three," he said, his voice choked with emotion. "Folks tell me you're a godly woman. I'm hoping you'll accept this and that you might be obliged to say a prayer for me now and again when you see it."

Ruth put the feather she was holding in her right hand into her left one and took the small package he was holding out to her. "Of course I'll pray for you," she promised, then heard the sound of Jake's cane hitting the ground close behind her. She turned, looked over her shoulder, and smiled when she noted the fearsome look on his face. "Everything is fine. I'm not in any danger," she assured him.

When she turned back to face Maxwell Flynn, however, he was not there, and she caught just a glimpse of him before he disappeared around the other side of the building.

Panting hard, Jake stopped just behind her. "Madam, have you entirely lost your mind?"

She whirled about and saw he was still wearing that fearsome look. "I beg your pardon?"

He pointed his cane to the place where Flynn had been standing. "Instead of charging the man who could have killed you last night, did it ever occur to you that you might not want to give him another opportunity by running ahead of me like that?" he snapped.

She tilted up her chin. "I'm not certain whom you're talking to, but I'm absolutely positive you cannot possibly be speaking to me. Not in that tone of voice."

He let out a long, deep breath and twirled the cane in his hand with his fingers. "You're right. I'm sorry."

"And well you should be," she argued. "But if you must know, I didn't run off because I was anxious to prove I could defend myself, although I believe I could have," she added and pointed the sharpened tips of the feathers at him.

When his eyes widened and he drew back, she said, "Precisely the reaction I was expecting from Mr. Flynn."

He snatched the feathers out of her hand and shook his head. "He could have disarmed you just as easily."

"Which would have given you the opportunity to prove you're still a man capable of defending a woman," she countered. "You might have won against him, but I daresay you'd have injured your back even more, which is exactly why I ran ahead of you. Not to save you from him. To save you from yourself."

The cleft in his chin deepened when he

pressed his lips together and appeared to clench his jaw as if struggling to accept her words.

Her heart trembled. "I'm sorry. I didn't mean to speak to you so bluntly or to offend you," she whispered, mindful of the way she had spoken to him yesterday at his cabin. "I think you're quite manly enough, just as you are," she blurted. Horrified that she had voiced her opinion of him so brazenly, she felt her heart begin to pound with the same embarrassment that warmed her cheeks, and she rushed to cover her blunder.

"Apparently, Spinster Wyndam agrees with me, or she wouldn't have tried to keep the two of us together at the church picnic, or invited us both to supper tonight," she offered. "She's rather well known for her matchmaking. If you don't believe me, just ask Reverend Haines when he gets back. She's been trying to match him up with any number of women for years now," she gushed, nervously twisting the package she held.

He cocked his head and studied the feathers he had taken from her. "Is that why she fashioned these and put them onto that bonnet she gave you? To give you something to defend yourself if I acted . . . improperly?"

She rolled her eyes. "Not you exactly. Anyone at all. And she wasn't the only one concerned about what happened to me last night. I received a whole basket of weapons today from other women, which I have stored upstairs if you'd like to see them."

"I think I'd rather see the damage done to the storeroom last night. If it's as bad as I have heard, I may need to revise my estimate for Mr. Garner."

She swallowed the lump in her throat and wished she could have taken her offer back. Caught between having this man downstairs in the storeroom or upstairs in the family living quarters, she opted for the lesser of the two evils. "You can wait in the storeroom if you like, but it's getting darker by the minute. I'll go upstairs and get an oil lamp so you can see the damage better. Just leave the door open," she said, rushing up the steep staircase as fast as she could without tripping over her skirts.

She stopped in her bedroom long enough to drop her gift onto the bed and take off her bonnet before she went to the sitting room to retrieve the oil lamp. Her hands were shaking a bit when she tried to light it, but when it failed to light, she realized she needed to pour more oil into the lamp's base. Frustrated when she heard him rattling around the storeroom, she quickly filled the lamp and lit it. The lamp was heavy, and she had to walk slowly while she carried it down the hallway. She was half afraid her aching arms would give out and she would drop the lamp, setting fire to the entire building.

She reached the top of the staircase, but found the door closed. She did not remember closing it when she came upstairs, but sighed and set the lamp down on the floor. She let her arms rest for a moment and prayed the bruises would heal soon. After she opened the door and saw that the storeroom was quite a bit darker, she sighed again. She hitched up her skirts and bunched them in the same hand she needed to use to hold onto the railing, took up the lamp with her other hand, and started very cautiously down the steps.

She could hear Jake still moving about the storeroom, but by the time she was three-quarters of the way downstairs, she had enough light to see him poking at the fallen shelf and pushing boxes away with his cane. "Is this better?" she asked as the lamplight filtered throughout the storeroom.

He kept his back to her but pointed to the shelves above his head. "Could you stay right there and lift the lamp a bit higher?"

She hesitated. Her arms were really sore now, and she barely had the strength to hold the lamp at waist level, let alone raise it any higher. "I don't think I should. Not until I get to the bottom of the steps."

He turned and closed the distance between them in a matter of heartbeats. Standing directly below her on the floor, he reached up and took the lamp from her after he leaned his cane against the outside of the staircase. "I'm sorry. I didn't realize you were still on the staircase." He looked at her with concern. "You're awfully pale. Are you feeling unwell?"

"I'm fine. It must be the light," she insisted, not wanting to tell him that her encounter last night had not left her as free from injury as she may have appeared.

"I'll keep the light on the steps so you won't fall." He kept his eyes locked on her until she reached the storeroom floor.

She dropped her skirts and gently rubbed her arms to get them to stop aching, but immediately recognized her mistake when his gaze hardened. "He did hurt you."

Not a question she could deflect with an excuse of some sort, his statement left no room for denial. With her cheeks burning, she shrugged. "It's just a few bruises. Nothing serious. But please don't tell anyone."

He lifted the lamp until the light fell full on her face. "Since you wouldn't favor the notion that I follow that brute and make him very sorry that he hurt you, give me one good reason why I shouldn't have him arrested."

"He came to give me something and apologize tonight because he's leaving at first light. For good."

He sighed and lowered the lamp. "I suppose that'll do, but the next time we're together and anyone —"

"I'll let you be gallant and rescue me," she promised, "as long as you let me say 'I told you so' when you end up crippling yourself for life. Agreed?" she asked, extending her hand.

He hesitated before he took her hand in his, then held it for just a moment longer than she thought necessary.

A warm sensation coursed up her arm and spread from limb to limb. But she dismissed her reaction as nothing more than the fact that she had never really held a man's hand before, other than her father's. His hands had been as smooth as her own, whereas Jakes's hand was rough with calluses.

"I've seen what I needed to see in the storeroom. I should go." His voice was husky, and his gaze simmered with something she had never seen before, though she assumed it was nothing more than a glint of hurt pride. "Stay here a moment," he said and started up the staircase, using the railing for support.

"Where are you going?"

"To put the lamp at the top of the staircase for you."

Once he had the lamp sitting on the floor in the hall at the top of the stairs, he started back down, blocking the light behind him so all she could see was his silhouette. She stepped aside when he reached the bottom step and he retrieved his cane.

"Tell Mr. Garner when he gets back that the price will be the same, and I'd really appreciate it if you could get him to commit to letting me do the work for him as soon as possible. I haven't had much work lately and I sorely need the wages."

"I will," she promised. Uncomfortable with the embarrassment she detected in his voice, she knew how difficult it must be for this proud man to ask her for help in finding work.

He cleared his throat. "I don't have to remind you to latch the outer door, as well as the door at the bottom of the staircase after I leave, do I?"

"No," she said, shaking her head.

"That's a relief. I'd hate to have to save you, especially from yourself, and injure my back even more," he said, turning her words back against her.

"Aggravating man," she grumbled after he had left, then latched the door and went upstairs. She picked up the oil lamp and started carrying it back to the sitting room. When she passed by her bedroom, she caught a glimpse of the package from Mr. Flynn sitting on her bed and quickly detoured. She set the oil lamp on a chest of drawers and sat down on the bed, anxious to see what he had given her.

When she unwrapped the package, which was no bigger than the palm of her hand, tears sprang to her eyes. Lying in the middle of the crumpled brown paper was a perfectly shaped white heart hanging from a worn strip of leather. She picked up the heart and held it to the light and realized it had not been carved from stone. The ridges on the heart suggested he had carved it from a seashell, similar to the ones she had seen along the shores of the river.

Ruth folded her hand around the simple token of affection Maxwell had made for his Abigail. She bowed her head and whispered a prayer for him, along with a prayer that she would someday find a man who would love her as much as he still loved his late wife.

She might even hope that Jake Spencer would be that man, until she realized that he could never love a woman who had wrongly accused him of lying, yet had lied to him over and over again from the very first day they had met.

TWENTY-SEVEN

The next morning, great rumbles of thunder shook the building and woke Ruth out of a sound sleep. She rose from her bed and looked out the window, but then leaped back a step when a bolt of lightning cracked the sky and startled her. She crossed her sore arms and gently rubbed them from shoulder to elbow while she watched the thunderclouds rolling in.

Within moments thick raindrops were pelting the window, and she sighed. The storm canceled her plans to spend the day in her garden and set the starter plants she had been given into the ground. "At least the rain will keep the roots moist," she grumbled and then slipped back under the covers. She considered how to spend her day but did not think very long before she decided that since every plan she had made for the past two days had led to one detour after another or some sort of disaster, she would simply let the day unfold.

Satisfied with her decision, she included Maxwell Flynn in her morning prayers and dressed quickly. She brushed her hair, parted it down the middle, pulled it back behind her neck, and held it in place with her comb. Humming softly, she made the bed and went directly to the kitchen to make something for breakfast.

By midday she had dusted and swept out the family's living quarters, save for the Garners' bedroom, as usual. She also finished the apron she was making for Phanaby. Eventually, the storm blew its way through the village and, tempted by bright blue skies and warm sunshine, she changed into a work gown and her oversized boots, grabbed a stack of old newspapers along with her silly bonnet, and headed to her garden.

Thankfully, she did not encounter the turkey hen either on the sandy path or the grounds surrounding the cabin. She was both relieved and a bit disappointed not to see any smoke curling up from the cabin chimney, which meant Jake was probably not around. Ruth found she was still sifting through her emotions after their time together the previous evening.

When she finally reached her garden, Ruth

found the ground very moist, but not the puddle of mud she had found there the other day, and the starter plants sitting in the bushel basket looked green and healthy.

After retrieving her garden tools from the shed behind the cabin, she returned to the finger of land she had claimed for herself and first arranged the plants out on the ground. Thankfully, each of the women who had given her these plants had given her the name of the flowers that would bloom before the end of summer. They had also given her some idea of how big to expect the plants to grow, which helped her to decide where to plant them in relation to each other.

Once she was satisfied she had every plant in its proper place, she folded the newspapers she had brought along to make a thick pad to use when she knelt down to dig.

Her gloves, boots, and the hem of her skirts wore a thick coat of wet dirt by the time she finished, but she had finally planted her garden. By midsummer, when the garden was in full bloom, the flowers would offer a contrast of yellow and blue blossoms. At the very center, several cup plants would have flowers similar to small sunflowers, which would be surrounded by a circle of daisies. Around those, bellworts with beautiful oval leaves already held yellow-orange flowers that would continue to bloom through the end of next month. And the border of the garden held bluebonnets and daintier bluets.

Ruth drew in a long breath. She had no idea when she first planned this garden that she would actually be here when the flowers would be in full bloom. In all truth, she was not convinced that either she or Lily would be able to stay here for very long. Not with the village so close to New York City and the scandal and notoriety that could still reach out and strangle both of their futures, especially with Robert Farrell planning to return before long.

After spending three days and nights without her little one, Ruth was growing anxious to have her home again. Her feelings for Lily were still confusing. So were her feelings for the man who lived in the cabin behind her.

For now, though, she was satisfied with the work she had done this afternoon. She was ready now to head back to the apothecary and change before everyone arrived home. She lifted the newspapers out of the dirt and dropped them into a hole she had dug beyond her garden. "A rather suitable resting place for you all," she murmured as she refilled the hole and stamped the spot down again and again with her boot. Then she hurried to the shed to store away her garden tools and leave before Jake returned home.

After a joyful reunion with Lily and the Garners and a fine supper, Ruth tucked Lily into the bottom half of the trundle bed and lay with her a bit longer, even after the toddler had fallen asleep.

Although she knew the Garners were waiting for her in the sitting room, and she was anxious to hear their explanation for extending their trip, lying here with Lily cuddled up against her again had vanquished any and all confusion in her heart. Reluctant to leave just yet, she leaned on an elbow and looked down at the little one sleeping so peacefully beside her, and smiled. Despite the hard work and the challenges she faced every day with Lily, she knew that innocence and purity existed in this world because she could actually see it in that little face. She knew that joy and happiness existed every time Lily explored the world around her. And she knew what it was to love another person because Lily offered that same love to her, freely and without condition, every time she wrapped her little arms around Ruth's neck and snuggled close for a kiss.

"I don't know why you came into my life, but I'm truly glad you did. We'll muddle through somehow until we figure out a way to stay together that will make us both happy," she whispered and slipped out of the bed.

She tiptoed across the room and eased the door open. After she stepped into the hallway, she turned and left the door open a crack, just in case Lily woke up and called out for her. Following the light shining into the hall from the sitting room, she made her way to where Elias and Phanaby were expecting her.

"I'm sorry if I kept you waiting," she offered, pleased that Phanaby was still wearing the apron she had made for her.

Elias had pulled one of the chairs that was usually nearer the fireplace to sit facing the settee where Phanaby was sitting. She patted the seat next to her and smiled. "I'm glad you had some time alone with Lily. She's missed you. Come and sit beside me. There's much we'd like to tell you about our trip."

"You said it went well," Ruth prompted, taking her seat. Earlier, she was relieved when Elias assured her that Farrell had proven to be nothing but a boring nuisance during their journey.

Elias nodded. "It did, but we . . . that is, we both feel uncomfortable being less than honest with you about why we went to Forked River."

Phanaby took Ruth's hand and held it. "We don't like lying to our friends and neighbors, but we do it because we have no other choice. But we can be and we should be honest with you because you're the only one here in the village who knows how important Reverend Livingstone's work was to him and to so many others who supported him like we did."

Suddenly, the weight of the lies she had told the Garners tugged heavily on Ruth's conscience. "You weren't simply visiting your friends?" she asked, looking from Phanaby to Elias and back again.

Elias shook his head. "No, we met secretly with a number of Reverend Livingstone's other supporters who traveled much greater distances than we to get to Forked River. A few were delayed by bad weather, which is why we had to stay a day more than we had planned," he explained. "For their sake, I don't believe it would be necessary or even well advised to tell you their names or where they live, even if we could, but we wanted you to know that a number of ministers have expressed an interest in continuing Reverend Livingstone's ministry."

Phanaby squeezed her hand. "We don't know for certain how serious any of them are, but we do have hope now that his work will live on and that young women and their children, like you and Lily, will find homes where they can be accepted and grow stronger in their faith."

Ruth swallowed the lump in her throat and managed a smile, in spite of the tears what welled in her eyes. "This is all good news, then," she whispered, knowing how pleased her father would be to know that his work would continue, despite his passing.

"Not quite," Elias said.

"Robert Farrell told us he's planning to spend the next week or two in Forked River looking for Ruth Livingstone," Phanaby said, her gaze troubled.

Ruth tried to focus on what Elias and Phanaby were trying to tell her. "But you said he was nothing but a nuisance during your trip."

"He wouldn't tell us why he thought she might be in the area," Elias said, "but his presence there, given the nature of the meeting we attended, was particularly troubling and made it all the more imperative for us to be very careful not to arouse his suspicions."

"But you said he was nothing but a nuisance during your trip," Ruth repeated.

"He was," Elias insisted. "It was only after we arrived and were disembarking that he told us the purpose for his journey there. And in all truth, I believe it was divine intervention that put him on the same stagecoach that we took to Forked River. It gave us fair warning that the press is not going to let go of the tragedy Reverend Livingstone endured during his last days any time soon, although I don't think we need to worry about Mr. Farrell returning to the area again."

"You don't?" Ruth said.

He chuckled. "Within a matter of days he's going to get a lead on Ruth Livingstone from one of our friends, which will send Farrell scurrying to Boston. Others there should keep him occupied for a spell before they send him elsewhere following another false lead."

"If other newspaper reporters are like Mr. Farrell, we can expect them to be just as determined and unprincipled," Phanaby offered. "We can't keep tabs on all of them."

"We discussed that very issue at our meeting," Elias countered, keeping his gaze on Ruth. "The longer the newspapers continue to focus on the scandal surrounding the Reverend's acquittal and promote the absurd idea that his daughter is somehow hiding evidence of his guilt, the more careful we all have to be. Unfortunately, it also means that the ministers who are considering taking over the ministry may lose interest. Without a leader, the network we belong to will quickly unravel, and frankly I fear it already has begun to do just that."

A sharp pain sliced through Ruth's chest, making it nearly impossible for her to breathe. "Is finding his daughter really that important?"

He snorted. "To the newspapers? I'm afraid there's no stopping them. I'm afraid the more they hawk their nonsense about the reverend's guilt and his daughter's complicity in the matter, the more the public demands to know about her and her whereabouts. And the more newspapers they sell, the more profit they make. That only makes it all the more difficult for us to find a new leader."

"What about the network? Does everyone involved think it's necessary to find her, too?" Ruth asked.

"I don't think so," Phanaby replied. "We're all agreed that the dear girl has fled to someone within the network who is protecting her, and whoever it is will pay dearly if Farrell, or any reporter, for that matter, finds her living with them, because their names will no doubt appear in the newspaper articles. We don't know who they might be, partly because we can't be exactly sure that we know everyone Reverend Livingstone recruited to help him."

Elias nodded. "And partly because he kept his life with his daughter so completely separate from his ministry. I don't know anyone within the network who has actually met her, although I've heard that several might have seen her years ago, as a child."

"He knew that since his work was so controversial, it was likely his name would eventually be associated with some kind of scandal his detractors would promote," Phanaby added. "He loved his daughter very much and wanted to protect her at all costs, which is why he never had her participate in his work in any way."

Ruth shook her head. As much as she wanted to accept what they had just told her, she simply could not and did not believe that either one of them knew her father well enough to be trusted with his private feelings or motivations. "How can you be so certain of what he thought or how he felt about his daughter?" she asked, looking from Phanaby to Elias, hoping for nothing but the full truth from them.

Phanaby paused and looked at her husband for a long moment before she said, "I'm certain because he told me himself."

Ruth's eyes widened and her heart started to pound in her chest. "H-he told you? You actually met him?"

Phanaby's eyes filled with tears, but she kept her gaze locked on her husband, who was looking at her with complete tenderness. "I met Reverend Livingstone nearly fifteen years ago when he visited the brothel where I had been working for a number of months. He helped me to find my faith again and sent me to live with an older couple in western Pennsylvania. They also welcomed me into their hearts when I later married their son. So you see, Ruth, I'm a Prodigal Daughter, one of Reverend Livingstone's daughters-in-faith, just like you are."

Stunned, Ruth could scarcely breathe, but the looks of devotion and love that passed between the couple who had welcomed her into their home only reinforced what she had known in her heart of hearts all along: Her father had truly loved her.

The only thought that troubled her now was whether she had the right to put the life that Elias and Phanaby had created for themselves in this village at risk by remaining here with them, or if she should contact Capt. Grant to see if he could help her find somewhere else to live.

Twenty-Eight

Jake left his cabin at first light on the Fourth of July, but he was in no mood to celebrate the nation's birthday. Not when he was no closer now than he was a month ago to claiming his own independence from the mistakes he had made two years ago.

Since Farrell had arrived in the village, Jake had spent every waking moment facing one frustration after another. He had received not one but three letters from Clifford. The most recent letter, which he received only days ago, contained a final ultimatum: Finish the story on Ruth Livingstone, with undeniable proof of her identity, along with whatever incriminating information she had hidden about her father, and report back to New York City by the end of July, or sign the documents relinquishing his interest in the *Galaxy*. Clifford had the audacity to send the papers along with his letter, almost as if Jake's failure was guaranteed.

Jake walked to the river and stared down at the water. It would not surprise him if Farrell showed up and ruined the festivities today. He'd need to keep a sharp lookout for the reporter, not to mention any other reporters who might appear to take advantage of the fact that everyone for miles would be in the village for the daylong celebration.

He turned to look at Ruth's garden, which was nearly in full bloom now, and caught the subtle fragrances in the air. For nearly a month now she had been coming to her garden every day, and he often ventured outside to talk with her. If she came in late afternoon, she would frequently bring Lily with her to play in the safe area he had fenced off while Ruth weeded or thinned the garden.

He flexed his thumb and clenched his fist. That little blue-eyed minx had turned out to be a charmer, and if he was not careful, he could easily lose his heart to two females, instead of just one.

"Another time. Another place. But not now," he vowed and refused to consider the possibility that it might be too late because they already threatened to steal his heart.

He squared his shoulders. Listening to his

heart, instead of his head, had cost him his career once before. He could not afford to make that mistake again any more than he could understand how he could redeem his reputation as a reporter, destroying the life she had created for herself here, and yet love her.

Stymied, he started down the sandy path to implement his battle plan for the day: Either get Elias Garner to finally commit to a day to have him replace the shelves in the storeroom, or wheedle an invitation from Phanaby Garner to come to supper within the next week. Jake had even made a special gift for Ruth, which he planned to give her tonight, and hoped it would go a long way toward getting even closer to her.

Either way, he would manage to get upstairs to the family's living quarters, find a way to search for that wooden chest, examine its contents to see if there was anything of value for his story, write the story, and then get back to New York City well ahead of his new deadline.

He stopped walking and gazed at the village stretched before him. If he failed to redeem himself by learning and printing the whole truth about Rev. Livingstone's daughter and the evidence she was hiding that had thwarted justice for Rosalie Peale, he had no future at all.

Unfortunately, Ruth had stopped reading the newspapers, which was about the only tidbit of information related to his secret investigation that he had been able to glean from her lately. He had not been able to engage her in any discussions of the news that might give him some additional clues, if not answers, related to a number of important issues. He needed to understand her motives for hiding in this particular village and her actual relationship to Lily, if indeed there was one. If not, he needed to correctly identify Lily, her parents, and the reason why they had given her to Ruth.

His only hope to do that was to pray that the nature of the celebration today would give him the opportunity to bait her into a heated discussion.

Confident that his redemption was still within reach, he closed his eyes for a moment, hoping God would forgive him for neglecting his prayers lately. Then he resumed his march and crossed the bridge that led to the village, as well as his destiny.

Red, white, and blue banners draped every storefront, the makeshift stage that closed Main Street in front of the bank, and an assortment of tables set up for dinner near the bridge. The American flag was flying everywhere, and ladies wore patriotic ribbons in their bonnets or pinned to their gowns.

By midmorning, after the militia had performed their traditional maneuvers and the ceremonies on Main Street had begun, Jake had successfully completed the first component of his battle plans for the day: He had found Ruth and she had agreed to spend some time with him.

Against his better judgment, however, he was standing next to Ruth now near the front of the stage where the band had assembled. He had little Lily perched on his shoulders so she would not be crushed by the crowd of villagers that surrounded them. Being this close to the stage would make it easier for her to see, but he was not as convinced as Ruth had been that the little girl would tolerate the noise of the music.

Long speeches followed a reading of the Declaration of Independence and the Preamble to the United States Constitution by local schoolchildren, and Lily was growing fidgety. He breathed a sigh of relief when Mayor George Washington Pendleton finally concluded the last speech of the day.

". . . and so my friends and fellow citizens, I remind you all that our battle for liberty

324

continues to this very day. Do not take your freedoms for granted. Embrace your responsibilities as good citizens. And be ever vigilant. Rise up and speak out against those who threaten your freedoms, so that truth and honor and justice, in the name of freedom, shall prevail for all the future generations who will call this chosen land their home. God bless you all, and God bless America!"

"Perfect," he murmured, certain that he could use this part of the mayor's speech to engage Ruth in a discussion like the one they'd had shortly after he arrived.

When the crowd roared, muskets fired into the air, and the band blared into full play, Lily began wailing, yanking hard on his hair, and kicking at his chest. He handed his cane to Ruth and lifted the child down and into his arms. He tried to hand her to Ruth, but Lily wrapped her arms around his neck and buried her face against the base of his throat.

Fearful that she might revert back to biting him, he held Lily close to him with his free hand. As they worked their way through the crowd, he whispered softly to the child to try to calm her, but she still cried every step of the way.

He was halfway through the crowd when

he spied Phanaby standing on the sidewalk in front of the general store with several other women. After quickly changing direction, the three of them exited the fringes of the crowd almost directly in front of her.

Phanaby waved and smiled at them. "Over here. I'm over here!"

After leaving Lily behind with Phanaby, along with his promise that he would have Ruth back within an hour and join them for the picnic dinner, he and Ruth started walking side by side toward Lawrence Street. They followed a herd of others who were headed for the church grounds, although he was not particularly interested in seeing the villagers' offerings that were due to be judged before the area was cleared for a variety of games to be played this afternoon.

He kept his pace slow, in part to accommodate her shorter strides, but mostly to allow the others to pass by them. Fortunately, she was not holding his arm as they walked, or he feared he would be too distracted to focus on his goal for the day.

He chanced another look at her. Like many of the women in the village, she wore a new gown today, but there was not another woman there who could wear a simple dark blue and gray gown with a tiny lace collar and look as stunning as she did.

In all truth, there was not a woman here or anywhere he had traveled who had her startling eyes, either, and he had a hard time making his heart beat normally instead of pounding against the wall of his chest until he kept his gaze focused on that silly bonnet she wore.

They had only covered half a square before she looked back over her shoulder for a third time. "You were right," she finally admitted. "We were standing much too close to the stage for Lily, but she looks very content now that she's away from the noise and the music."

He chuckled. "Either that or she feels safer being away from those dangerous weapons you've got stuck on that bonnet you're wearing again today, although the ribbons add an interesting touch."

She looked over at him and narrowed her gaze. "My bonnet would look much better if you'd remember to return the two feathers you took home so I could put them back where they belong."

"I'm sorry. I'll try to remember them tomorrow and drop them off at the apothecary before I go to the Swains'." He pointed to the northeast with his cane. "They live about half a mile past Spinster Wyndam's cottage and need me to repair their front steps," he explained, grateful for the opening he needed to pursue a more important topic. "After that, I haven't got any work, so I'd like to fix those shelves for Mr. Garner," he said, hoping to remind her that she had promised to speak to the man on Jake's behalf.

Ruth sighed. "He's been so busy lately that he's been content to have everything where he can find it, even if it's all such a mess. Maybe you should ask him about it today when we all have dinner together."

He shrugged, hoping to appear nonchalant. "It's a holiday. Tomorrow will do just as well."

"Actually, any conversation you start at the picnic dinner might be better than focusing on Mayor Pendleton's speech today, given your views on principles like truth and honor," she quipped.

He moved a bit closer to her when a couple of boys ran past them, chasing each other, before putting a more proper distance between them again, which gave him a bit of time to choose the proper bait to lure her into a discussion. Drawing in a long breath, he glanced down at her. Her gaze was focused straight ahead, but her steps were quicker now. "I should have known that the mayor's speech would end up as a topic of conversation today, one way or the other, since it hits very close to the pointed discussions we've had about newspapers and the articles they print," he ventured.

"On the contrary," she argued. "I have no desire to discuss his speech or anything relevant that's been printed in the newspaper with you or anyone else. And in all truth, the few discussions about newspapers we've had weren't all pointed. We obviously disagreed at first, but —"

"As I recall, that's an understatement," he noted, trying to keep his voice firm but calm.

She stopped and looked up at him, forcing him to stop walking. "Nevertheless, I still consider the argument you made that day to be superficial. And I still believe that newspapers and the men who own them or write articles that appear in them can't use principles like truth or justice as a pretext to print everything and anything they like simply because it appeals to the more prurient interests of the public. There's still no honor in doing that as far as I can see, which I thought you understood, considering the last time we talked about a specific article, you actually agreed with me that it was inappropriate. Unless you were simply trying to placate me."

He cleared his throat. He found it difficult to pose a single argument that might provoke her when she was looking up at him with those dazzling eyes and tempting him to kiss her instead of arguing with her. Instead, he tried to refocus their conversation if only to give himself the time he needed to redirect his thoughts from personal to professional.

"Are you suggesting I was being less than honest when I agreed with you?" he prompted.

She dropped her gaze, shrugged, and resumed walking again. "No, but as I recall, you were sitting on the floor in a great deal of pain at the time. Now that you're recovered, I wouldn't be surprised if you changed your mind and decided that the reporter had every right to print those horrid allegations about that minister's daughter. So I think it's probably pointless to discuss anything else," she whispered.

Her voice was laced with emotion. She was still no doubt grieving for her father, which made her all the more vulnerable. This made him question the kind of man he must be to take advantage of that vulnerability for his own purposes. He guided her away from the walkway, but waited until they were under the shade of an old maple tree before he reached out and touched her arm.

She stopped but did not look up at him. "I haven't changed my mind," he insisted. "Not at all, and I should hope you know me well enough by now that if I did have an opinion or if I changed my opinion about something, I'd tell you. I told you my opinion of that silly bonnet you wore when we went to supper with Spinster Wyndam, and I told you again today that I thought it was silly, didn't I?" he added with a smile when she hesitated to respond.

She sighed, but when she looked over at him, her gaze was misty. He knew she was battling tears, which added yet another layer to the guilt he was already carrying. "Yes, you did," she admitted. "I'm sorry. You've always been very open and honest with me. I shouldn't have assumed the worst of you."

He swallowed the lump of guilt in his throat, but it lodged in the middle of his chest.

"I've been awfully busy for the past few weeks," she continued. "Although I have little interest in the newspapers, I really haven't had any time to read them. Perhaps you've read something recently you could tell me about that we could discuss."

"It's a holiday. Maybe we should just think

about enjoying the festivities and have a discussion of the news another day, perhaps while you're working in your garden," he suggested.

She smiled and her eyes sparkled. "I expect to be at my garden tomorrow morning to see if the fireworks later tonight did any damage."

"Tomorrow it is," he replied and nodded toward the church grounds. "We'll need to hurry if we expect to get back in time for our picnic dinner." He guided her toward the first row of tables, where the women had set out their best pies to be judged.

Walking beside her, Jake's dreams of professional redemption suddenly felt selfish. Was he willing to destroy the future of the woman by his side and the little girl she protected? His worries exploded into outright fear, however, when he spied a man standing across the street, in the alley where they had argued last month, watching them from afar.

With his heart racing, he deliberately dropped his cane and took a quick step to the side to block Ruth's view and prevent her from seeing something that made it all the more imperative for him to stay by her side today: Robert Farrell, the scoundrel, had finally come back, just as he had vowed he would.

TWENTY-NINE

Like most of the men he saw escorting women up and down the rows on the church grounds, Jake followed along behind Ruth. He left her to survey the entrants to the competition without rushing her or offering his own opinion about the wares, all the while keeping a sharp lookout for Farrell, who seemed to have disappeared.

He watched Ruth study the pies as they passed by them, but she waited until they were at the end of the row and starting for the next one before announcing her choice for the blue ribbon. "Mrs. Toby should win. Her apple pie looked the best, but Mrs. Ayers will take home the blue ribbon," she whispered.

When he gave her a questioning look, she leaned closer. "Apparently, she wins every year. Don't ask me why, but I overheard someone say it has to do with the fact that Mr. Ayers contributes a sizable donation for the fireworks display later tonight."

"That's a good example of not being truthful . . . or perhaps it's more like a breach of honor. You might want to mention that to some of the folks who organized the contest. What do you think?" he teased.

When she glared at him, he chuckled and let his remark stand as they started up the second row of tables, filled with an assortment of cookies ready to be judged informally by the crowd. He still had not seen any sign of Farrell again, but spied the Jones cousins up ahead and watched them for a moment to make certain they were not headed this way. He stopped abruptly when he realized that Ruth had gone ahead to the next row, where he saw a blur of red, white, and blue decorations. He hurried to catch up with her.

He slowed his steps, however, and stopped under the shade of a maple tree where he decided he could both observe her and watch for Farrell. For her part, Ruth scarcely noticed he had stepped away. In fact, she was surrounded by a group of women standing in front of a display that would only seem odd to anyone in the village who had been living under one of those docks at the river's edge.

As it stood, he was more than glad he was

nothing more than a distant observer when the women urged Ruth closer to the display, chattering at her like a flock of squawking sea gulls chasing after a single gull with a fish in its mouth.

"Come and see!" "We were hoping you'd agree to be our judge." "It's all in good fun. Please don't be offended." "The general store sold out quickly, so we had to change the rules and let women enter their used ones, too."

Even when Jake strained his neck, he could not see Ruth's face, but her back was as stiff as if her spine had been replaced with one of those gaily decorated brooms leaning against a small fence positioned on top of the table. He was half afraid she would refuse to be a part of anything even remotely related to the nickname she found so annoying or speak her mind and offend the women.

That is, until he heard her laugh and clap her hands, exactly like Lily did when something truly pleased her.

Some minutes later, after she had chosen a winner and he had still not seen any sign that Farrell was close by, she looked around and smiled when she finally spied him. She said something to the other women that he could not quite hear, but judging by the laughter coming from the other women, he had a sinking feeling he might somehow be involved. He promptly deemed the idea ludicrous. They were probably just teasing her that she needed to do something to get him to ask if he could court her — an idea he had briefly considered but dismissed as taking his investigation over the line that separated honor from dishonor.

She walked over and joined him under the tree, and he was grateful she could not read his thoughts of just a moment ago, or even now when all he could concentrate on was the sight of her soft, smiling lips. Her pale gray eyes were sparkling with merriment, and her cheeks were flushed the color of the red stripes on the many flags that were flying throughout the village.

"I was hoping you'd help me choose the winner, but I couldn't see you anywhere," she said with a glint in her eye.

He held up his cane defensively in front of him. "There were too many women and too many brooms over there to suit me. Besides, I wasn't quite sure how you'd react when you saw all those brooms decorated in your honor, and I'd rather not be anywhere near you when you're upset and doubly armed with those feathers and a broom," he teased.

"You're armed with that cane you have there, and you can easily defend yourself now that your back is healing so well. But since you didn't bother to come with me or to help me choose the winner, you've lost any right to complain later."

His heart thumped in his chest. "Complain about what? I didn't have anything to do with the idea of decorating those brooms," he argued.

She laughed. "Perhaps not, but you do now."

"Why? Because I just happen to be spending a little time with the Broom Lady?" he quipped, finding her gaiety at his expense as unnerving as the matchmaking fever that had struck nearly everyone in the village where he and Ruth were concerned. He, however, found the notion all too distracting and had actually turned down several invitations to supper lately if Ruth had been invited, too.

"No. Guess again."

He narrowed his gaze and tightened his hold on the cane. "I sincerely hope this isn't some sort of joke —"

"It isn't a joke at all. Apparently, the women who decorated those brooms all paid an entry fee, which will be donated to the church. They all took their work very seriously because they each wanted to win very badly. Would you like me to tell you who the winner is, or would you rather be surprised at dinner? No, now that I think about it, you can't wait. I really need to tell you now."

He snorted. "I think I'd rather wait, at least until you stop jabbering nonsense and speak plainly so I have some notion of what you mean."

"Fine," she said. "Plainly speaking, the broom I picked to win was the one Lorelei Jones decorated, although I didn't know it at the time. You'll be sharing the picnic dinner today with her, much to the dismay of the other unmarried women who entered the contest, because along with winning a blue ribbon, you were the additional prize given to the winner."

Jake looked into her eyes, saw them twinkling with sheer merriment, and nearly choked. "I'm the *prize?* In that broom-decorating competition?"

Her grin widened as she took his arm. "Don't be a spoilsport. It's all in good fun, and those women raised quite a bit, considering they only had their pin money to use for their entrance fees. I'll make your excuses for you with the Garners, too, and don't worry about being alone with her and the broom she made," she assured him before she leaned closer to him and lowered her voice to a whisper. "I heard from a very reliable source that she plans to share you with her cousin, too, but don't say anything. I think it's supposed to be a surprise."

Most of the ribbons had been awarded, but the picnic dinner had not yet started when Ruth approached the table where Jake sat alone while his two companions waddled up to the judges' stand for Lorelei Jones to accept her blue ribbon.

"You've managed to smile more than once or twice so far. Don't stop on my account," she teased when he got up from the bench to greet her.

"I wasn't smiling. I was smirking," he insisted, quite certain Farrell had good reason to disappear from this part of the festivities. "Contrary to all those ladies' good intentions, I'm about as embarrassed right now as I was when I was seven years old and my schoolmaster, Mr. Ephraim Pitts, forced me to wear a toga costume for a play about Rome at the end of the winter session."

She chuckled. "That doesn't sound so awfully terrible."

He snorted. "Trust me when I tell you

that it was," he argued, but for propriety's sake he didn't add that when the toga fell off, he ended up standing in front of the schoolroom wearing nothing but his night-shirt in front of everyone.

"Did you dig in your heels then, too? Or did you go straight to fuming and fussing and downright refusing to be in the play before he bribed you to participate, like I had to do?" she countered.

"If you need to know, Mr. Pitts didn't try to bribe me. He had a very intimidating strap that I'd felt once too often. And in case you're interested in being fair, wearing that costume may not sound too awful to you, but being a prize for anything or anyone, especially a ridiculous broom com-petition won by one of the Jones cousins, is a bit hard to swallow."

"But you did it, even though you made me promise to do a whole list of things," she said and pouted her lips. "I should think letting you escort me to the fireworks display tonight and allowing you to walk me home afterward would have been enough. You can drive a hard bargain, Mr. Spen-cer," she teased.

Jake smiled. He looked forward to spend-ing the entire evening alone with her and decided he deserved to be with her tonight, without any worries about Farrell or his assignment or even his brother. For this one night, he wanted to be with Ruth as the man he wanted to be, rather than the man he would turn out to be in the end: her nemesis.

And he knew just the man who could help him make that happen.

THIRTY

The festive celebrations had replaced more than the humdrum of daily life in the village. For one entire day, villagers set aside their disappointments and disagreements, their sorrows and sins, to revel in the joy of simply being alive in the greatest nation on earth, where they were free to acknowledge their blessings, their love for God, and their belief that the government their forefathers created would protect their freedoms.

When darkness finally fell, all the preparations for the grand finale that would mark the end of the day were done. The air itself was thick with expectancy, as well as the realization that dawn would signal the return to the ordinary trials of life.

Most of the men, women, and children normally abed at this hour had gone down to the open land below Dock Street, a fifteen-minute walk east of the village, to view the fireworks display. Others who would not or could not walk that far crowded together on the bridge at the western end of Main Street. Yet a number of men remained in the village, just in case one of the fireworks went awry and landed on a building instead of fizzling out when it hit the river.

Ruth, however, was anxiously waiting for the darkening sky to explode with color. She was on board the *Sheller,* the very ship that had brought her here, with the captain who owned and commanded the vessel, and the man so often in her thoughts, Jake Spencer.

The night was perfectly clear, the river calm, but Ruth's heart was racing with anticipation. Quite certain she was the only one on board the ship, if not the village itself, who had never viewed fireworks before tonight, she stood at the railing nearest the bow with Jake to her right and Capt. Grant standing next to him.

While the two men bantered back and forth about the future prospects of the village and the decline of available cedar wood needed to build masts for ships, she studied the two men. Since the differences in their ages and physical appearances were rather obvious in the full light of day, she detected more subtle differences now that they were shadowed by the evening's darkness.

While Grant's voice was raspy, he spoke with the assurance of a man accustomed to having his every word obeyed and his wisdom honored. Jake, on the other hand, had a rich, deep timbre to his voice, and he listened more often than he shared his views.

Still, the two men seemed to have much in common. She suspected each had a gentle heart beating beneath their manly demeanors, and there was an aura of mystery about each of them, too. She did not know much about Capt. Grant, but assumed he had a lifetime of experiences at sea she would find fascinating. Despite the hours she had spent with Jake, she knew just as little about him. He had never shared much about his life before coming to Toms River, and she had never questioned him because she could ill-afford answering questions he might have for her.

She also detected just a hint of familiarity between the two men, a certain level of easy comfort that seemed unusual to the point she wondered if they had known each other for a long time. She also considered her lack of experience being around men to be a detriment to fully understanding the camaraderie between Capt. Grant and Jake Spencer. Because her father rarely, if ever, had

anyone call on him at home, even his closest friend, she had never been around men
when they were having a conversation
between themselves.

A soft whoosh, followed by an enormous
burst of dazzling white stars, lit the sky
directly in front of the ship and promptly
ended her woolgathering, as well as the
men's conversation. Before the falling stars
disappeared, an explosion of blue lights appeared, followed by a red umbrella of light
that twinkled in the sky for several heartbeats before disappearing with a hiss as the
particles hit the surface of the river.

When a barrage of very loud sounds that
resembled the volley of cannon fire tore
through the air, she leaped straight up from
a sense of wonder and awe. Heart pounding, she gasped and grabbed hold of the railing with one hand. Fearful that a cannonball
might actually hit the ship, she clapped the
other hand to her heart, her thumb landing
on top of the shell heart she wore every day
now.

Jake moved closer to her and laid his hand
on top of hers, but his touch was more unnerving than reassuring as warm sensations
coursed up her arm. "Apparently, Lily isn't
the only one who dislikes loud noises. If
you'd mentioned it earlier, we could have

watched the fireworks from the bridge, but it's not too late. If you like, I can row us to shore if you think you'll be more comfortable a bit farther away."

"No. I'd rather stay here. I-I just wasn't expecting the fireworks to boom like that," she blurted and gently withdrew her hand, hoping the reactions his touch inspired would quickly ease.

He did not reply until another wave of color hit the sky. "You're serious? I thought you said you lived in New York City before you moved here. I saw the fireworks there a few years ago. As I recall, the display was more boom than anything else."

Capt. Grant grunted. "That's true enough. They don't take enough precautions to protect the ships in the harbor, either, which is why my first experience at anchor there on the Fourth of July was my last."

"I-I wouldn't know. I've never seen fireworks before tonight," she admitted.

"Never?" Jake asked incredulously.

"Not once," she replied, praying he would not ask the reason why, and then tensed when another volley thundered overhead.

"Were you always afraid of them, or not interested for some reason?" Grant asked when the noise abated.

347

"My father was a . . . a hawker. He sold . . . trinkets so he worked a lot, especially on holidays like the Fourth of July," she said, voicing the first idea that popped into her head that made any sense. She could hardly tell them the truth.

Holidays were the few times when men who frequented brothels on a regular basis could be counted on to be with their families, which meant her father had more time to preach to the women who sold their bodies to survive. "Was your father a sea captain, too?" she asked the older of the two men when there was a lull in the display, if only to keep herself out of the focus of the conversation.

Capt. Grant yawned before he answered. "All his life, which included very little of mine," he offered before he yawned again. "I've got some record keeping to finish before I fall asleep standing here, so if you folks don't mind, I need to get it done if I expect to sail at first light. Assuming my crew makes it back in time," he added with a snort and clapped Jake on his arm. "Let me know when you're ready to row back. I'll help with the dinghy," he offered and promptly took his leave.

Series after series of impossibly beautiful displays of color, followed by loud bangs, kept Ruth too enthralled to ask Jake any questions about his life before he came to the village. Later, however, when he was rowing her ashore, she was able to gather her courage. She sat in the stern of the boat, holding his cane for him, while he sat in the middle, and their knees almost touched. Although the dark of night kept her from seeing his features clearly, she was close enough to hear him take a breath over the sound of the oars gliding in and out of the water.

"I don't really know very much about you, beyond the fact that you injured your back in a fall from a roof you were repairing. I can only assume you're a carpenter by trade," she prompted, in part to keep her thoughts from focusing too completely on the man so near to her.

"That I was," he replied, his voice straining as he pulled the oars through the water. "With my back healing as well as it is, I expect I'll be leaving within the next few weeks to go back to the old homestead, but I'm inclined to choose another livelihood when I do. Painful mistakes can force a man to think long and hard about his future," he murmured.

She shuddered, just imagining the painful recovery he had endured before he came to

Toms River. "Do you have family waiting for you?"

He paused so long she regretted the question and sighed with relief when he finally answered her. "My parents are gone now. I have one brother, but we haven't been close for a couple of years now."

"Growing up, I used to wish I had a brother or sister. I still do," she mused, but when she caught the scent of the flowers in her garden and saw a glimmer of light near his cabin, she tightened her hold on his cane. "Why are we going to the south side of the river? The apothecary is on the other side."

"That may be true," he said as he leaned forward to pull the oars through the water again. "But the seaman who was guarding the cabin on the odd chance that part of the fireworks display misfired is waiting for us on this side of the river. He's going to row the dinghy back to the ship while I walk you home."

She smiled and shook her head. "You really didn't have to go to all this trouble, although I truly enjoyed being on the ship tonight. But we could have watched the fireworks with everyone else. It would have been much safer for you, too. All this rowing can't be very good for your back."

"My back is fine, and I don't have one or two but three bottles of Mr. Garner's remedy, just in case I need it," he countered. "Hold onto the sides of the boat. We're about to hit shore."

The boat no sooner scraped the sandy bottom when the glimmer of light grew a little brighter. By the time Jake had pulled the dinghy to shore and helped her stand on solid ground again, the young seaman arrived holding a rather dim lantern. After a brief exchange, during which Jake handed over a few coins, the seaman pulled the boat back into the water, leaving Ruth alone with Jake.

Completely alone. In a bubble of gentle light. Surrounded by total darkness. With a man who made her heart race when he looked at her, captured her gaze, and held it for almost an eternity.

"I wanted to show you something. It's right over here." He carried the lantern as he led her to her garden, where she found a lovely wooden sitting bench with a high back and wide seat. He had it positioned so that she would have a close view of her garden, but a panoramic view of the river, too.

Rendered speechless, she watched him set the lantern on the ground and his face light up with delight. He slid the hinged back of the bench forward while the seat remained stationary, transforming the unique gift he had made for her from a high-backed bench into a bench with a narrow table.

"I only finished making it yesterday. I know you like to spend a lot of time here. Now you have a place for you and Lily to have a picnic, even if the ground is too wet."

"It's amazing," she whispered. Overwhelmed by his skill as a carpenter and his thoughtfulness, she walked over to the bench, stood next to him, and ran her hand over the wood he had sanded to a smooth finish.

Blinking back tears, she dared to hope that this man might be the one man she could trust to help her protect Lily, the one man she could trust — someday — with the truth about who she really was.

She touched the shell heart she wore beneath her gown, fairly certain that if he had not captured her heart before tonight, he surely had stolen it from her now.

When she saw the tiny cross carved into the middle of the back of the bench, she blinked back more tears. "Is this your mark?" she asked, pointing to the carving beneath it that looked like a cane turned upside down before she realized it was the letter *J*, his initial.

Feeling a bit foolish, she looked up at him when he did not answer her and lost all thought and all sense of time or place. He was gazing at her with such longing, she could scarcely breathe. Her heart nearly stopped beating when he bent his head close and kissed her.

Very gently. Very tenderly. And only once, which was more than enough to let her know that he might be falling in love with her, too, because the dazzling burst of emotions that filled her entire being, from the top of her head to the tips of her toes, made the display of fireworks tonight pale by comparison.

The only question that exploded in her mind, with all the force of a cannonball, was whether or not he was also the one man who would forgive her for all the lies she had told him . . . or if he'd reject her as unworthy of his love and devotion.

After escorting Ruth home, Jake took his time walking down the dirt path that led from the back of the apothecary to the base of the bridge on Main Street. The village was quieter now, and without the fireworks he had little to light his way. He had no regrets about kissing Ruth tonight, if only to have one very special memory of her that would have to last a lifetime unless he found a way to finish his assignment and redeem himself without losing her.

Forced to choose between his career and a woman he had quite unexpectedly grown to care deeply for, he was deeply troubled and nearly oblivious to his surroundings.

Until a dreaded voice rang out from behind him.

"Too busy chasing skirts to care about your career. Pity. Your brother will be so disappointed when I give him this news tidbit."

Jake whirled about and glared at Robert Farrell, who was standing in the path, just beyond arm's reach. Otherwise Jake might have used his fist to make the man swallow his own words. Truth be told, he was just as angry with himself. He should have suspected the cad would be lurking about, hoping to talk to him at some point. "What are you doing here?"

The reporter shrugged. "I could ask you the same question, although after the kiss you stole from Widow Malloy back by your cabin tonight, I can only assume you were hoping for another."

Outraged by the man's audacity, Jake hissed, "You were there? Watching us?"

The man took a step back. "Of course I was there. I take my orders seriously. Or have you forgotten that I work for your brother, and since he's the one in charge of the *Galaxy* at the moment, he's the one I take orders from, not you."

"What orders?" Jake tightened his grip on his cane. "Clifford just sent me a letter that I received only a few days ago. He can't possibly have changed his mind about my assignment yet again."

"He sent me to make sure you understood what's at stake."

"I understand what's at stake," Jake countered.

"Do you? Unless your brother told you what I've discovered about Ruth Livingstone, which I learned on a rather lengthy trip to Boston, where she resided until very recently, and what I expect to confirm in Philadelphia, I don't think you have any idea how close I am to writing the full story of what that young woman kept hidden to keep her father from being convicted."

Jake was tempted to tell the man that his information was dead wrong, but decided his own interests would be better served by having Farrell chase down leads that would take him far from here. "Don't let me stop you," he snapped. "Just be on the stage when it leaves tomorrow morning."

Farrell snickered. "I'm traveling by private coach now, which is waiting for me over the bridge as we speak. By the way, I actually do have a rather odd message from your brother."

Jake stiffened his back. "What's the message?"

"He said to tell you he's removed the cot in the storage room at the newspaper office. It doesn't make any sense to me, but he said you'd know what that means."

"I do," Jake said, without explaining that Clifford was making it very clear that there was no room for Jake at the newspaper anymore if he failed his brother again. There was no room in Clifford's heart for forgiveness, either.

THIRTY-ONE

Ruth soon found she had neither the time, the energy, nor the inclination to keep wondering if the first kiss she had shared with Jake Spencer would be her last. For the third night in a row, she spent the wee hours before dawn wearing down the floorboards in her bedroom trying to comfort Lily while Elias tended to his wife, who had been ailing for a few days. Now that dawn was finally breaking, she was too exhausted to take another step. She stopped pacing and swayed from side to side since any motion at all seemed to help the whimpering child lying in the crook of her arm, and she prayed the little one would finally drift off to sleep.

Poor Lily. Her eyes were swollen from crying all night, her cheeks flushed, and the curls that framed her face wet from her tears, which had dampened the neckline of Ruth's nightdress. Softly, Ruth began to croon the lullaby she had sung so often during the night. " 'Hush, my dear, lie still and slumber, holy angels guard thy bed. Heavenly blessings without number, fall in kisses on thy head.' "

As Lily grew limp and quiet, her breathing slowed, but Ruth continued to sway and hum the melody. She did not dare stop and put Lily back into bed before she was in a deep sleep. Unfortunately, none of the remedies from Elias worked as well as simply holding the teething child, although Ruth was not certain how much longer she could hold the little girl without dropping her unless she sat down.

Her arm was nearly numb, her shoulders and back were throbbing, and her head ached unmercifully. "If I had my way, babies would be born with a full set of teeth." She looked over to the empty trundle bed and sighed. "All I want is to put my head on my pillow, draw up the covers, and sleep until you're old enough to go to school."

The sound of footsteps out in the hallway and light trickling into her room from beneath her door made her pulse quicken. When she heard a soft rap at her door, she ever so gently laid Lily into bed, tightened the belt on her robe, and tiptoed quickly across the room to open the door.

Elias Garner looked every bit as weary as she felt, but the concern she saw in his eyes that had troubled him for the past few days had deepened to fear. "I need to fetch Dr. Woodward," he whispered. "I know you've been up most the night again with Lily, but if you could sit with my wife —"

"Of course." Ruth slipped into the hallway and eased the door closed. "Is there anything I can do for her until you get back?"

"If she wakes up, give her some water, if she'll take it, and change the compress on her forehead as soon as it warms. Otherwise just . . . just pray," he urged and hurried off.

Swallowing hard, Ruth crossed the hall and entered the couple's bedroom. The light from the oil lamp sitting next to a small wooden chest on the dresser to her right was dim, and the air in the room was heavy with the unique scent of the remedies Elias had used to try to cure his wife's illness. If Elias felt it was necessary to get the doctor, Ruth was afraid that Phanaby was far sicker than any of them had anticipated.

Ruth tiptoed to the chair sitting at Phanaby's side in front of the bed table and eased into the seat. The older woman appeared to be sleeping, yet she looked far worse than when she had first taken to her bed. Her face was flushed with fever, her lips were dry and cracked, and her breathing was so shallow, Ruth had to hold her own breath to hear the woman draw in any air.

Ruth removed the compress from Phanaby's forehead and her fingertips brushed the woman's skin, which was far hotter than she expected. She poured fresh water into the basin on the bed table, rinsed the compress, and wrung it out before gently laying it back in place.

Phanaby stirred. Without opening her eyes, she lifted a hand from beneath the covers and grew restless until Ruth covered her hand with her own. "I'm here," she whispered. "Just rest. Dr. Woodward should be here soon."

Phanaby blinked several times before she opened her eyes, but when she tried to speak, her voice was too soft to be heard.

"Would you like some water?"

An almost imperceptible nod.

After taking two awkward sips, however, she closed her eyes, and Ruth used the handkerchief in her pocket to wipe away the water that trickled down the woman's chin. She held Phanaby's hand and bowed her head. Completely exhausted, Ruth found she did not even have the strength to think of any words to say. So she prayed with all she had to offer: the silent words of her heart.

Elias returned half an hour later to tell her that Dr. Woodward had been called to an accident down at the mill in Double Trouble late yesterday and had not yet come home. He was clearly upset, and Ruth grew increasingly worried about him when he left again every few hours to go to the doctor's home to inquire if he had returned, even though the doctor's wife had promised to send him to the apothecary the moment he rode back to the village.

Finally, in late afternoon, when Elias returned with Dr. Woodward, Phanaby was much worse. At that point, Elias was frantic with worry, and Ruth feared that the Prodigal Daughter who had reclaimed her faith in God and served Him so well for the past fifteen years would be with her beloved Savior before the sun rose again.

While Lily was napping, Ruth kept a tense vigil with Elias, who paced up and down the length of the hallway. Finally, Dr. Woodward stepped into the hall. Grim-faced, he closed the door behind him when Elias was at the end of the hallway near the staircase door.

Elias froze in place and hesitated for just a moment, as if he was afraid to hear the doctor's diagnosis, before rushing to the man. "What's wrong with her? Can you help her? Tell me you can help her. Please!"

An exhausted Dr. Woodward put his hand on Elias's shoulder. "I'm not entirely certain what's wrong, but I've bled her and she's resting a bit more comfortably now. I'll stop back later tonight and check on her," he offered before turning to Ruth. "In the meantime, since nothing else you've done has helped, you might want to see if she can take some bark tea made from white willow. It would likely help if you could bathe her with cloths dipped in that tea as well."

"I can do that," she assured him, certain that Elias would have the herb she needed downstairs in the apothecary, if not the storeroom.

Elias clenched his fists. "But what is it? Why is my wife so ill?"

"We'll know more tonight. Hopefully, she'll be much improved by then," the elderly doctor replied and left both of them standing there, silent in their private petitions to God.

Ruth touched Elias's arm. "If you could go downstairs and find the white willow bark, I'll start heating the water to make tea," she said, gently prompting him. When he started to shake his head, she assumed he did not want to be that far away from his wife. "Just tell me where to find it, instead," she suggested, aware that he could save her from wasting valuable time trying to find it.

His eyes glistened. "I can't. I sold the last of it to Mrs. Sloan just last week, and it's not something other folks normally keep around because it's imported from Europe and very expensive," he murmured, and his voice cracked with every word he spoke.

"How much did you sell Mrs. Sloan?" she asked, but she had to repeat her question several times before he answered her.

"I told you. All that I had."

"Which was probably twice what she needed because she always insists she have extra on hand. Am I right?" Ruth asked.

As he blinked his tears away, his eyes sparkled with hope. "Y-yes. As a matter of fact, she does."

"You stay here with your wife. Since Lily's still napping, I'll go down to the general store and talk Mrs. Sloan into giving me whatever she has left," she insisted. She was halfway down the staircase when he called out to her.

"Stop. You can't go outside."

Startled by his sharply spoken words, Ruth halted and looked back over her shoulder. "I can't go outside? Why not?"

He motioned for her to return, and she mounted the stairs quickly. Once she was back in the hall, he shut the door behind her and his gaze darkened. "When I was looking for Dr. Woodward today, I overheard people talking about a reporter who arrived yesterday afternoon from New York City. I'm sorry — I nearly forgot to tell you. The man's registered right up the street at Burkalow's. I don't think it's safe for you to go outside until he's finished up his stay here and leaves."

Her poor heart dropped so fast and so hard, she feared it would hit her feet and burst.

"I'm sorry, Ruth. He's a reporter for the *Transcript,* and he's reserved accommodations at Burkalow's for the next two weeks. From what I could gather, he's already been holding court at the tavern and entertaining folks with stories about Reverend Livingstone's trial and the search that continues for his daughter. He claims he's followed a number of women who worked in Mrs. Browers's brothel to find out what they knew about Rosalie Peale. If by chance he's followed you here because he thinks you might know something about her, or recognizes you since you worked in the city —"

"His name," Ruth managed. "Did you

learn his name?"

He raked his fingers through his hair. "I think they said his name was Porter or Potter or . . ."

"Porter. His name is Eldridge Porter. I think I know exactly who he is," she whispered. She found it hard to believe it was mere coincidence that one of the few reporters who had actually seen her when her father granted a number of interviews at home before his arrest would have chosen to come to Toms River.

More likely, he had somehow traced her here, and she knew beyond any doubt that she had no choice but to remain inside these living quarters just as Elias had suggested. Once she helped nurse Phanaby back to health, she would have to take Lily and leave the village. But without a single coin to her name, she had no idea how she could afford to leave, or where she would go, or how she would support them both — unless she could somehow find a way to reach Capt. Grant and convince him to help her.

THIRTY-TWO

Forced into exile from the village proper, Jake stood outside his cabin and watched the hot summer sun edge closer to the western horizon at the head of the river. He was so furious he could not decide whether to direct his anger at himself or Clifford, but settled on Eldridge Porter, the reporter for the *Transcript* who had taken up residence at Burkalow's several days ago.

He had been well acquainted with Porter until leaving two years ago, and there was not a doubt in Jake's mind that Porter would recognize him. Unable to monitor the reporter's activities, Jake could only imagine what progress Porter was making in pursuing the story he claimed to be writing about the late Rev. Livingstone and his daughter — the only tidbit of news about the man Jake had been able to glean before hibernating in his cabin.

Unfortunately, Porter was not an inexperienced reporter like Robert Farrell, and Jake knew only too well that the man was too driven and too anxious to make a name for himself not to have come here to Toms River without a good reason. Jake now faced the very real possibility of failing to complete his assignment before the *Transcript* ended up printing the story he needed to write for the *Galaxy.*

He tore back into the cabin and slammed the door behind him. The fire, which he had started before going outside, was now blazing. Although the heat it provided made the air in the cabin unbearably sultry, he did not have any choice. The only way Jake could be certain no one else would read the information contained in the letter Capt. Grant had secured inside one of the newspapers that his seamen had delivered just an hour ago was to burn the letter.

He tossed Clifford's letter into the fire. As flames began to lick at the missive, he watched it ignite. For good measure, Jake added every piece of correspondence he'd received from his brother, along with the legal papers relinquishing his share of the newspaper so Clifford could find a suitable investor to replace him.

Still, his anger and disgust remained, along with his fear that Porter might have uncovered the same information that Clifford had reported to him. If he had, the small fortune Clifford had paid to guarantee the information was exclusive had been wasted.

The information itself, however, was so explosive, he knew his brother would have paid any price to get it from his source, Evelyn Billings. She was the sister of a woman who had worked as Peale's maid in Mrs. Browers's brothel. She claimed the child Ruth was raising now as her own was in fact Rosalie Peale's daughter, Lily, a child who had been raised in secrecy by Billings herself. Even more scandalously, Billings also claimed that Lily's father was the same man who had argued with Rosalie Peale and killed her in the midst of the argument, the same man who had rifled through the prostitute's room and stolen a number of items, and the very same man who had sent his older daughter into hiding with the evidence he had stolen that would have convicted him: Rev. Gersham Livingstone.

Clifford also ordered his brother to confront Ruth with Billings's allegations and return to New York City by week's end with a full article ready to be set to print. Jake's anger at his brother raged anew. But as the letter burst into an orange ball, he came to realize he had no one to blame but himself. He was the one who had slowly developed a relationship under the guise of undercover reporting, when truth be told he was far more interested in the captivating woman instead of the scandal he was to reveal. And he was also the one who had taken that one final moment they shared together for himself as a man, rather than as a reporter, and kissed her.

Just one kiss.

One soul-wrenching kiss.

That was all it took for him to know there would not be another time or another place for him to fall in love.

The time was right now.

The place was right here.

And as much as he had tried to deny it, he knew in his heart that Ruth was the only woman he would ever love, just as he knew that by loving her, she was the one woman who could cost him the one thing he so desperately wanted to achieve: his redemption.

He watched the letter slowly blacken into ash, a troubling symbol of his efforts to deny his love for her. He had tried working from dawn to dusk, doing odd jobs throughout the village for the past two weeks, so he would not even be tempted to see her when she worked in her garden.

He ended up dreaming about her every night.

The ashes began to drift to the hearthstone, and he sighed heavily. He would never be able to write the story he knew his brother expected him to write — indeed, a story he had expected himself to write. Unless he could find a way to fall out of love with her.

Sweating profusely, he turned his back to the fire, walked away, and started pacing from the front of the cabin to the rear and back again. Regardless of what he did or did not do about his feelings for Ruth, he had no time left to wallow in self-pity or what might have been. He had to choose what he wanted and act decisively now, or he would lose both the woman he loved and the career he wanted to reclaim, ending up with nothing at all.

He carefully weighed his options. If he followed his heart and turned his back on his career, as well as his brother, he could wait for Ruth to come to her garden tomorrow morning and confess all the lies he had told her. By some miracle, if he could convince her that he had fallen in love with her, they could take Lily, run away together, and settle down as a family somewhere far away.

"Not a good idea," he whispered, kicking at the dirt floor with the toe of his boot. He'd already made the mistake of running from a problem instead of facing it. Taking Ruth and Lily into hiding with him would not help either one of them, either. Sooner or later, a reporter would find them, and they could not spend their lives constantly relocating, running away from a past that would eventually catch up with them.

Jake stopped in front of the ladder to the loft, lifted the cane he had hung from one of the rungs, and threw it across the room. He watched the cane bang into the table before it flipped, end over end, and landed in the fire.

He walked over to the hearth and braced both hands on the edge of the mantel. He let the cane burn, knowing the ruse he had concocted to fool everyone, especially Ruth, would haunt him for the rest of his life.

He ignored several sharp knocks at the door, but when the cabin door opened, he whipped around and saw Capt. Grant closing the door behind him. "As warm as it is outside, you've got a fire going? It's hotter than Hades in here," he complained.

"Hades sounds about right," Jake quipped and shook hands with the older man. "I didn't think I'd see you tonight."

"Given that your brother was unusually snappish when he handed me the letter to bring to you, I suspected he didn't have good news. So . . . since I had the chance to pick up some cargo that needs to be in Baltimore tomorrow afternoon, I thought I'd better stop by tonight. I'll be back here on Thursday, though, and then sail to New York City on Friday."

Jake swallowed hard. "My work here is finished, so I'll be needing passage with you on Friday. What do you want me to do about the cabin?"

Grant let out a sigh. "I've got a couple of folks in mind who might be able to use it. Stop by the livery tomorrow and ask for Ned Clarke. Tell him to ask his father if he'd like to move closer to the village now that his boy's working here and he's working at the mill in Double Trouble. Just don't mention my name. Nobody around here knows I actually own this cabin and the land it sits on. I'd like to keep it that way. You can let me know on Friday if they'd like to use the cabin."

Jake nodded, hopeful he could slip into the livery in the early morning hours before Porter would be up and ready to start the day. "Passage back to New York City for me won't be a problem, will it?"

372

The captain walked over to the window facing the river, swung the shutter open, and stood by it as fresh air blew into the cabin. "Not for me, but it looks like it might be a problem for your brother — unless there's someone else who's responsible for that peevish look on your face."

Jake ran a hand through his hair. "Can you stay for a while or do you have to get back to the ship?"

Capt. Grant looked out the window and shrugged. "It's already dark. I've got about five minutes, maybe less if the fool waiting for me in that dinghy out there takes one more swig from that bottle of hard cider I bought for myself. So speak fast and don't dawdle on details."

Jake cleared his throat. He probably needed a good hour, just to lay a proper foundation before he could ask this man to help him make the right choice. With only five minutes, he had to go straight to the core of his dilemma, but had difficulty choosing the right words. "What matters more? A man's principles? Or his work? Or . . . or his —"

"Or his heart?" The older man chuckled for a moment, but when he turned to face Jake, his expression was sober. "If a man has the right principles, he invariably

373

chooses the right work to do. His heart will lead him to the one woman who will help him to be true to both." He walked to the door and opened it.

Looking back over his shoulder, he smiled. "Perhaps you might consider a more important question that makes all the others seem irrelevant: What could possibly matter to any man if he spends even a single day of his life without serving God? Answer that question correctly, and you won't have any trouble knowing what to do. He'll show you." Then the captain walked out the door and closed it behind him.

Dumbfounded, Jake could not move a muscle. By the time he recovered his wits and rushed out of the cabin to the shore of the river, the captain and the dinghy, along with the seaman at the oars, had all but disappeared into the darkness. He waited until he could no longer hear the oars swiping through the water before he turned and started walking along the shoreline.

The air outside was warm, but it was a far sight cooler than the heat in the cabin. He fumed as he walked. When he grew weary of his anger, and his disappointment that Capt. Grant had left him to ponder such a provocative question, he walked over to the bench he had built for Ruth and found that pesky turkey sitting there.

Annoyed, he shooed it off and sat down, then became even more annoyed when the bird decided to stand a few feet away watching him, as if ready to reclaim its spot when he left. He had built this bench to encourage her to visit her garden more often or to stay longer when she did. She had never returned to use it, not even once, but he hardly wanted the bench to end up as a place for that turkey to roost. He glared at the bird, getting only a few squawks for his effort, and dismissed it as far too inconsequential to worry about when he had his future, as well as Ruth's, to ponder.

As Grant's words echoed over and over again in his mind, he looked up at the night sky. Thick clouds obscured any view of the moon and the stars, yet he knew they were there. He had seen the sun disappear at sunset more times than he could remember, but he never doubted that the sun would return to shine light upon the world the next day.

Yet somehow, in his search for success and his need to prove himself to his brother and the world itself, he had lost sight of His Creator and had doubted Him more often than not. He had forgotten to faithfully love and serve the very God who had created the moon and the stars and the sun, and more important, the God who had created him.

Humbled, Jake grew desperate for the redemption of not his career but his very soul. Bowing his head, he prayed, truly prayed like he had done as a child: with a faith that was strong enough to resist the temptations of this world, a heart that was open to the wonders of His love and the power of His mercy, and a spirit yearning to serve Him and Him alone. He prayed exactly the way Capt. Grant had encouraged him to do each time he had given him one of the seashells stored now in his trunk, seashells bleached white by the sun, just as the stains of his sins had been bleached white by God's grace when he asked for God's forgiveness.

When he was done, when his heart and his soul were completely at peace with God for the first time in many, many years, it was not the image of his brother that flashed through Jake's mind.

It was the image of Ruth. The grief she hid behind her smile. The tiny freckles sprinkling the bridge of her nose that crinkled when she laughed. Her small hands holding Lily's hand as they walked together down the sandy path toward her garden or the planked sidewalk on Main Street. And her eyes. Her beautiful, haunting, soulful eyes, sparkling up at him when she told him he was a prize at the Fourth of July celebration — eyes that simmered with emotion just before she closed them to kiss him.

And it was not the echo of his brother's voice that he heard, either. It was Ruth's voice, echoing the challenge of holding true to principles like truth and honor while reporting the news, and having the strength to resist the public's thirst for scandal that overwhelmed the rights of innocent people caught on the fringes of that scandal and victimized.

Principles he had once embraced just as passionately as she did, before his ambition had blinded him.

Innocent people like Ruth. And Lily, the most innocent victim, and the one who would be hurt the greatest if he chose to write the article Clifford expected him to produce and deliver by week's end.

THIRTY-THREE

"There's still hope. She's no better, but she's no worse."

Ruth sat by Phanaby's bedside at mid-morning on Tuesday, her spirit clinging to Dr. Woodward's parting words an hour ago and her faith in God resting in endless silent prayers she said for Phanaby's recovery. Her heart was still heavy with disappointment that she had not been able to respond to Jake's note to let him know that she would not be able to meet him at her garden at dawn today or any morning until Eldridge Porter left the village, but the tiny blue flower he had picked from her garden and left with his note was pinned to her collar.

When Phanaby grew restless and stirred awake, she took the woman's hand very carefully to calm her and tried not to disturb the bandages on her arm that covered the several places where Dr. Woodward had bled her.

"Elias?"

"He's downstairs with Lily in the apothecary. Would you like me to get him for you?"

Phanaby tried to moisten her cracked lips with her tongue, but shook her head instead of voicing her answer.

"Drink some more tea. Dr. Woodward seems to think it's helping you," she urged. She managed to get the woman to drink nearly half a cup of tea, and she was pleased how little of the dark liquid had trickled out of the corners of her mouth before Phanaby pushed Ruth's hand away.

"Please," she whispered and weakly pointed to the dresser where the wooden chest was sitting next to the oil lamp.

Ruth furrowed her brow. "Would you like me to light the lamp?" she asked, fearful that Phanaby's vision had been affected, because the natural light in the room was quite sufficient to see, even with the curtains drawn.

Phanaby closed her eyes for a moment as if trying to garner the energy she needed to speak. After she opened her eyes again, she managed to say one word: "Chest."

"You want me to bring you the chest?" Ruth asked, certain she had misunderstood, since Phanaby had reacted so strongly when she had merely moved the chest to dust the top of the dresser some weeks ago.

A single nod.

Still confused, Ruth retrieved the ornately carved wooden chest. It was a bit bulky to carry with one hand, but it was light, and she wondered what type of sentimental keepsakes Phanaby had stored inside.

Phanaby's eyes widened, and the fever-bright glaze to her eyes grew brighter still once Ruth placed the chest on the bed. "Would you like me to open it for you?" Ruth asked, but the lid refused to lift, and she barely took note of the keyhole when Phanaby lifted one of her hands, reached out, and flipped the chest over before collapsing back onto her pillows again.

Ruth separated the key on the bottom of the chest from something that looked like red sealing wax and slid the key into the keyhole. Before she could turn the key, Phanaby placed a hand on top of Ruth's to stop her. Once again she closed her eyes, and it was a good bit of time before she opened them again. When she spoke, her voice was barely a whisper and her words were clumped together in phrases, although they were clear and plainly uttered. "I received that chest . . . from Reverend Livingstone . . . several days before . . . you arrived," she said and paused to rest for a moment. "Open the chest. . . . His note to me is lying . . . right on top."

Ruth's fingers trembled as she unlocked the chest. With the key still in the keyhole, she lifted the lid, praying she might also find a letter inside that her father had written to her. With one glance, her hopes soared. A stack of papers was piled neatly inside the chest.

Once she lifted the small note lying on top, she saw the faded green ribbon that tied the rest of the papers together. With her heart throbbing in her throat, she unfolded the note, which was dated two days before she had left, and read it silently:

My dearest daughter-in-faith,

Within days, Capt. Grant will bring to you Widow Malloy and the precious child entrusted to her care, whom she can now claim openly as her own, precisely as planned. Circumstances dictate that I must send this chest to you immediately, and I trust you will guard it well until she arrives and can guard it herself.

With faith in His wisdom and mercy,
GL

Blinking back tears, she ran her fingers

381

over the words her father had written and
rested her fingertips on the fancy initials
her father used for personal correspondence, as well as the notes he would leave
for her if he left the house in the morning
before she woke up. She was not certain she
understood his message entirely, but the
date alone told her that he had sent this
wooden chest to her and not to Rosalie
Peale, who had already been murdered by
the time he had written the note.

"He meant this wooden chest for me," she
murmured. Although she was highly anxious
to read the other letters her father had
stored inside, she wondered even more why
Phanaby had not followed her father's
wishes and given the chest to Ruth months
ago when she first arrived. She looked to
Phanaby for the answer, but found the
woman was weeping silently, with her hands
steepled at her waist, lying on top of the
sheets that covered her.

"Forgive me," Phanaby whispered.
"Please . . . forgive me."

Ruth swallowed the lump in her throat. "I
forgive you. Just tell me why you waited so
long to give this to me. Please tell me why."

She had to wait a good while until Phanaby stopped crying, then waited even
longer before the woman found either the

courage or the energy to answer. When she finally did begin to speak, Ruth leaned closer to capture every softly spoken word.

"Please don't blame Elias. He . . . he thinks it's mine . . . He doesn't know the chest belongs . . . to you."

"I'm not fixing blame on anyone," Ruth insisted. "Just tell me why you never did what my fa . . . Reverend Livingstone asked you to do until now."

Phanaby's bottom lip trembled. "Those first few days were so hectic . . . you seemed so . . . overwhelmed, and Lily was so fussy. . . ." She stopped to draw in several shallow breaths of air. "Once we all . . . settled in together . . . I kept putting it off because . . . because I was afraid . . . so afraid," she whispered and closed her eyes.

When she appeared to be drifting off to sleep again, Ruth took her hand. "What made you so afraid?" she whispered.

Phanaby sighed, and she did not open her eyes when she started to speak again. "I was afraid you'd read something inside . . . take Lily and leave us . . . We'd both come to . . . love the two of you so much . . . I didn't want you to go."

Ruth understood now why Phanaby had been so upset when she had found Ruth holding the chest while she had been dusting. "Then why give me the chest now?" she asked, although she had a good idea of the answer she would receive.

"I'm afraid . . . I'm not going to get well . . . and you'd never know . . . the secret I'd been keeping from you."

Ruth smoothed the woman's troubled brow, alarmed by how warm she was, and wiped away her tears. "Shhh. Rest now. Just rest," she said.

Ruth stayed by Phanaby's side until the poor woman finally drifted off to sleep, without telling her that as soon as she recovered, the fear that had driven her to keep her secret would become real. As much as Ruth wanted to stay, she knew she had no choice but to take Lily and leave. Even if by some miracle the reporter from the *Transcript* left empty-handed, another reporter would appear in the village sooner or later and threaten the life and the love they had found here. That reporter would pose a threat to the life Elias and Phanaby enjoyed here, too.

Unless by some miracle there was something within the wooden chest that would allow them both to stay.

THIRTY-FOUR

Ruth had to wait until early afternoon to find out if the wooden chest contained a miracle of any kind. Although she doubted it contained anything of value to anyone else, she was incredibly curious to find out exactly what her father had sent to her.

After dinner, Elias closed the apothecary again in order to spend the rest of the afternoon with his wife. Lily actually crawled into her bed for her afternoon nap and fell asleep almost as soon as her little head hit the pillow, leaving Ruth the free time, and the privacy, to investigate the contents of the chest.

Ruth sat on the bed next to Lily. While she waited to make absolutely certain the child was asleep before she moved an inch, she repeated the most plaintive words that Phanaby had spoken that morning. *"We'd both come to love the two of you so much,"* she whispered and wrapped one of Lily's curls around her baby finger.

The truth was that during the course of the past three months, Ruth had come to love the Garners, too. And she could scarcely remember life before she had Lily, and she could not imagine life without her now. "I love you, baby girl," she whispered. "I love you, and I won't ever let you go. Never. God will find a way for us to be together, if only I trust in Him." She leaned down to kiss her sweet cheeks.

While checking to be sure the door to her bedroom was securely closed, Ruth paused to listen. When she heard Elias softly singing a hymn to his wife in the bedroom across the hall, she knew she had more than enough time to read the letters, so she sat on the upper bed and opened the chest. She set Phanaby's note on top of her pillow and removed the letter below, breaking the sealing wax with the tip of the scissors she had slipped into her apron pocket earlier.

Her eyes opened wide when she saw that beneath the stain of the wax, her name was scrawled on the letter lying on top. Before she opened the letter, she closed her eyes for a moment to pray that her father had either sent her some funds or would tell her if he had made other arrangements for them.

Although she realized the letter itself was extremely long, the sight of so many words he had written with his own hand rekindled the deep grief lying just below the surface of her sorrow. She wept until her vision was clear once again before starting the letter. The date was the very same date as the note he had written to Phanaby, erasing any doubt that he had meant for Ruth, not Rosalie Peale, to receive the wooden chest.

Next, she started reading the entire letter, but with each word she read, her heart began to race a little bit faster. By the time she finished the letter, her head was spinning and her heart was beating erratically. She took a deep breath and began to read the letter again, taking the time to read each paragraph very slowly in order to absorb what her father had written.

My beloved daughter, Ruth,

If you are reading this letter, then you have arrived in Toms River with Lily. I pray that I will be able to send for you both in a matter of days, but I could not risk putting this letter or the wooden chest into your hands before you sailed, for fear that you would not leave my side, as charges against me seem imminent.

She moistened her lips, recalled how hard she had fought against leaving him, and shook her head before she continued:

I have never kept a diary or journal, so I have now written down an account of my life before I married your mother. The rest of the contents of the chest I only discovered myself several hours ago when Rosalie Peale gave it to me some moments before she died. Once you read my account, I pray you will forgive me for what I've done and what I've failed to do over the course of my life . . . and that you'll love me as completely as you always have and as I have always loved you.

Pausing, she found his words confusing and continued again:

I also ask that you keep all that you learn from being used to exploit or destroy an innocent child, and while we are both waiting for God's plans for each of our lives to unfold, I ask you to trust in Him. Always.

Your loving father,
GL

Blinking back tears, Ruth refolded the letter and laid it alongside the note he had written to Phanaby. Perplexed by the notion that her father could have possibly done anything that would require her forgiveness or that could be used to hurt Lily, she was convinced that her father must have exaggerated some unusual situation to prepare her for some sort of upsetting news.

She spent the next hour reading a detailed account of the time he spent in western Massachusetts as a newly ordained minister, as well as the rest of the letters in the chest, most of which turned out to have been written by her father many years ago to Liza Adams, the young woman who had claimed and broken his heart while he had been living there. All carried the signature she knew so well: *GL*

But only by reading a number of other letters, written by Liza herself, did she learn that Liza's family had objected so strenuously to the match that they had forced Liza into hiding with distant relatives in Connecticut. From her father's poignant account, Ruth further discovered that he had spent two years searching for his beloved Liza before giving up, moving to New York City and eventually marrying Ruth's mother. He had been completely unaware that Liza had borne him a daughter, Rosalie, who carried her cousin's surname, Peale, or that Liza had died nearly eighteen years later, still single and still very much in love with him.

And it was only then that Ruth knew that her father had not exaggerated at all. The painful, even shameful events he had described were indeed difficult to believe of the faithful man she had known her father to be. But she also knew that he would have turned to his Father for forgiveness for the sin that had set the tragedy of his life, as well as Liza's and Rosalie's, into motion. She could not deny him her forgiveness as well.

Ruth set all the letters aside, along with any judgment of the star-crossed lovers or their illegitimate daughter. She placed the delicate miniature she had found wrapped in faded cloth at the bottom of the wooden chest into the palm of her hand — the very miniature her father had had made of Liza and given to her so many years ago. The resemblance between Liza and Lily was undeniable, and she also knew that this miniature held sentimental value now to the one person who was far too young to understand the implications it held: precious Lily.

She closed her hand and wrapped her fingers around the miniature. She found it hard to believe that her father's ministry working with the city's fallen angels had coincidentally led him to his own daughter, Rosalie Peale. A woman who had run away from home at age seventeen, after her mother's death, to search for the father she had never known, and then been forced to turn to prostitution to survive.

When her father had helped Rosalie reclaim her faith, she had become a Prodigal Daughter, his daughter-in-faith like Phanaby and so many others. But she had died before she was able to share the secret she had kept from him in life for reasons that would never be known. Like Ruth, she was his very own daughter.

To say Ruth was stunned would be entirely fair, because she felt too many emotions all at once to be able to sort through them. To say she was outraged or disappointed by what she had learned would be entirely within reason, but it would not be fair at all. She was simply overwhelmed to learn that despite her father's passing, she was not alone, without any family in this world.

Rosalie Peale's child, Lily, was not simply an orphan who needed protection and a home. Lily was Ruth's blood relative, her niece and her father's granddaughter, and she had all the proof she needed right at her fingertips.

She doubted anyone would challenge her

father's relationship to Lily, as well as her own, but she was absolutely certain that any number of reporters, including Eldridge Porter, would exploit it for one reason: profit.

Her fingers tightened around the miniature so hard that the edges bit into her palm. She no longer had any personal concerns about protecting her own identity, but she had even more reason now to leave the village as soon as Phanaby was well again. Otherwise she had little hope of protecting the innocent one sleeping so peacefully next to her, a child who was too young to protect herself, a child who was her very own niece.

Sighing, she carefully folded the cloth around the miniature and placed it back into the chest. Her fingers lingered on the gift her father had given to Liza, a woman who had trusted him with her heart and had never given it to another because she loved him so completely.

If Ruth dared to do the same, if she trusted Jake with her heart and loved him as completely, then she knew she would also have to trust him with the truth and take the risk that if he walked away, she would never be able to give her heart to another man.

But she had more to worry about than her own future if he betrayed her trust. She had Lily's future to consider, too. Lily was far too vulnerable as it was. Ruth would not complicate her life any further by putting her own needs ahead of her niece's.

Determined to turn to the one person who might be able to help her, she waited until later that night to search out Capt. Grant in hopes of avoiding an encounter with the reporter for the *Transcript*. After Lily was fast asleep and Elias had gone to bed, insisting he would care for Phanaby if she awoke and needed care, Ruth slipped out of the apothecary. There was little moonlight to guide her way, but she knew the back alleys well enough now to be fairly confident she could reach the dock area without getting lost.

To avoid being recognized, she draped her shawl around her head and shoulders and kept her face downcast. She managed to reach Dock Street without passing anyone, but hesitated and remained standing in the shadows when she realized she had no way to reach the ships at anchor in the river. It was also too dark for her to see if Capt. Grant's ship was even there. Entering the several well-lit taverns that were frequented by the seamen to inquire about Grant, even if she were escorted, would be highly irregular and inevitably lead to gossip she could ill-afford to ignite.

Frustrated that she might have made a mistake by coming here, she was ready to turn around and go home when she spied an elderly man exit one of the taverns and walk in her direction. She waited until he had nearly passed her by before calling out to him. "Sir?"

When he paused and looked about, she stepped far enough out of the shadows that he could see her.

He looked at her, shook his head, and lifted a pint of spirits he was carrying. "If it's company you're seekin', missy, you'd best try one of those younger lads in the taverns. I've got all the company I want right here."

Her cheeks flamed hot. "No, sir. I-I . . . that is, could you tell me how to get in touch with Capt. Grant? His ship is the *Sheller.*"

"Sailed this afternoon. So did the *Primrose Lady* and the *Annabelle.* If it's passage you want, you might try —"

"No, I really need to speak to Capt. Grant," she insisted. "Have you any idea when he will be back?"

He shrugged. "Coupla days, I suspect.

Maybe less. Wouldn't know," he said and then walked away.

"A couple of days," she echoed, and started back to the apothecary, praying she and Lily might be safe enough staying with the Garners for a little while longer. She had no one else to turn to who would help her to find another place where she and Lily could hide.

THIRTY-FIVE

Miracle of miracles, Phanaby's fever finally broke Wednesday night.

By the following afternoon, she was still very weak, but she was feeling well enough to take some broth along with her bark tea and shoo her husband back downstairs with orders to leave her in peace. By Thursday night, after Lily had gone to bed a bit earlier than usual, she was sitting in a chair in her bedroom, wearing a fresh nightdress and robe and talking to her husband, who had brought another chair into the room for himself.

Ruth walked back into the room with a fresh pitcher of water and set it on the bed table before she stooped down and picked up the soiled linens she had set on the floor earlier before she put fresh ones on the bed. "As long as the weather is still fine, I'll launder these in the morning. Is there anything else you'd like me to do?"

Elias took his wife's hand. "No, thank you, Ruth. You've done so much already."

"I don't know what I would have done without you," Phanaby offered. "You've been a blessing. Truly," she added, glancing over at the dresser where the wooden chest had once been before she met Ruth's gaze.

"I'm just glad you're recovering," Ruth said.

"Almost as quickly as I took ill," Phanaby replied.

Ruth managed a smile. "Since you're feeling better, I think I might just go to bed early tonight. I'm a bit tired," she confessed, though it was really only her heart that was weary.

Jake had left her a note at the apothecary every night this week, along with a flower from her garden. She had not been able to meet him at her garden as he kept asking her to do, for fear of encountering that reporter. Hopefully, he had heard of Phanaby's illness and assumed Ruth was too busy caring for her and Lily to leave, because he could not possibly know she was a virtual prisoner in this home while Eldridge Porter remained in the village.

"Before you go, we need to discuss something with you," Elias said.

Instinctively, Ruth hugged the sheets

close, but automatically assumed Phanaby had told her husband about giving Ruth the wooden chest. Neither of them could possibly know the very intimate information the box contained because the wax seal on the ribbon tied around the letters had not been broken. But until Phanaby was completely back on her feet again, Ruth did not have the heart to tell either of them that she and Lily would need to leave as soon as possible, and that she was hopeful Capt. Grant would be willing to help her.

Instead, Ruth's mind latched on to her more immediate concern. "Have you heard anything about the reporter? Has he left the village?"

Elias sighed. "According to the latest gossip, which the Jones cousins carried into my apothecary this morning, Porter hasn't shown any indication that he's planning to leave any earlier than expected. But in fact, Mr. Burkalow stopped in later and told me himself that Porter had paid him today, in advance, for a third additional week. Beyond that, no one really knows how long he'll be here but Porter himself."

"Another week? Why must he stay so long?" Ruth groaned and plopped down onto the bed.

"I'm so sorry. I know how stressful it is

for you to have him in the village," Phanaby said.

Elias cleared his throat. "Unfortunately, ladies, he's made it clear that he's here because he thinks he will be able to learn all the information he needs for the article he's writing about Reverend Livingstone and Rosalie Peale. I think it's obvious he's willing to stay until he does." He paused and gazed lovingly at his wife. "As hard as it will be, I think it's best that we find new living arrangements for Ruth and Lily."

"Yes, I-I think it's best if I take Lily and leave," Ruth murmured. Although she was surprised Elias had brought up the subject of her leaving, she was reluctant to explain how urgently she needed to take Lily, as well as the wooden chest, as far away from New York City as possible to protect her niece. She also needed to protect the couple sitting across the room, who had no idea they were providing safe refuge for Rev. Livingstone's daughter and also his grand-daughter. "How quickly do you think I'd be able to leave, if I must?" she asked, hoping she did not hurt their feelings by sounding overly anxious.

Phanaby started weeping, and her husband put his arm around her shoulders. "We should be able to put you and Lily on a stagecoach or on board a ship within a day or two, assuming fair weather, but I don't think it's necessary for you to leave that quickly."

Ruth's eyes grew big. "But how — ?"

"Reverend Livingstone's network of supporters is organized rather well," Elias explained. "Every time he sent one of his daughters-in-faith to one of us, he had at least one other household willing to accept her, just in case the first one didn't suit either her or the people who took her in. He asked that we keep that arrangement to ourselves, because if the young woman had trouble adjusting to her new life, he was afraid she'd give up trying if she knew she had someplace else to go."

Ruth nodded. If what Elias had just told her was true, Phanaby was right to be afraid that Ruth would leave once she had given her the wooden chest. "Do you know if he made those same arrangements for me?" she wondered aloud, grateful she would not have to rely on the hope that Capt. Grant might have been willing to help her.

Elias let out a long breath, his gaze grew misty, and he leaned closer to his wife, who was still quietly weeping. "He did. All I need to do is talk with one of the folks in Forked River to find out what those arrangements are, but I'd rather not leave for the next day or two. As long as you stay inside, I think you'll be safe for a few more days until I'm able to get the information we need and know where you can go. But we don't want you to leave until it becomes absolutely clear that you should pack up, take Lily, and say good-bye." He bent his head low to comfort his wife.

Ruth quietly left the room without telling Phanaby or Elias that the need to leave could not be any clearer to her. The time to pack was now. The time to take Lily away was now. And it was time to say good-bye to the new life she had found here in Toms River and the couple she had grown to love who had made it all possible.

For the very first time, Ruth truly understood how important her father's work had been to the women he had served through his ministry. Because of his commitment to them and the network of believers he had developed, she would find another home for herself and Lily with people who would help them. Without their help, she would be forced to live on the street, like Rosalie and many other women who found themselves in such desperate straits.

Humbled and ever grateful she would never face the same fate, Ruth carried the soiled linens down the hallway while fingering the tiny carved heart she wore around her neck. She knew she would probably have to leave without saying good-bye to Jake. She also knew she would leave behind her heart, because he had already stolen it. But she would always have the little notes he had left for her and would keep them always, just as Liza Adams, Lily's grandmother, had done.

Jake armed himself with a slingshot and a pocketful of tiny seashells he had gotten from Capt. Grant during his travels over the past few years.

He charged up the sandy path that led to the village, with the pesky turkey hen right on his heels, as fast as he could in the dark of night. He had barely an hour left before he needed to be on board the *Sheller,* which would set sail at first light with or without him. His trunk, which contained everything he owned, as well as the articles he had finished writing last night, were already stored there in Grant's cabin.

He did not know why Ruth had ignored the notes he had left for her the past four nights. In all truth, he did not care why she had not returned to her garden or that she had never seen how he had weeded the garden and watered it every night after dark, with only the meager light of the moon to guide his work.

When he tripped over something in the middle of the path, he nearly lost his footing. Panting hard, he slowed his steps but nearly fell again when the turkey hen swooshed across the path in front of him before disappearing into the brush. "Stupid turkey!" he snapped and hurried along.

Step after determined step, he kept his focus centered on his mission. Ruth may have abandoned her garden. She may never have sat with him on the bench he had made for her. She may even have decided to abandon any interest in him, too. But he could not and would not leave this village without telling her the truth about himself and assuring her, in spite of his lies and his betrayal of her trust, that he intended to do everything within his power to protect her and the child she claimed as her own.

When he reached the bridge at the head of the river, he stopped before he crossed it, looked around, and listened hard. The entire village was in a deep, silent slumber. Even Burkalow's Tavern and Inn was dark, which meant the reporter who had taken up residence there was abed. With the singular sounds of the crickets chirping and the cicadas buzzing, forewarning a sultry day ahead, he crossed the bridge and disappeared down the alley that led to the rear of the apothecary.

When he reached the building itself, he planted his feet on the ground below her window and drew a deep breath. He felt a little foolish using the slingshot, but if it was good enough to slay Goliath, he hoped it would be good enough for him to slay the demons of all the mistakes he had made. He pulled the slingshot he had made out of his pocket and then took a small seashell out of another pocket.

He paused to draw a deep breath, but he did not need to pray.

Not now.

He had spent every waking moment praying as he wrote the articles he was taking back to New York City with him, just as he had prayed every night while he practiced using the slingshot, again and again, until his aim was sure. He was fairly confident the seashells he selected for his ammunition were light enough to stir Ruth awake when they hit her window, hopefully without waking Lily, yet not heavy enough to break the glass.

"She'll forgive me," he whispered, and shot the first seashell at her window. After it hit the glass with a *ping,* he waited, but got no response.

"She won't forgive me." The second seashell hit the frame of the window, but again no response.

By the time six seashells went unanswered, he wondered if Ruth was in the room at all. He felt around in his pocket. He had one seashell left, the largest of the bunch he had brought with him. This time he did pause to say a quick prayer before he sent the seashell flying through the air. He cringed when he heard it hit, then groaned when he heard the telltale sound of cracking glass.

If that did not wake her up, he feared nothing would, short of banging down her door.

It was too dark for him to see anything through the window itself, but he did not expect her to light as much as a candle since Lily was sleeping in the same room.

He held his breath for a moment, cocked his head, and listened. Nothing. Not a sound. Not a shadow of movement.

"Come to the window, Ruth. Please. Just come to the window and open it," he said as loudly as he dared, and then he simply waited.

THIRTY-SIX

Another summer storm?

The first pelt of heavy rain that hit the window roused Ruth from a fitful sleep. Waiting for the rumble of thunder or the sizzle of lightning, she huddled under the covers, but then bolted from her bed when she heard the glass in the window actually crack.

Without bothering to put on her robe, she thought twice about lighting a candle and tiptoed to the window and carefully felt the glass for cracks to be certain she had not simply been dreaming. "Ouch!" she yelped and pulled back her hand. "Not carefully enough," she grumbled. She tasted just a bit of blood when she sucked her throbbing index finger. She did not think the cut on her finger was very deep as she furrowed her brow and looked out the window.

It was too dark to see much of anything, but she was more concerned about what she did not see and leaned closer to the window. "There's no rain at all?" she murmured.

"Ruth! Open the window!"

Startled, she looked down, saw the vague outline of a man, and drew back. She had foolishly opened the door to a man in the middle of the night once before and ended up needing to defend herself. She had little desire to invite a similar ordeal, even though she was safe on the second floor of the building.

"Ruth!"

This time she heard her name, recognized the man's voice, and opened the window. After kneeling down to keep him from seeing that she was in her nightdress, she poked her head through the opening. "Jake? Is that you?" she asked, only able to see the barest outline of his body.

"Yes, it's me. I need to see you. We have to talk."

"Now? Are you addled? It's the middle of the night!"

"I'm sorry, but I'm sailing for home in the morning, and I can't leave until I talk to you. Please. I promise I won't keep you long."

It was so dark that she had no worry that anyone, particularly Eldridge Porter, would see her. Still, she was not about to go outside at night again, wearing nothing more than her nightdress and her robe, to meet any man for any reason, most especially Jake Spencer.

"I'm sorry. I can't," she whispered. "I'll try to think of a way to meet you later."

"I told you. I'm leaving at first light."

His voice sounded desperate, but she dared not relent. "Then I'm sorry. You should . . . you should go."

"I'm not leaving until I speak my piece. If you won't come outside, then I'm going to stand right here and say what I have to say because you need to hear it from me."

His voice was no longer desperate, but very determined. She knew him well enough to suspect he would do exactly what he said, and when Lily started to stir, she knew she had no other choice but one. "Hush! You're waking Lily. If you're so determined to talk to me, then you'll just have to wait until I can get dressed. Now be quiet!" She closed the window before he could argue with her and rushed over to pat Lily's back until she stopped whimpering and fell back to sleep.

It only took her fifteen minutes to get dressed, but a full half hour had passed before she slipped out the back door. By then the darkness was less opaque and she was able to see him standing a few feet away, although it was nearly impossible to distinguish his features or gauge his expression until she was standing directly in front of him. When she saw the tenderness in his gaze, she swallowed hard.

"I hope you have a good reason to come calling at this hour," she said, a bit more flippantly than she intended.

"I left notes for you, but you never came to your garden to meet me. Did you get them?"

"Yes, I have them, but you must have realized I couldn't go anywhere. Between nursing Phanaby and taking care of Lily, I haven't had a moment to spare," she explained, unwilling to admit she could not leave because of Eldridge Porter.

"Phanaby's been ill?"

"Nearly all week, but she's doing much better now. You hadn't heard?"

His gaze darkened. "No, I've been out at the cabin," he said, looked east toward the river. "I haven't much time, but I needed to see you before I left. There's so much I need to say, that you need to hear. From me," he said, lifting his hand as if to take hers, then letting it drop.

Ruth's heart swelled with the hope that he might declare his feelings for her and ask her to leave with him. She reached up to touch the small carved heart she was wearing and wondered if she had the courage to tell him her real identity if he did.

"I love you, Ruth, and I think you have feelings for me, too," he whispered. "If I could, I'd ask you to leave with me this morning and have Capt. Grant marry us before we reached the mouth of the river. But I can't do that any more than I can ask you to allow me to help you raise Lily."

She blinked back tears, struggling to understand his reluctance to ask her to marry him. "I love you, too," she whispered. "Why? Why can't you ask me? If it's because of your back and how difficult it is for you to earn —"

"No," he said firmly. He squared his shoulders and tilted up his chin, looking far more formal in demeanor than she had ever seen him. "In all truth, my back is perfectly fine. I've spent the past two years working in small towns and villages along the coast, but I've never fallen off a roof or hurt my back in any way," he began, his voice growing steadier as he spoke. "I returned to New York City several months ago to work with my brother again. We own a newspaper there, the *Galaxy*. My real name is Tripp, not Spencer. And though I've always gone by Jake, I use Asher Tripp as my professional name —"

"No. Th-that can't be true," she argued, instinctively taking a step back from him as his words sliced through every hope and dream she had ever wrapped around the man standing in front of her.

"I'm afraid it's true. I came here to investigate you for a story. I know that you're not Widow Ruth Malloy. You're Reverend Gersham Livingstone's daughter, and Lily is not your child. I know it all, Ruth, every last detail of the proof you've been hiding, which is likely stored in that wooden chest your father sent to Phanaby Garner several days before you arrived here."

She dropped the heart she had been holding to let it hang free again and clapped her hand over her mouth, too horrified to scream, let alone speak. She was also far too devastated to cry, but she had the presence of mind to put two more steps of distance between them.

"I'm not proud of who I am or what I've done since I've met you, but I promise you —"

She held up her hand, saw how badly it was shaking, and used her other hand to steady it and form a shield in front of her.

"Just leave. Don't say another word — just go," she spat.

She turned her back to him and started walking back to the door with her head held high and her back stiff, more determined with every step she took that she would not shed a tear in front of that . . . that reporter . . . that horrible, lying, sneaky excuse for a man!

Not one tear. Not now. Not ever.

"Don't go. You don't understand," he argued, following her. "I'm not going to write an article that will hurt either you or Lily. I'm going to do everything in my power to protect you both."

Holding onto the door, Ruth turned just enough to glare at him. "Protect us? Just exactly how do you expect to do that in your article when every word that's been printed in your newspaper or any of the others has done nothing but hurt us with lies and innuendos that are blatantly false and odious to anyone familiar with the truth?"

Breathing hard, she huffed, "By the time your article reaches the pathetic public that worships every word they read in your newspaper as the gospel truth, Lily and I will be gone from here, far enough away that you can't hurt us anymore. Feel free to print whatever version of the truth that sells the most of your precious newspapers. You will anyway."

Jake glared back at her. "You actually think that I'd write an article that would subject Lily to the shame of knowing that she was the love child born to a prostitute who was murdered by her own father? She's your half sister, Ruth. Even if I didn't give a whit about that child, which I do, I could never do that to you. I love you."

She dropped her hand from the door and whirled around to face him. "Wh-what did you say?"

"I said exactly what you know is true. My brother's already confirmed the fact that your father and Rosalie Peale were lovers and had a child together. When she threatened to tell their secret, he killed her, and he was only acquitted because he hid everything he had ever given to her, letters or trinkets or whatever, in that wooden chest and then sent you away with Lily."

She struggled and struggled to breathe. "You . . . you're . . . despicable. You're beyond despicable. How could you possibly think that . . . that disgusting story is true? And even if it was, how can you possibly justify printing it in your newspaper? Rosalie is dead. My father is dead. But Lily and I are still very much alive, and neither one of us deserves —"

"You both deserve much more than I could ever give you, but I won't break my vow to protect you both because I do love you, Ruth," he murmured. "Both of you. Please, won't you try to understand and forgive me for lying to you?"

When he reached out to her, she slapped his hand away. "Your profession of love is just as perverted as your vow. You don't deserve forgiveness," she snapped, turned her back, marched inside, and slammed the door in his face when he tried to follow her.

Body trembling, she collapsed against the door. With her fist pressed hard against her lips, she did not utter a cry until she heard him walk away. Deep sobs tortured her body, and she wrapped her hands around her waist. The depth of his betrayal was so overwhelming and the pain so excruciating, she did not know if she could bear it.

When her sobs finally eased into weeping, she sat down on the bottom step, removed the carved heart she was wearing, and shoved it into her pocket. Alone in the dark, she doubted she would ever find the strength to smile or to trust anyone ever again.

Moments later, too weak to cry and too disappointed to pray, she started back up the steps. She was halfway to the second floor when she realized she had no one but herself to depend upon and decided she would have to wake Elias and beg him to go to Forked River today.

By the time she closed the door at the top of the steps, she had also decided to tell them that it was useless to worry about Eldridge Porter, because he was not the only reporter here in Toms River who posed a threat to her and Lily.

Ruth reached their bedroom door and had lifted her hand to knock when she heard Lily whimpering. Anxious not to delay speaking to the Garners, she slipped back into her room, hoping to urge Lily back to sleep again. She found Lily lying in Ruth's upper bed, but when she picked her up to soothe her and place her back in the lower bed, she grew terrified and all thoughts of Jake quickly disappeared.

Poor Lily was burning up with fever.

THIRTY-SEVEN

Within hours of his arrival in New York City, Jake was tempted to get back on the *Sheller,* sail to Boston with Capt. Grant, and disappear again.

He balled his hands into fists, ready to charge over the desk that separated him from his brother at the *Galaxy* office, if that was what it took to get a clear, forthright answer from him. Instead, he tried giving his brother one last chance to respond honestly before he resorted to physical intimidation.

"No," Jake repeated. "I haven't read what the other newspapers reported, Clifford, because I'm only interested in what's printed in the *Galaxy.*" He pointed to the front page of the paper he had purchased as soon as he debarked the *Sheller.* He hadn't been able to read more than the first page before he stormed into the office less than five minutes ago, infuriated. "Now, for the last time: This headline and the articles below it. Are they based on provable facts or not?"

Clifford glared back at him. "There's no need for a show of temper. Of course they are," he stated. He sorted through the papers stacked on his desk, chose several, and threw them onto Jake's desk. "If you don't believe me, sit down and read those. There's a copy of the actual deathbed confession, which I paid dearly to get and paid even more dearly to guarantee that none of the other newspapers had a copy of it in time for today's issue; a statement from all of the witnesses who signed it; and notes from my interview with the constable, as well as Reverend Livingstone's lawyer."

Clifford paused to clear his throat. "I'm not as irresponsible as you apparently think I am. I know what I'm doing — and I did it every day while you were off nursing your wounded pride for two years before you decided to return and redeem yourself."

Satisfaction was hardly the word for the feelings that churned in Jake's gut and colored his opinion of his brother. While his brother continued to glare at him, he stood at his desk and read every single document. By the time he finished, he was able to control the urge to literally strangle his brother, but only barely. "Since it appears that someone else is actually responsible for killing Rosalie Peale, and not Reverend Livingstone, how do you explain what you wrote to me in your last letter — which, as it turns out, I was fully justified to toss into the fire?"

Clifford replied, "At this point? It's irrelevant."

Jake's pulse went straight into a gallop. "Irrelevant? That's the best you can offer as an excuse for the misinformation you sent to me? What excuse would you like me to give to Ruth Livingstone to explain why I told her that I had proof that her father had killed Rosalie Peale because he had fathered her illegitimate child? Or should I just tell her to forget it because it's 'irrelevant' now that the real killer has confessed?"

Clifford's eyes glittered. "Then you confronted her. Excellent! Based on these new developments, you'll need to alter your article, of course, but we'll still have an exclusive that will have the other newspapers on the defensive. We'll tease the readers, perhaps with just a few tidbits for a week or so," he mused, talking more to himself than to Jake. "Then we'll publish the full article you've written, just as we promised."

"Promised? When?" Jake demanded, fearing the nightmare he was having had somehow just gotten even worse.

Clifford opened the newspaper on his desk and pointed to an announcement placed prominently on the third page. "I had every confidence you'd come through with a good article, but since you were actually able to speak to Ruth Livingstone, the revised article will be better than good. It'll be great."

Jake read the announcement, squared his shoulders, and stared at his brother. "You shouldn't have promised to write the truth about her. Anything and everything about Ruth Livingstone is now 'irrelevant,' " he argued, tossing his brother's own word back at him again. "Her father has been completely vindicated, once by a jury, and now by the actual killer's confession."

"That may be true," his brother countered, "but the public's fascination with him is ongoing, perhaps even more so now with that woman's dramatic confession. I'm going to use that fascination to my advantage. Think about it, Jake. It's entirely possible that at least some of the information I was able to uncover about Peale was based on fact. If Peale actually had a child, and Ruth Livingstone can offer any kind of proof, perhaps something her father hid in that wooden chest you mentioned —"

"Stop!"

Clifford looked at Jake as if he had grown a second head. "Stop?"

"You're not going to print anything about any child, if one even exists," Jake said firmly, determined to keep his vow to protect Lily as well as Ruth. There was so much more he wanted to do for them, if Ruth would only give him another chance.

"You don't make the decisions about what I decide to print in the *Galaxy*," his brother argued. "I do, and I'm going to pursue this story and print what I can until the readers tell me they're not interested anymore. The public has a right to know the truth —"

"The *truth?* The *public?* Listen to yourself. You can't seriously think the truth is best served by exploiting that woman and opening her life for public scrutiny. She's as much a victim in this whole sordid affair as Rosalie Peale, and public demand for —"

"I don't want to argue with you, Jake. A successful newspaper meets the public demand or it folds, which is precisely what would have happened if I hadn't saved it two years ago," Clifford said, his words laced more with anger than disappointment. "I need to print the story I asked you to write about Ruth Livingstone. Beyond that, it's entirely up to you. Stay and help me continue to build the *Galaxy,* or go. I've got any number of investors ready to buy out your share of the paper. But if you decide to stay, be prepared to loosen up those principles of yours. They're far too rigid for you to be successful in this business."

Jake swallowed hard. Completely disillusioned by the divide that existed between them, which was based more on principles of faith than the principles men had built upon them, he stepped through and beyond his brother's shadow for the first time in his life to stand alone, beneath the shadow of his Creator. "I don't want to argue, either. I've written an article about Ruth Livingstone that I'd like you to print. In return, I'll sign whatever documents are necessary to give you full title to the newspaper, which will also assign my original investment to you."

Clifford shook his head. "While your offer sounds generous, I doubt very much I'll be interested in what you wrote. Maybe it's best if you just leave and think my offer over."

"I don't need to think it over. I know exactly what I want. Will you at least read the article before you reject my offer?"

Clifford sighed. "Give me a few days. I just hope you know what you're doing."

"I do. Let me show you the article," Jake offered, praying God would intervene and soften his brother's heart.

When he left the office two hours later, he found Capt. Grant waiting for him in the oyster bar down the street, just as he had promised.

"Well?"

"He's agreed to *consider* printing my article," Jake replied.

The older man nodded. "Then there's hope yet. I hope you're as hungry as I am," he said when the waiter suddenly appeared with a tray of food that would feed half the captain's crew.

Jake leaned forward and lowered his voice to a whisper. "Now will you tell me how you got so involved in Reverend Livingstone's network?" he asked, anxious for the captain to keep his promise and explain the mystery of the role he had been playing.

Grant smiled. "Later. After we eat and we're back on board again. And after you tell me what you're going to do to win that young woman's favor. But there is one thing I can tell you now." He placed half a dozen boiled oysters onto his plate.

Jake leaned closer still.

"It's not Reverend Livingstone's network," Capt. Grant whispered. "It's always been mine, and I have great hope that you'll join us."

THIRTY-EIGHT

For two straight days, Ruth only left Lily's bedside for a few brief periods — to make certain Phanaby was still regaining her strength and good health, or to prepare a meal. But there was never a single beat of her heart that did not contain a prayer for God to spare Lily.

By the time the sun rose on Sunday, the third full day of Lily's illness, Phanaby was well enough to resume her household duties again, although she felt incredibly guilty that her illness had spread to the little girl she loved as her own. Ruth was free to devote every moment, day and night, to her niece.

In addition to her prayers, she even tried to bargain with Him, offering to exchange her life for Lily's. She thought about offering the life of the man who had betrayed her instead, but thought God would find the idea too self-serving.

Although Dr. Woodward had refused to bleed Lily because of her tender age, he had prescribed nearly the same remedy for her as he had for Phanaby. Ruth had bathed Lily's fevered body several times a day with cloths dipped in the same white willow bark tea, which she diluted and sweetened with honey to entice the babe to drink more. She had rocked Lily in her arms and walked her and swayed with her when she was too exhausted to take a step. Whenever Lily did sleep, albeit fitfully, Ruth had lain by Lily's side in the lower bed, cradling her in her arms.

On Monday, Lily finally fell asleep at noon. Ruth's fears for Lily had distanced her from the shock and horror of Jake's betrayal. All that remained now was a deep anguish and more heartbreak.

She still found it difficult to accept that Jake Spencer, the tenderhearted man she had come to love, and Asher Tripp, the villainous reporter, were one and the same man. But Ruth decided not to share this truth with Phanaby and Elias unless it became absolutely necessary.

Unsure of how much time she would have before Lily awakened, Ruth was anxious to freshen up a bit in the hope she might feel slightly human again if she did. Although she was tempted to open the window for some fresh air, she was afraid the draft might be harmful to Lily, so she tiptoed across the room to the chest of drawers instead. After slipping out of the clothes she had worn for the past twenty-four hours, she washed up and changed into the clean gown Phanaby had laundered and set out for her.

"Bless you, Phanaby. You even remembered a new ribbon for my hair," she whispered and tied a clean apron at her waist. She left the room just long enough to carry the soiled clothing to the back of the hallway. When she found Lily was still sleeping, she went to the kitchen and indulged herself with a rather thick slice of bread slathered with molasses.

Once she finished, she returned to the bedroom, removed the tired ribbon she had worn to keep her hair pulled away from her face, set it aside, and started brushing her hair. The small cut on her finger from the broken glass had nearly healed. Not so the wounds to her heart. She brushed harder and harder, unable to bear the thought of the hateful lies that would soon be in the newspaper, if indeed they had not already been put to print. Lies that would vilify her father's name. Lies that would shame Lily's name. And lies that would make it nearly impossible for Ruth to challenge them without revealing the truth — a truth that would still shame Lily's name.

The sharp rap at her bedroom window startled her so badly she yelped. With her heart pounding, she whirled around and saw Mr. Toby standing on a ladder and staring at her through the cracked glass, motioning for her to open the window. Directly over his head, a blanket of storm clouds darkened the horizon. She hoped that Elias, who had left early that morning for Forked River, had not run into bad weather.

Groaning, she remembered too late that Elias had told her that he had arranged for Mr. Toby to come over this afternoon to replace the glass in the windowpane. Otherwise she would have put Lily to bed in the couple's bedroom, which would have given her an opportunity to change the bed linens, too.

Grateful Mr. Toby had not appeared half an hour earlier when she had been changing, she pressed her finger to her lips and rushed over to the window. She opened it just wide enough that he would be able to hear her. "I'm so sorry. I forgot you were coming this afternoon," she whispered and pointed to the bed on the opposite wall.

"Lily's sleeping right over there."

"Still sick, is she?" he asked and craned his neck to look past Ruth.

Ruth nodded. "Would you mind so terribly if I asked you to come back later today?"

He rolled his eyes. "You mighta poked your head outside and said somethin' earlier, say, when you heard me set the ladder against the buildin'."

She cringed. "I'm sorry. I must have been in the kitchen then. I'm just afraid you'll wake her up, and I'm not sure it's a good idea to have the window open, either. Her fever's already so high, and with the draft that will blow in . . ."

"There's a storm brewin'. I'll come back tomorrow morning. Just open the window a little wider so I don't have to carry these back down with me." He lifted a hand from the side of the ladder and held up his fist.

Ruth nudged the window up higher. When he handed her a handful of seashells, instead of some sort of tool or whatnot he was going to use to remove the cracked pane of glass, she furrowed her brow.

"I found those on the ground right below the window. From the looks of things, somebody needed a good arm to toss these shells up to your window on the second

428

floor and break the glass."

Ruth shoved the shells into her apron pocket and frowned. She did not know how strong Jake's arm was, but she had seen the slingshot he had been holding the night he had cracked the window and ended up breaking her heart. She also suspected he had gotten those seashells from Capt. Grant, since they looked very much like the two seashells he had given to her and Lily.

"Can't imagine anyone hereabouts who'd risk annoying the Broom Lady," he teased, "but Avery's got somebody new workin' at the livery. Mighta been him."

"Ned! Ned must be working there now," she gushed as Mr. Toby started down the ladder.

"That's his name. Ned Clarke. He's been workin' there 'bout a week or two now. I'll head on over and talk to him for you, if you want," he offered, without stopping his descent.

"No. He didn't crack the window. I'm certain of it," she blurted. She could not let that boy take the blame for something Jake had done. She simply said the first thing that popped into her mind. "I'm afraid I'm the one who cracked the window . . . with a slingshot. I just haven't told anyone."

He stopped, looked up at her, and

grinned. "You are one dangerous woman, Widow Malloy, which poor Maxwell Flynn found out too late — not that he didn't deserve what you gave him." He pointed his finger at her as if she were a child being scolded. "You might wanna reconsider things a bit so the next time you got a man like Jake thinkin' about courtin' you, he won't hightail it outta here like Spencer did. I heard tell that Ned and his pa —"

"I'll try to keep that in mind," she quipped before the man could offer any more gossip as she shut the window, along with any hope he would keep his mouth shut about what she had told him.

She tiptoed over to the bed to reassure herself that all the commotion had not disturbed Lily, but fortunately, Lily was still sleeping peacefully. She went straight to the chest of drawers to put away the seashells Jake had shot at her window and sighed. The wooden chest was locked, and she had left the key in the soiled apron she had carried out into the hall.

Once she retrieved the key and had the seashells stored safely inside, she looped the new ribbon Phanaby had left for her hair through the key and tied it around her neck. "Much safer," she whispered and tucked the ribbon and the key beneath the bodice

430

of her gown. She gave her hair a final quick brush and bypassed using the frayed ribbon in favor of using her comb again. Yawning, she lay down on her bed to rest, just for a little while until Lily woke up, falling asleep as she prayed that God would help Elias find a proper place for her and Lily to make a new life for themselves.

THIRTY-NINE

"Ruth! Wake up, Ruth!"

Ruth batted her eyes, but when she fully opened them, she had to blink several times to clear the sleep away. It took a moment before she recognized the face that came into focus. "Lily!" she croaked.

When she tried to turn to see if she had been sleeping too soundly to hear Lily wake up, Phanaby urged her out of the bed. "Lily's still asleep. Elias is back with news. Wonderful news," she whispered, her gaze teary.

Ruth rubbed her eyes, but the room still seemed awfully dim. "What time is it?"

"I think it's finally time to rejoice," Phanaby murmured. "Go on. I'll stay with Lily. Elias is waiting in the kitchen to share the good news with you. You can have a bite of supper, too."

Ruth shook her head to clear the daze she was in. "It's time for supper? Already?"

Phanaby chuckled. "It's seven o'clock and it's time to rejoice," she insisted and ushered Ruth out of the room and into the hall before she closed the door.

Ruth wandered down the hall. By the time she reached the kitchen, her mind, as well as her vision, was clear again. She found Elias standing next to the kitchen table, but she blinked hard the moment she saw the several newspapers spread out on the table.

Her mind raced from confusion straight past joy to fear — then back to confusion again when Elias greeted her with a broad smile. "Praise God, Ruth. He's been cleared. Reverend Livingstone's finally been cleared! Come. See for yourself. It's true!" he exclaimed.

With her heart racing, she joined him at the table and stared at the headline he pointed to in the *Transcript: Deathbed Confession Renders Justice for Rosalie Peale.*

"I heard that Eldridge Porter was so distressed that he missed reporting this story, he bought a horse and rode straight back to the city," he said, chuckling. "Here's another," he said, pointing to a headline in another paper before she had the chance to read a single word in the article below the first headline. The bold words on the first page of the *Sun* were just as unbelievable:

Brothel Owner Confesses to Killing Rosalie Peale.

"And another," he said, reading the headline in the *Herald* out loud: " 'Reverend Livingstone's Verdict Affirmed by Deathbed Confession.' I've read these three papers already. Every one of them says pretty much the same thing, although none of them had the decency to apologize for ruining Reverend Livingstone's name with innuendo and gossip they passed on to the public as fact," he noted sadly.

Nearly overwhelmed, Ruth eased into the nearest chair. Her tears flowed so hard and so fast, she doubted she would be able to read anything for a good while. "Please. Just tell me what the papers said," she managed, afraid to believe that her father's good name had been restored to him.

Elias started folding up the papers. "Rosalie Peale worked on King Street at Mrs. Browers's brothel, which is old news, where the poor young woman apparently was the highest-earning woman at the establishment, something we didn't know," he said, his cheeks turning pink.

He cleared his throat. "Apparently Rosalie told Mrs. Browers that she was leaving, and the woman tried to convince her to stay. When Rosalie refused, the woman flew into a rage and attacked her, shortly before Reverend Livingstone arrived. At least that's what the woman confessed to Reverend Wells when she called him to her deathbed. At her request, he drew up a statement to that effect for the authorities, and she signed it in front of witnesses right before she died. One of the papers, the *Sun* I believe, also mentions something about a maid, who admitted stealing money from Rosalie's room, but —"

"I'd like to see that newspaper, too," Ruth said, when she saw him put the other three newspapers on top of it. "Is that the *Galaxy?*"

"Yes, but it says pretty much the same as the others," he said.

Convinced he was trying to keep something from her, she slid the *Galaxy* free. Battling more tears, she read the headline *Justice for Rosalie Peale and Reverend Livingstone,* skimming the article that covered the entire front page. Relieved she found nothing amiss in the article itself, she opened the four-page paper, saw a large box bordered with thick black lines at the top of the second page, and froze when she read the information inside the box, set in bold type:

IN A FORTHCOMING ISSUE, THE *GALAXY* WILL PROVIDE A DETAILED ACCOUNT OF REV. LIVINGSTONE'S DAUGHTER, RUTH, AND THE LIFE SHE LED WHILE IN HIDING. WE TRUST OUR READERS WILL BE MOST INTERESTED IN THE INFORMATION WE HAVE UNCOVERED DURING OUR PROLONGED AND EXCLUSIVE INVESTIGATION.

"It's not over. It won't ever be over. Not for me. Not for Lily. Not even for you or Phanaby, as long as we're still here," she whispered. When Phanaby came running into the kitchen carrying Lily in her arms, Ruth dropped the newspaper and leaped to her feet.

"Her fever's broken!" Phanaby cried and handed the sweat-drenched child to Ruth. "Praise God. It is truly a day to rejoice."

Ruth cradled the child in her arms. Her nightdress was soaked, but her eyes were clear, her cheeks no longer flushed, and her skin was as cool as Ruth's. "Thank you, Father," she whispered, nuzzling the little girl's face with her own as she broke into weeping.

With gratitude for God's mercy and His

healing of this precious child.

With joy, now that her father's name had been cleared.

And with the certainty that this day would not end with rejoicing.

Tonight, she needed to tell Phanaby and Elias that she was definitely leaving as soon as Lily was well enough to travel. Regardless of where Elias would tell them their new home would be, they were going to sail directly to New York City first. Somehow, even if she had to beg, she was going to make certain that Jake did not print the forthcoming article mentioned in the newspaper — for her sake, for Lily's sake, and for the sake of the couple who had opened their home and their hearts to them.

She did not know exactly how she might do that, but she had a drawerful of weapons she was going to take along with her — just in case she needed to prove to him that in addition to being the very naïve, trusting woman he had so easily fooled, when it came to protecting the people she loved, Mr. Toby had been right.

She could be one very dangerous woman, too.

FORTY

As it happened, it was not Lily's illness nor waiting for her full recovery that delayed Ruth's departure, but a combination of factors well beyond her control.

The storm brewing on Monday afternoon developed into the strongest bout of bad weather she had experienced since moving here, keeping all the ships at anchor until Wednesday morning and forcing Ruth to remain inside. Fierce winds damaged many of the buildings on Main Street and littered the sidewalk and the roadway itself with broken glass and splintered wooden shingles.

Ruth stayed to help with the village-wide effort to clear the debris and repair the damage on Wednesday. Elias had been unable to book passage on any ship for Thursday, but when the *Sheller* sailed downriver the following day at midmorning, rather than at first light, Ruth and Lily would be on board.

Ruth arrived at the private sanctuary she had created for herself shortly after dawn on Friday, expecting to find her flowering plants strangled by weeds and her memories of the hours she had spent here with Jake a haunting reminder of his betrayal. Instead, the garden was a brilliant collage of yellow and blue flowers, and there was nary a weed in sight. Just as surprisingly, her memories of Jake were difficult but more sweet than bitter. But the bench he had made for her was nowhere to be seen.

"Jake . . ."

Standing in front of the garden, facing the river, she whispered his name and her love for this man soared throughout her entire being in the space of a single heartbeat. Devastation, however, pained her heart as she fingered the key she wore on the ribbon around her neck. Several months ago, when Rev. Haines asked her, when the time came, to bring fresh flowers to church services, she never thought she would be here to see them bloom. But she never dreamed that love would also bloom, only to be destroyed long before frost would claim the last of her flowers.

Ruth experienced a heightened sense of déjà vu when she detected the smell of burning wood and turned to see smoke curling skyward from the chimney in the cabin. She looked through the copse of trees and saw a figure of a man emerge from the cabin, then gasped when he limped toward her, leaning heavily on a cane.

Struggling for control of her emotions and her traitorous heart, she shook her head. Why had Jake chosen to reappear today, using the very guise he had used to snare her attentions on the first day they had met?

She clenched her fists as he approached and readied herself to give the speech she had prepared, but had not expected to deliver until she arrived in New York City this afternoon. When he finally emerged from behind the trees separating them, she clapped her hand to her heart. The face before her was of a much younger adolescent standing a few paces away, timidly smiling at her.

"Ned?"

"Yes, ma'am. Been meanin' to stop by to see you, but I banged up my knee real bad a few days back tryin' to get back to the cabin before that storm hit."

"You're living here?"

A wide grin. "Yes, ma'am, me and my pa. He's all healed up and workin' down at the mill. Mr. Avery's been lettin' me keep

Shortcake stabled at the livery. That mule's happier there than those bees that feed on the flowers in that garden, but my pa's hopin' to build a lean-to before winter sets in."

"But h-how did you . . . when did you . . . ?" Blushing, she paused, unable to speak without stammering or forming a complete question. "I'm sorry. You caught me by surprise. How did you and your father come to stay at this particular cabin?"

He shrugged. "I'm not sure. Mr. Spencer talked to me and my pa first, then I think he had to talk to somebody else. But it's a whole sight better than what we had, and we don't have to pay no rent, neither."

She lifted a brow. "No rent?"

"Not a single coin," he said proudly. "All we have to do is take real good care of this garden. It's real pretty. I heard you planted it. That right?"

Her heart warmed to the idea that Jake had made certain her garden would survive, even if she did not return there because she could not bear to be near the place where they had spent so much time together. "Yes, I did," she murmured and recalled the promise she had made to Rev. Haines to give him flowers from her garden for the church. "I wonder if you would do something for me," she ventured.

Ned smiled.

"When Reverend Haines comes back in a few weeks, would you cut some of these flowers and give them to him to put in the church for Sunday services?"

"Yes, ma'am. I surely will."

She smiled. "Thank you." Ruth looked around. "You didn't happen to notice a bench sitting out here, did you?"

His eyes sparkled. "Me and Pa use it inside 'cause there wasn't nothin' to sit on 'cept one old chair that's so warped, it looks like somebody set it into the river behind you."

More bittersweet memories.

She looked up and saw that the sun was rising too fast for her to stay any longer. She bid him farewell, but he called to her before she reached the sandy path.

"Ma'am?"

She looked back at him over her shoulder.

"You wouldn't know nothin' about that wild turkey hen that stays around here, would you?"

She saw the turkey hen standing a few feet behind the boy and smiled through her tears. "Does it bother you overmuch?" she asked, realizing the bird had been so much a part of her relationship with Jake that she

442

would never be able to eat turkey again.

He shrugged.

"I believe it'll make a good pet for you," she murmured and then walked toward home.

Ruth shared a tearful good-bye with the Garners before leaving for Dock Street, and she was surprised to see a good number of the villagers gathered along Main Street to wish her well. No one here, other than the Garners, knew she would not be arriving in the small hamlet of Alleluia for at least a week. She was not entirely pleased she would be living in one of the many towns along the Erie Canal, but she was grateful she had somewhere to go.

She trusted God would provide an alternative if He did not mean for her to be living in Alleluia, just as He had provided for her to be in Toms River and had guided her to her niece.

Lily fell asleep before the *Sheller* sailed from the Toms River into Barnegat Bay. Ruth was tempted to crawl into the bunk with her and take a quick nap herself, but wondered if she should go up on deck to ask Capt. Grant about the arrangements Elias said the captain had made so she could spend the night in New York before boarding a packet boat that would take her the rest of the way to Alleluia.

She answered the rap at her door, saw Grant standing there, and smiled. "What a coincidence. I was just thinking about going up to the main deck to see you."

"It's a long way to the city. I thought you might like something to read," he offered and held out a newspaper.

She swallowed hard, especially when she saw the *Galaxy* masthead at the top, but took the paper anyway.

His gaze softened. "While you're reading, you might want to keep one thing in mind," he cautioned gently. "There are no real co-incidences in life for those with faith strong enough to recognize coincidences for what they really are: intricate pieces of the providential design God created for each of our lives. I have a Bible in my cabin. I'll bring it to you in a spell. I suggest the story of Ruth." He left her standing there, convinced the past few months of her life would have been easier to bear if he had shared his wisdom and his faith with her when she had first sailed into Toms River, instead of now when she was leaving.

She held his advice close to her spirit and carried the paper over to a porthole to read it in the best light. Oddly enough, the newspaper was dated for tomorrow, the four-teenth of August, but the article, centered on the first page directly below the mast-head, immediately captured her attention. She skimmed through some sections and read others aloud.

The reporter, identified as Asher Tripp, claimed he "interviewed Ruth Livingstone at great length" and argued with great force that "any and all skepticism about Reverend Livingstone's innocence and rumors that his daughter had hidden some sort of evidence of his misdoings, even after Mrs. Browers's deathbed confession, should be laid to rest."

With her heart pounding, Ruth read that he suggested readers would be much more interested in reading about "Reverend Simon Hart, most recently of Boston, who has resumed the very important ministry begun by the late Reverend Livingstone and is already tending his new flock: the fallen angels of this city."

Tears blurred her vision to the point Ruth was unable to read any further, and she stopped to wipe away her tears before she continued, anxious to read the final para-graph, which contained a personal message from the reporter:

While this report is my first article to appear in print for several years, it will also be my last. Following publication of this issue of the *Galaxy,* my brother, Clifford Tripp, will assume full ownership and editorial duties associated with this newspaper, while I leave to pursue other interests outside of the city. It is my fervent prayer that the *Galaxy* will uphold the finest principles of truth, honor, and justice in future publications, inspiring readers' confidence in the news reported therein, as well as the blessings of Providence. In saying farewell, I would also ask all of you, faithful readers, to pray for me as I allow God's plan for my life to unfold and for Rev. Livingstone's daughter, who is living in a town that will remain unnamed and enjoying quiet anonymity with the man she recently wed.

Bowing her head, she wept as Jake Spencer and Asher Tripp became one and the same man in her heart and mind — the man she loved. Jake had done much more than keep his vow not to write anything that would hurt her or Lily.

The article he had written had given both of them the protection and the freedom to enjoy the days and months and years ahead without fear that their identities would ever be revealed, although she found it rather odd that he had written that she had gotten married.

Another rap at her door sent her scrambling to wipe her face free of tears after setting the paper aside. Although she would have given anything to be able to see Jake at this very moment, she knew Capt. Grant was simply returning with the Bible he had promised to bring to her.

When she opened the cabin door, however, she looked into the eyes of the man she loved. The emotion in his gaze was almost overpowering. "I waited as long as I could. Did you read what I wrote?"

Captivated by the love brimming in his hazel eyes, she was unable to speak but managed to nod and moistened her lips. For every lie he had told her, she had told him two, but in the end it was the truth of their feelings for each other that mattered most of all.

"Would you care to discuss it?"

She shook her head and embraced the events some would call coincidences that had brought her to this moment in time with this man, events she saw clearly now as providential. Her father's dedication to a ministry for which he was often ridiculed yet which led him to the daughter he never knew had been born. His insistence that Ruth and Ruth alone protect an innocent child. The specific reporter who had found them, but had protected them instead of exploiting them. And a sea captain who seemed to be the only common link to them all.

"Ruth?"

The sound of her name startled her and ended her musing. "I asked if you'd care to discuss anything I wrote."

When she shook her head again, he cocked a brow. "No? I'm surprised. I don't seem to recall a single instance when you didn't complain about something printed in the newspaper."

She shrugged. "Now that you mention it, I do have one complaint."

He started to smile. "I was hoping you might."

"This recent marriage of Ruth Livingstone you mentioned in the article. For a reporter committed to reporting only the truth, I'm afraid you fell short. As far as I know, she isn't married at all."

The cleft in his chin deepened. "Very true, but since the paper is dated for tomorrow, there's still time to rectify that mistake."

"Really?" she said, feigning indifference,

although her heart was racing so fast she felt faint.

"Marry me. Let me spend the rest of my life proving to you that I'm the man who will love you the most, because I'm finally the man you encouraged me to be." He cupped her cheek. "Join with me to continue your father's work. Capt. Grant is waiting for us in his cabin. Say you'll have him marry us. Right away."

Her heart leaped with joy as she leaned her face against the palm of his hand. "I do believe I've heard that the captain of a ship can perform marriages at sea, but are you certain it would be legal?"

He tilted up her chin and kissed her. "It doesn't matter," he said. "Capt. Grant's an ordained minister, too." He then lifted a sleeping Lily from her bunk and turned to face Ruth again with the little girl in his arms. "Marry me. Make us a real family."

Ruth blinked, fresh tears coursing down her cheeks. "Did you say the captain is an ordained minister?"

He smiled and held out his hand. "I'll explain it all to you after the ceremony."

When he kissed her again, she slipped her hand into his and held on tight to the loving man in front of her, and the ever-loving God who had brought him into her life.

THE SEASHELL

Seashells are homes for some of God's many treasured creatures. Although the shells are quite colorful, once the creatures within them die, strong currents carry away the shells. Many of them will be much paler by the time they crash upon distant shores, but even the most colorful shells will be bleached white by the sun before a sheller comes along to collect them.

As human beings, we are the most precious of God's creatures, and we are very much like those seashells. Within our earthly bodies, we have a spiritual soul that is a home for our faith and our love for Him. Whenever we commit a sin, our souls become very colorful, perhaps turning green from being envious or red from being angry or purple from being jealous or gold from being consumed by a thirst for wealth or fame.

If we turn to Him and ask for His forgiveness, His grace can purify and whiten even the most sinful and colorful of souls. When death comes and our souls wash upon Heaven's shores where He waits to collect us, I pray that He may find our souls have been purified by His forgiveness and grace, just as the seashells that land upon our shores have been bleached white by the sun.

Love Him. Serve Him. And trust in Him always as you await the glorious day when the greatest of all shellers, Our Lord and Saviour, welcomes you Home.

Rev. James Christian Grant,
written aboard the *Sheller*
February 1808